Bury the Demons

Michael Ghosh

Copyright © 2020 MR Ghosh

All rights reserved

When the lights go out and silence fills the cold room, I lay my weary head on the pillow and appreciate the warmth of those who make me feel so grateful.

For my beloved wife and darling daughter.

An Affair to Forget

It took me a few years to make that long awaited call to my mother. Racked with shame and guilt, I nervously picked up the phone and dialled the number, my hands shaking uncontrollably.

"Hi mum."

"Bobby, is that you? Oh, my God, you're still alive! What have you done son? The police are looking for you. Where are you?"

Before I could answer, I found myself slamming down the handset. I wasn't ready to tell her my side of the story. It all still seemed like a bad dream. I needed to run through the series of events in my head first, perhaps to a stranger, maybe that stranger could be you? I don't want to burden you with my demons, I'd just like to present you with my sorry tale and ask for a fair hearing. I'm not flipping a coin to see which side it lands, I'm throwing my entire overdrawn bank account at you with the hope it buys me your sympathy.

Before I start, let me guess, you're probably sat on the sofa, maybe tucked up in your bed, perhaps on holiday and reclining on a sun lounger. There's a chance you're on a plane, a train or the back seat of a car. It doesn't really matter. Wherever you are, I'd wager on you being there through choice. You might prefer to be somewhere else but no one is forcing you to stay. Am I right? Well, I wish I could be in your situation. How I long for the simple things in life. The creature comforts that we all take for granted. The truth is, I am in a place, both in body and soul that I really don't want to be and there's nothing I can do about it. "Why not?" I hear you ask. Well, the slippery slope of my downfall began by simply trusting the wrong people at the wrong time. People who I embraced as they stabbed me in the back. I never thought that I was gullible or naïve but I do realise I've made my mistakes and bad errors in judgement.

It all started in the early throws of the summer of 2017. A summer that would turn my life upside down. As I walked into my back garden and watched the butterflies flutter amongst the summer flowers as they began their long-awaited bloom, I reclined in my newly acquired back yard bench and gathered my thoughts. Sipping on a large glass of wine from a bottle that had been gathering dust under the kitchen sink, I couldn't help but bask in the warming air and consider that my life, to that point, had been pretty damn good. I was single and carefree.

No wait, hang on. That was the problem, I didn't want to be single anymore. I craved for the love of a good woman. Oh, here we go I hear you cry, another tale of unrequited love. Well, I don't want to give anything away so I'll let you be the judge of that, but let me assure you, if you are one of those readers who tries to guess the ending to this story, I was no easy target, so please, cut me a bit of slack and hear me out. Oh sure, I had the confidence and maturity of a mildly successful man who had just turned thirty. I was living in a decent suburb of London, had a pretty steady career and my bank manager didn't give me any grief, but the one box that lay empty was the one concerning my love life. Single for some time, I was under pressure from friends and family to take out the pen of happiness and get that damn box ticked. I knew that it was a numbers game. I had to play the field, throw a hundred darts at the board and surely one would hit the bullseye. I can assure you that I was on the case, effort deserves reward, right?

It was a Friday, the first one in June, and I had lined up a date but the events of this particular night would change my life forever. Half an hour before she was due to arrive at my humble home, I'd brushed my teeth twice, put on my finest evening attire and finished a large glass of Dutch courage in preparation for an evening of high jinks and optimistic romantic gratification.

After last week's dating disaster, I was a little nervous, a tad bruised but not disheartened, only more determined. That particular failing happened to be my best friend Julie's fault. Bless her, she had set me up on a random blind date with her hairdresser's sister and made me promise to send a text message to let her know how it was going at the first possible opportunity.

Julie and I went back years. We first met whilst working together at a motorway service station. I was cleaning tables to fund my way through university while she was fuelling a rather innocuous gambling habit. After a few weeks sharing pleasantries, I found her outside the main entrance in sobs of tears. Between sobs, I ascertained that she had been sacked for stealing from the till and with some gentle prodding, she opened up further. We hugged and cried together, cementing a friendship that would stand the test of time. "Oh, how lovely," I hear you whisper. "Why aren't you guys together?" Well, we probably would have been if it wasn't for a six foot five, cage fighting lunatic called Rodney. They've got four kids together now so that ship has well and truly sailed. To be completely honest, we would have never worked out anyway. She has rather large hands and not wanting to go into too much detail, I prefer girls with smaller ones!

Anyway, I digress. Back to my faux pas. After arranging a suitable place to meet, I arrived at the pub near her work early and secured a table in the beer garden. I'd gambled on a bottle of rosé. Why not? It was a lovely summer evening and I felt that a drop of grape juice would make me seem classy and sophisticated!

Julie had described her to me. "I've been told that she's an Amazonian beauty!" What she clearly hadn't been told, or omitted to tell me, was that she had the biggest set of ears I've ever seen on a human! A slight wiggle of them and she would have vertically taken-off.

It wasn't the poor marketing that got my goat but the fact that I'd given up a curry night with the lads to be there. After ten minutes of polite chat, she went to powder her nose. I took the opportunity to send that text. "You are a numpty! You've stitched me right up. You know I don't like Toby Jugs! I'm going to get you back for this! X"

Whoops, I'd only gone and sent it to my date! I knew that the error of my mobile mastery would not go unpunished. As she was still inside the pub, I weighed up my options. My choices were simple, endure the beating like a man or take the easy way out. Without warning, I got up and ran into the nearest underground station. When I resurfaced, the pings on my mobile signalled my fate. After a bumbled apology, in no uncertain terms, I was informed that I should have more respect for women and was an obnoxious loser. She was right and a valuable lesson had been learnt.

After the dust had settled on last week's debacle, it was time to move on. Today was a new day and I was full of optimism. I poured another glass as the doorbell rang. The girl behind the door was called Sarah, she was my flatmate Martin's work colleague. Her final work meeting of the day was perhaps well organised. A research firm a stone's throw away from my flat. Who was I to complain? One final look in the hallway mirror and I was ready. I was nervous but quietly excited and on opening the door, this time, my shallow being was not disappointed. Her slender frame supported a beautiful mop of curly blonde hair. Her bright blue eyes radiated her animated soul and her friendly smile burst through her fragrant smell.

"Alright chuck!" She said, announcing her arrival! Oh, excellent, a northern lass with a glint in her eye. I knew we would get on and instantly relaxed. She'd clearly arrived straight from work in a very glam pin striped suit. "Ok if I get changed before we go out? I just need five minutes to put my face on."

About an hour later, we headed into town. The suburb of Ealing could not be described as a cool and trendy part of London, but there were three half decent bars that served prosecco and a couple of swanky restaurants, plenty enough to warrant a decent first date. The ten-minute stroll into town was spent talking about her stressful day at work.

Six back to back meetings, two of which were meetings to discuss upcoming meetings!

"After the day I've had, I really need a stiff drink," she exclaimed. As if on cue, we darted into the first pub available, the town's obligatory Irish bar.

So, it turned out that she was a girl from the Yorkshire Dales, had two brothers, grew up on a cattle farm, had fostered numerous pets through her childhood, been through three long term relationships, travelled to four different continents and owned an electric scooter.

It took three rounds before she asked, "so tell me about yourself. Why do they call you Bobby when your name's Simon? It makes no sense to me." The direct question and change of focus caused me to spill a little beer down my shirt as I stuttered into life. "I err, grew up in a small err town outside of err Manchester, everyone had a nick name at school back then. Mine was Bobby Brewster the Paxo Rooster. Apparently, I ran like the bird on an old TV commercial for gravy granules at the age of ten and it stuck! It was a primary school friend's father who gave me the tag. It spread like wildfire and the rest is history. I'm sure he's unaware of the damage he caused. I tried to shake it off a few times but I'm used to it now."

I gave her my well-rehearsed backstory. One that was short, sharp, tried and tested, I'd stumbled into a banking job in "The City" ten years ago, promising myself that I'd return back 'up north' on 1st Jan each year. I guess that secretly I enjoyed living in the nation's capital. I knew this, as when I went home to visit family, I'd get restless within twenty-four hours. I certainly wasn't built for the City but then again, who is? London had enticed me with its riches, stroked me with its passion for life, fed me with its opportunity and tamed me with its unfathomable depth of cultural beauty.

"So, what makes you tick?" She asked. I should have given her chapter and verse on how I loved extreme sports, adrenalin fuelled crazy stuff but found myself uncomfortably slipping into complete honesty.

"I'm a bit of a nerd really. I enjoy watching and playing football like most lads but my real passion is losing myself in films. I'm a massive film buff. Last year, I rewatched the top one hundred rated movies on the IMDB review website, in reverse order! I'll understand if you'd like to leave now." I said laughing, but soon stopped as she stood up and walked away. After she came back from the bar with two sambucas and a cheeky grin, I sensed that the date was going well. Especially after she said that I looked like a taller version of Tom Cruise. To which I replied, "yeah, if he grew a beard and put on a couple of pounds." It wasn't long before we got into the "so why are you still single" chat to which I gave the standard, "I guess I haven't been lucky enough to meet the right girl" answer. I was a little surprised when she said with a glint in her eye, "you'd better crack on as you ain't no spring rooster, Mr Brewster!"

We grabbed a bag of chips and curry sauce on the walk home. She didn't let me have many as I'd made a big deal of her 'selling out' by not ordering gravy. When I opened my front door the lights were off, Martin was clearly either out partying or in bed. Sarah, asked whether it was ok to crash round as it was getting late. "Of course!" I replied slightly too enthusiastically. It was Friday after all, and I was hoping for a positive result.

"Do you want some water?" I asked as she entered my boudoir.

Now, one of my all-time favourite old films is An Affair to Remember. At that precise moment, I could hear Deborah Kerr offering up one of her classic lines. "I'm not prudish or anything but my mother warned me not to enter a man's room first in any month ending in R!"

"Fuck that, where's my dress?" She shrieked!

"Eh, what are you talking about?" I called out from the kitchen.

"I left it on your desk chair." The delicate tone in Sarah's voice was no more.

"Wait, are you sure? Let me check around the place for you." The flat was Victorian, full of charm and I loved it but it was not much bigger than a tennis court. Within thirty seconds, the communal spaces had been checked thoroughly and the garments in question were nowhere to be seen. With only one more room left, I knocked on my flatmate Martin's bedroom door to see if he knew anything about the mysterious disappearance.

"Come in!" It was Martin's girlfriend Poppy. She'd heard the commotion, knew what the drama was about and so pulled back her duvet to reveal a sight that I was not expecting! Martin was lying comatose, wearing the skirt and jacket. The ensemble seemed to fit pretty well but to be fair to Sarah, he was training for a marathon.

"I'm so sorry." He's blind drunk and must have been sleep walking again" she confessed on his behalf.

At that moment, Sarah burst into the room and discovered exactly what had happened to her outfit. "OMG! What the hell? Is this some sort of weird joke? This can't be happening to me!"

"I'll sort it in the morning?" I said hopefully, as I gestured her to my bedroom.

After a little smooth talking and reassurance that Martin meant no harm, she took off her jeans and jumped on the bed. "Shit, the bed's wet!" She shouted.

Poppy was up now and was listening to the commotion from the kitchen. "Oh dear, I am sorry, Martin does have a habit of peeing when he sleep walks." She said almost unashamedly.

I took a deep gulp and expected the worst but couldn't believe my luck when Sarah said, "we need to turn the mattress over. You get one end and I'll get the other. One, two…" Three naughty paperback magazines which were hidden under the bedding slid across the room.

"You have got to be kidding me. That's it! I've had enough! Get me a taxi!" I tried to defend myself and claimed that the dubious picture books were Martin's, but she wasn't having any of it and I could hear her muttering something about camels, straws and dry cleaning.

Ten minutes later, the front door slammed and that was that. I slept on the sofa that night. I had no choice. The smell of Martin's indiscretion tainted the air with the same contempt as the disastrous end to the date. As I lay awake and thought of what might have been, I couldn't control my anger. "How could he do this to me!" Deep down, I knew that this wasn't Martin's fault. There was no malice behind his actions. He didn't have a bad bone in his body. No, I knew exactly why the evening had ended so badly. It was karma. It was my punishment for treating my last date so badly. God, I couldn't even remember her name. Who was I to judge another human being? How must I have made that poor girl feel? She didn't ask for elephant ears when she was ordered up on a silver plate in the maternity ward. I felt ashamed. Ashamed of the way I'd behaved and ashamed of the person I'd become. My father, who had passed away a decade ago, a man of many morals, had not brought me up to disrespect women. A promise to myself to be humbler and more genuine allowed the dark cloud of self-loathing to disperse as I drifted off.

Martin was mortified in the morning. He never usually made me breakfast and the bacon butty was little consolation but I couldn't really be too annoyed with him for too long. We'd only just hugged it out after I upset him last month.

When he started dating Poppy, I literally didn't see him for two months. He spent every night around at hers. When he announced that he was bringing her to the flat to meet me, I felt a childish prank in the offering. I printed off loads of half-naked pictures of men and scrawled on comments like, 'thanks for the memories, lots of love. Trevor' and 'miss you big boy, luv Jeremy' across them in black marker pen. I framed them all over his room and bought a rainbow flag to drape over his bed. Poppy creased up, but Martin didn't see the funny side. He door slammed seven bells out of the flat to make his feelings clear and then didn't return for another two weeks. After witnessing Poppy's big brown

eyes and perfect olive skin first hand, I understood his
infatuation but it was too late, the damage was done.

The next few days were fairly standard. I converted a
couple of good deals at work which inched our department
past its quarterly sales target. The business of trading
stocks and shares was fairly straight forward to me
although the current financial uncertainty had made things
a little more complex. The investment rule book might as
well be ripped to shreds when economic unpredictability
throws its shadow of darkness. Still, that being the case,
we'd made it through most of the fiscal year unscathed and
the traditional 'tools down' Friday lunchtime drinks
awaited.

I didn't mind working for Myles Goldstein Investments.
I'd been there a few years and had locked down a fairly
decent reputation. A couple of promotions had seen off
many of my competitive colleagues and kept me on the
straight and narrow. I'd made a few friends by pandering
to their inadequacies and a few enemies by stealing their
sales leads, but it was all part and parcel of a dynamic office
environment. As the years ticked off, I took less orders and
made less tea. If I'd been more ambitious, I'd have taken
the many calls from head-hunters but I wasn't. The job
suited me and I suited the job.

I was just logging off when my manager tapped me on
the shoulder with a startled look on his boat race. "There
are some cops waiting for you in reception Bobby.
Everything ok?" Before I could offer him any meaningful
reassurance, I was hit with some predictable office banter.

"Been flashing down by the canal again son?" A comment thrown by a member of the 'New Business' team along with a screwed-up paper ball.

"Oh look, he's already trying to get out of buying a round!" Shouted one of the HR team. Now that might have been a little unsympathetic in some office environments but not ours.

"Clear off and line me up with a pint of the black stuff, I'll be with you in ten!" I retorted. I wasn't sure what to expect and my mind was working overtime trying to unpick the reason for this unwelcome visit. There were two of them. One plain clothed female, who was short, had long brown hair tied in a ponytail and the darkest eyes I have ever seen. Alongside this fairly attractive middle aged lady was a portly uniformed chap, who looked quite senior and weather worn by years on the beat.

"Hi, I'm Simon Dingle. Can I help you?"

"Hello Simon, my name's Officer Mary Blackthorn and this is my colleague, PC Mick Dibley."

If I'm sincerely honest, I was half expecting someone to jump out with an old school ghetto blaster playing 'Vogue' by Madonna while Mary threw herself into a provocative dance but alas, it wasn't my birthday and certainly not my stag do.

"We'd like you to accompany us to the police station, we've got some questions to ask, concerning the disappearance of Sarah Ann McKay."

"Excuse me! I don't know anyone of that name," I answered nervously.

The reply was a little sharper and had more authority. "We believe that you know exactly who this person is and may be able to help in our enquiries!"

I sheepishly followed them out of the building, the six floors of undiluted silence were awkward but gave me the opportunity to work through who they were talking about. By the time I was sat in the back seat of their patrol car, I'd fathomed the subject matter.

The drive to the station gave me the time I needed to fully recall the evening in question. Some of which I'd tried to bury but certainly not in the way they suspected. Slumped on an uncomfortable chair in the interview room, I gave my account of the events of our date.

"We met, had some drinks in town, got on fairly well, walked back to mine, decided that there was no chemistry and she left in a taxi." I didn't mention that my flatmate had humiliated me and caused her great distress. The officers asked me how I felt about being rejected and that it must have made me feel anger towards her.

"You didn't like being spurned, did you Simon?"

"Please do call me Bobby, everyone else does. Listen, you know how it goes, you win some and you lose some. Are you implying that I had something to do with her disappearance? What exactly is going on here? Do I need a brief?"

"No, we are just ascertaining Sarah's movements at this stage. You are free to go but we will be in touch!"

It was over before my anxiety really got the better of me. Why did they need to bring me in? Was I a suspect? Why were they firing a warning shot across my bow? Oh, and what the bloody hell had happened to Sarah? She might have been a forgetful dating statistic to me but I liked her and cared for her welfare.

As I was leaving, I called Martin and asked him to meet me in 'the local.' I told him that I'd had a 'mother' of a day and was in need of some light liquid refreshment to clear my head. Martin was always late. I was two pints in by the time he arrived with his girlfriend. Why did he have to bring Poppy? I really needed a friend's shoulder to lean on without it being taken by someone less destitute.

I relived my horrific 'brush with the law' experience and asked him what people were saying in his office about Sarah.

"Oh mate, I should have told you. It's nuts. She's been missing for a few days. No one seems to have heard or seen from her. Family, friends, neighbours, nobody. Her bank cards and mobile haven't been used. The whole thing is very distressing. Some of the chaps think it might be suicide. If you ask me, I think she's just gone on some kind of wild bender. I've heard that she's got form. She's always been a bit of a loose cannon."

"You know that I had nothing to do with it, don't you?" I said over enthusiastically.

"Of course, mate, I'm sure she'll turn up. Don't worry, she's not your problem."

I was a little taken aback by Martin's unsympathetic nature, but I was sure that he was just trying to make light of the situation. He was always a bit clumsy with his words in sensitive situations. When he nipped outside for a smoke, I asked Poppy what she thought about the drama. I liked Poppy and felt that Martin had hit the jackpot with this one. He was definitely punching. She had long brown hair and the eyes of a siren. She dressed like a rock chick but had the sophistication of somebody who organised and hosted fancy dinner parties. You always feel a little guilty when you fancy your mate's girlfriend but the beers were kicking in and her figure was looking amazing in her glittering tight top. She sighed and simply said that the whole matter was just terrible. She then randomly flipped the conversation.

"Can I ask you something in confidence?" After my confirmation, she randomly asked whether I thought Martin had been seeing someone else.

A little taken aback by the abrupt nature of the change in direction, I leaned forward and looked directly into her dispirited eyes. "You must be kidding! He's wrapped in you. You're all he talks about. Anyway, he'd be an idiot if he was. You are beautiful!" For some instantly regrettable reason, I threw her one of my cheeky grins. A grin that many a fine female had experienced before. "Why do you ask?"

"He keeps cancelling on me and going out with mates instead. It's so out of character. He never used to be like that. Oh, ignore me, I'm just being paranoid! But, you would tell me if he was, wouldn't you Bobby?"

"You have my word. Now come on, it's me who needs cheering up!"

When Martin returned, they made their excuses and left. Their reasons still hovering over me like a dark cloud. They'd booked a newly opened Mexican restaurant a while ago and didn't want to miss out. I wouldn't have joined them but an invite wouldn't have gone amiss. I knew that I should have called Julie instead, but it was too late now. In all fairness to Julie, she might have had her problems in the past, but she was definitely a good listener. I had used her services before and at times you'd be convinced that your mumblings would go in one ear and flush out through the other side, still tainted with worry. Then, at the end of your rant, she'd offer a diatribe of useful, heartfelt advice that would put your worst fears at ease. I picked up my mobile to call her but as it lit up, the displayed time, forced it back on the table. "I might wake one of the kids up." I stayed for another drink alone and pondered over what could have potentially happened to poor Sarah.

I didn't leave the flat the whole weekend. I guess that I thought it would be inappropriate to go out and enjoy myself when someone was either lying dead in the proverbial gutter or being locked up against her will. Surely the cops didn't think I was involved. After speaking to my mother, I felt 'a large bag of potatoes' better off. She reassured me that the boys and girls in blue were simply questioning anyone who had met her recently and were just doing their jobs.

Feeling a little more reassured after the spoonful of my dear mother's verbal medicine, I rummaged through my admin drawer and pulled out a list of side-lined DIY jobs that I had written some months ago. I'd been putting off the catalogue of home improvements for far too long but now, feeling relieved that I had something to focus my mind on, I began polyfilling holes made by wayward darts, hammering in nails meant for dusty forgotten canvasses and turning screws on wobbly wardrobe doors. Lightbulbs were changed and squeaky doors were silenced. I even brushed off a large cobweb that had been developing in a corner of the lounge and been, quite literally, bugging me for the last few weeks.

Hiding away and busying myself was all very well, but word of my police visit was getting around which forced me into fielding off a few calls from nosy colleagues and concerned friends. They all knew that I wasn't capable of pulling a leg off a spider, let alone ending someone's life. Of course, nobody thought that I was involved in the vanishing act of a young lady but that didn't stop the 'fear' of walking into the office on Monday morning.

"Alright Bobby Bundy, who's next on your list?"

"What's that in your bag, a dead body?"

"Have you sent the ransom note yet?"

"Watch out girls, Bobby the Ripper's on the loose!"

After a morning with my head down, things got back to normal, but I was relieved when the closing bell rang.

"Say hello to Sarah from me."

The guys just wouldn't let it lie, forcing me to close my ears to the barrage of banter until the lift doors closed.

That night, while I was preparing my 'go to' school night meal, chicken drummers, oven chips and baked beans, I overheard Martin on his mobile in the hallway. "I can't see you on Wednesday honey, I've got football practice. I don't want to let the boy's down. I'll make it up to you sweetheart, don't you worry."

With an accentuated frown, my thoughts turned to my awkward conversation with Poppy. Surely not! Was she right? Martin didn't even play football and certainly not for an organised team." I'd had a kick about with him before and I can assure you that there isn't a team in the civilised world that would accept him. And, if there was, he certainly wouldn't be letting them down by not turning up. This particular sportsman hadn't got two left feet, he'd got a couple of slippery eels attached to his legs!

After his call, he wandered into the kitchen with the sole purpose of scrounging some of my fine feed. After unsuccessfully fending him off, I thought it time to interrogate and explore my suspicions. If Martin was lying to his girlfriend, he'd be sure to tell me his motives. We had no secrets. Why would we? There were no locks on our bedroom doors.

"Oi fella, never mind pinching my food, tell me why you are feeding Poppy a load of porkpies? The only football you'll be playing is on that damn PlayStation of yours!"

"Eh? Oh! You heard me? Well err, there's Champions League football on mate. We are playing Barcelona."

To be fair, Martin had clearly played a blinder! He was a self-proclaimed Arsenal glory hunter who only watched high profile football games, so the sporting calendar management error had been justifiably corrected. "Oh yeah, great shout fella. Let's hope 'The Arsenal' have their underpants pulled down and get a good old-fashioned hiding, eh?"

The next day at work, I took the call that I'd been waiting for. It was the one and only Officer Blackthorn. A woman who had gone from being a complete stranger to giving me nightmares. "Thank the Lord!" They wouldn't need to see me again. Mary went on to claim that they had some 'strong leads of enquiry' and I was no longer on that particular list. I wished them well but felt a sadness that Sarah was still missing. I'm not religious but when I went for my three pm proverbial in trap two, I said a little prayer for her. Feeling a little lighter, perhaps due to the heavy burden being lifted, I paraded around the office, updating anyone who would listen and thus confiscating them of their poison arrows. Strangely, nobody seemed that interested, some were actually disappointed. Understandably so, what soldier would go into battle without any ammunition. Surely it was over. A terrible experience but one that would not scar me for life. Surely Sarah would resurface and when she did, I promised myself to give her a call and ask for a second date.

Wednesday couldn't come by fast enough. As a Spurs fan, I hoped that 'The Gunners' would take the Barca beating they deserved. I bought a four pack on the way home and secretly looked forward to the game. I wouldn't admit this to anyone but I did enjoy watching Arsenal's brand of exciting football.

I walked into our flat while belting out…. "Barcelona, it was the first time that we met. Barcelona. How can I forget."

Martin was in the kitchen. "Change of plan pal, I've got to take some shopping over to my dad's house. He's had a fall. It ain't great. He's broken an ankle and is completely bed bound." He spoke with emotion while squeezing two full carrier bags of food into his gym holdall.

"Oh mate. Sorry to hear that. Here, take these beers from me." With such a sensitive subject, I didn't want to say anything but I'd known Martin for over eight years and knew that he wasn't very close to his father. Hazy drunken conversations sprang to mind. I'm sure he'd ditched the family for his bosses wife who was twenty years his junior. Lost his job on the back of this. The relationship didn't last long as she went back to her husband and he turned to the bottle. But the damage was done and he was basically expelled from the family.

Something just didn't add up and recalling Poppy's concerns, I mentally questioned his reasoning. Has he really reconnected with his father after so much water had travelled under the creaking family bridge? Or, had he really got two girls on the go? I considered his intentions, as I slipped my Apple watch into the side pocket of his bag. After wishing him a fond farewell as he rushed out of the flat, I sat down and loaded my tracking app.

It wasn't the first time I'd used this low budget surveillance method. Whilst living at my family home after Uni, I treated myself to a fancy leather jacket using the proceeds of my not so hard earnt dole money. After taking it on a few casual weekend outings, I noticed that the damn thing stunk of weed. I knew the cause of this stench belonged to my younger brother but he denied this vehemently. He had a long history of procuring my fine wears. Not wanting to be used and abused, I snuck my Apple watch into one of the pointless zip sleeve pockets and the following night, traced it to my brother's mate Duggo's pad. Boom! Caught red handed. On his return, he found me waiting on the front wall outside our house.

"Alright bruv?" The boy was so stoned that he forgot he was wearing it and threw his hand up for a high five. Not only did I deny him but I served him up like a common bitch for the week by threatening to report him to the folks for blowing on the illegal bagpipes. Tea, laundry and a tidy room. Too easy.

Martin was on the move and heading out of town along the A40. There was no point tailing him tonight. He worked for a market research company and was on the road a lot. The buggers had given him a fairly rapid BMW which he liked to throw around. I decided to let him get to where he was going, the dirty dog, and then quiz him on his whereabouts when he returned. Hopefully he'd be back before the end of the second half. Three nil to Barca with only twenty minutes gone. Surely, I wouldn't have to miss out on some serious gooner baiting.

I had always been a light sleeper, so when the front door slammed shut around midnight, I sat bolt upright.

"Martin? Everything ok?"

"Yo, all good cheers buddy."

"Six nil at home. My granddad's old peoples home's mixed fourth team would give you lard arses a good game!" How was your night? Dad ok? Where's he living these days?"

"Fuck about! I'm not worried, we'll turn it around at the Neu Camp ha-ha. Don't worry about my pops. He lives with a couple of his pals in St Albans. He's fine, just a little sore. Well, good night, catch you in the morning."

I was never in the boys brigade and if you threw me in the middle of a jungle I'd still be there now but I did know that you would not drive along the A40 to get to St Albans!

"Ok Martin, see you in the morning."

Animal Pig Farm

I only had one job to do the following morning. The new starter induction session would only take a couple of hours. I took a deep intake of air and puffed out my chest as I walked into the boardroom. As a senior member of staff, I took my training responsibilities seriously. After some intricate company and market analysis, I took the nerdy looking graduate through the basics of making a shit load of moola for the company, or at least, how to give them the perception that it was in the pipeline. I was surprised, the fellow's arrogance and cockiness ruffled my managerial feathers but it did. He was clearly only interested in which company perks would float his boat and when his salary would be reviewed, which pushed me down the cliched abyss of self-indulgence. Having taken as much as I could handle, I gave him the false impression that if he wasn't driving a Ferrari within five years, I'd be eating my bowler hat. Nothing wrong with having a little fun at the jumped-up megalomaniacs expense, particularly one who wouldn't even pass his probation. Fortunately, he spilt his coffee on his badly ironed white shirt which allowed for a natural end to the meeting and his audacious behaviour.

I couldn't be bothered to go to the gym or have a bevvy at lunchtime. My mind just wasn't in the right place to be sociable and I wasn't in the mood to wiggle my beef jerky in the mirror. Maybe that was just an excuse and I was still feeling a little sore after my emotional heart strings had been pulled. The whole 'Sarah episode' was still playing on my mind. I knew that there was no point placing a plaster over my open wound. It was a terribly sad misadventure but it was one that didn't concern me. Nevertheless, the freedom of my lunchbreak now gave me the opportunity to continue the investigation into my flatmate's potential deception and indiscretions. With nobody in the office, I logged onto my 'app' and analysed the information that it presented. The tracker gave his destination as Horsleys Green, a hamlet located off the A40 between Piddington and Stokenchurch in Buckinghamshire, about a forty-five minute drive from London. I could have worked through the magnificence of modern technology in my mind but all I could think of, was what would any posh totty see in a lad from Grimsby!?

It took a couple of nights of asking before Martin said that he was visiting his sick father again. I didn't have any plans that evening. The fact is, if I'm honest, I didn't have any plans until Christmas. Tonight, would be filled with getting to the bottom of Martin's misdemeanours and having a relaxing drive to the countryside. I couldn't help but be excited to visit a place where drivers didn't stick their fingers up at you for having the wrong model of car. Or beeping at you for allowing an old lady to cross the road. How refreshing it would be to drive through a town that wouldn't turn you invisible simply because you wanted to join a roundabout or God help you, turn right at the damn thing!

My Apple watch was still hidden in Martin's bag which he again crammed with groceries. Whoever he was seeing, certainly wasn't being treated. The bags were filled with unbranded packets with reduced price tags. I felt an excitement that I hadn't experienced in a long time. This was going to be too easy. Was the sixty-mile roundtrip akin to the one hundred and fifty foot bungee jump I'd done last summer, probably not, but the adrenaline rush and apprehension was certainly similar. Three, two, one and let's jump off into the unknown.

I only got to drive my new Evoque once a week. Generally, that involved popping down to the local supermarket situated at the top of my road. Owning a Range Rover had always been a dream of mine. It was second hand and had a couple of minor dents, but it made me feel like I was someone special. I think it's because lots of British gangsters drive them in tough guy films. Before you ask, yes, I am that stereotypical male who ranks The Godfather as his number one watch.

Martin had already set off by and the time I left the flat, I was buzzing. This was an adventure not to be underestimated. I'd even prepared a couple of ham and cheese sandwiches and a flask filled with sweetened tea. Surely a stakeout feast would keep me satisfied if I had to wait outside the fancy woman's house in order to obtain the photographic evidence Poppy required. One made the assumption that a disgruntled scorned girlfriend would probably require proof of any extracurricular indiscretions. "If she's not prettier than Poppy then I'm going to drive off Buckinghamshire's equivalent of Beachy Head," I thought to myself as I set off on the tail of my friend, Martin Juan, the unlikely Casanova of the North. "As it's a land locked county with limited suicide potential, a small stream next to a thatched cottage might be the only option," I chuckled to myself.

My tracker highlighted the fact that Martin was in a hurry. This unsurprising information didn't perturb me. Through personal experience, I knew that a man driving to the beat of his own gear stick would always break speed limits. Without the same motivation, I felt the need to take my time and enjoy the ride out. It was always a pleasure to exit the madness of the city. A couple of sheep and the frivolous beauty of a galloping horse rolled the green carpet out for my arrival into the countryside.

I was about an hour behind Martin, enough time for him to sharpen his pencil, burn his sexual calories and complete his deed of decadence. Probably twice knowing him. I wasn't an expert on his love life but certainly had a degree of insight. The walls in our flat did not give the Victorian build justice. Martin once brought a heavily pregnant girl back. As his story goes, she'd had an argument with her husband, stormed off in a rage, met Martin in our local and ended up at our place. The two of them gorged on dirty kebabs and then slyly slipped into the bedroom. Obviously, I turned the TV volume down while clearing up the mess they'd left before it stunk out the place. The headboard's knocking rhythm suggested that Martin was on form, but it didn't last long. The short silence was broken by the expectant girl's voice.

"Talk dirty to me big boy."

After a moment of unhealthy anticipation, Martin resurfaced. "I've never tried that. What would you like me to say?" Almost pleading, I could hear her suggesting that he use his imagination. I doubled up in silent hysterics on hearing Martin's response. "Fuck off you fat bitch and bend over like a dog!" There are somethings that you can never unhear and some images that you want to erase. I quickly grabbed the remote, but it was too late.

"Excuse me? What did you just say? You do realise I'm pregnant? Err, no, I don't think so! Just get off me! You've ruined it now!"

I meandered into the village and spotted Martin's pristine company car at the side of a quiet country lane next to the entrance of what looked like a disused ramblers pathway. Bags of scattered rubbish and abandoned white goods lined the hedgerows with rose bushes, wild and unkept. The place looked lost in time; an epicentre of a once idyllic masterpiece of English heritage. I bore witness to a handful of once loved old farm houses, window boards hiding their former glory.

I'd parked up in a layby, about fifty metres further up from Martin's car and took stock of the situation. I questioned my whereabouts. "Surely nobody lives around here anymore?" My tracker pinpointed a location about a quarter of a mile away. It appeared to suggest that Martin was in an adjacent farm field.

I have to say, George Orwell's Animal Farm is a far better book than it is film but the 1999 adaptation featuring the voices of Kelsey Grammar, Patrick Stewart and Peter Ustinov is one of my go to hangover movies. One classic line entered my head as I sat and contemplated my next move. "Man serves the interests of no other creature but himself."

"Martin you filthy boy. How could you? And a bit of the outdoor action to boot, wow just wow!"

Not wanting to catch him with his old todger on display, I reached for my lunchbox from the back seat but as I blindly searched, my curiosity got the better of me and I decided to make my move. I had planned on taking a quick photo of the two of them together, preferably with their clothes on before getting the hell outta dodge, then blackmailing him into shouting me a curry from the local Indian. After all, it would be madness to not cash in on his infidelity. There was no doubting that Martin's best life lessons were executed by lightening the load of his underused wallet.

The sun was beginning to set so I knew that I had to be on my toes. As I ploughed forward and on closer inspection, I could tell that I wasn't standing on agricultural land, more of a woodland area. I crept through the undergrowth, trying not to make any sound, but just like in the movies the constant cracking of twigs and the rustling of leaves seemed to be magnified. As I weaved through the thicket, I could sense movement in the distance, between a couple of threadbare trees. I took out my phone. Full camera zoom at the ready when I froze at what sounded like a rather large animal bounding towards me. I felt nervous, slightly intimidated, the thought of a wild boar gnawing at my leg didn't seem too appealing. Not wanting to take any chances, I knew that I had to climb to safety. Looking around for potential options with sheer panic running down my spine, I decided that the silver birch right next to me would have to do. I gripped hold of its flaking bark with my hands as I looked to get some footing on a low-level knot. The magnifying sound of the beast was getting closer. Its gathering momentum grew louder. This wasn't going to work. I couldn't get any footing. If only I'd worn my trainers! I needed to run but where? I turned one way and then another but it was too late, I could feel the cold shadow of the beast upon me.

"What the hell!" My head was pounding so severely and the left side of my body ached. Now, I've never been ten rounds with Rocky Balboa, I've never even experienced one round with any boxer, real or fictional. In fact, I've only ever had one fight in my life. I remember it like it was yesterday, I was thirteen and attending secondary school at the time. Griffo, who was a well-established bully in the year above was throwing some rather salubrious racist language in my direction. Having a Mediterranean background, I had a little colour to my skin and up until this point, I had always been proud of my father's ancestry but I was a bit of a geeky swot back then and felt the heavy weight of the bigoted insults. Word was getting around the school that I was a soft touch. The taunts continued for a few weeks until I'd had enough. There were only three non-whites at our school. A Cambodian lad whose parents escaped from the tyrannous Khmer Rouge back in the seventies, a Chinese boy whose family ran the local chippy and me, a slightly overweight half Italian kid who always tried to keep out of the limelight. As the other two were younger than myself, I knew that I had to stand-up for our constitutional rights. Across this arduous and tortuous period, I saw Griffo every morning before assembly. The insults kept coming and the crowds kept laughing. I knew that I had to act now or forever be the victim. As our registration classes were next to each other, I selected the morning of battle, swallowed five spoons of sugar before leaving the sanctuary of home and was silent in the car en route to my destiny. My thoughts were gathered and as I marched to our porta cabin classroom, I was ready. Sure enough, Griffo was there, waiting.

"Ooh, Ooh monkey boy, give us a bite of your banana!" The shock in his eyes, as I swung that first punch was priceless. I proceeded to kick the living daylights out of him. He ran, I followed, he pleaded with me to stop, I continued. He cried. I'd won.

There were lots of witnesses that morning and the story quickly spread. I became a hero and Griffo became my bitch. It was my David and Goliath moment. A vital life lesson, a time to treasure and be proud of my stance. But where was I? Why had this memory entered my mind?

I certainly had some sense of how Griffo felt after I'd finished pounding his face and body with brute herculean force. Struggling to focus my eyes and in my state of discombobulation, I felt a soothing wetness on my facial wounds. Was it the wild boar? Had I stumbled and knocked myself unconscious? I must have been lying here for hours as darkness smothered my predicament. A rambler must have found me and I was now recovering in hospital with a nurse mopping my brow with a sterilised warm cloth. I could hear the tickle of voices. Were my friends and family surrounding my bed regurgitating stories of my amazing and successful existence? I was a great son, brother and friend. Never forgetting any birthdays or anniversaries, my last pennies would always be spent on presents. They must have gathered, praying for my survival and fretting that life wouldn't be as enriched without me in it!

"You fucking dick!"

"Eh! What?" That wasn't the sound of a loving family member and our national health service has got one the best patient care records in the world! So, surely a nurse or doctor would have more apathy than this! "Who said that?" I screamed.

Cool Hand Bobby

As my eyes started to regain their purpose and the dust began to settle, I realised that I wasn't on a warm hospital bed recuperating from the madness of my misadventures and the feeling on my face wasn't a warm damp surgical cloth. I was actually laid bare on a hard-stone floor and being licked by a mangy dog, but where was I? It was the stench that caught my attention first. So familiar, but not in a positive way. It didn't take my senses long to recognise it, tinned tuna and it was being warmed up in a pan. This revolting aroma meant only one thing, Martin was in the kitchen cooking up his favourite meal. So, was I back at the flat and why had he brought a dog with him?

Stirring as my mind continued to focus, I mustered the strength to gain some clarity. "Martin, what happened? How did we get home?" His response was as cold as the floor against my face. "You absolute knob! Why did you have to follow me?" Maybe Martin was right but the meandering path of human boredom often takes us places that we shouldn't go. In an attempt to further familiarise myself and grasp my uncomfortable situation, I found myself easing through the pain and sitting upright. My eyes started to adjust to the dim flickering haze of candle light. The realisation hit me hard. Surely my imagination was running away with itself. The blow to my head had cast a spell of treacherous mind-bending chicanery.

I could make out an eclectic mix of shadowy figures. Their eyes staring at me, their faces full of fear. They were statuesque, almost frozen in time. Between them were bars, lots of them. I felt anxious and confused as my mind played even more abominable tricks on me. Martin slid a plastic bowl of his tuna pasta underneath the bars of my cell. Yes, a cell! I was in a bloody cell, a prison cell!

"Eat that Bobby. You won't be getting anything else for a couple of days."

None of this was making any sense. I wanted to shout out but didn't know what. Was this some sort of demented joke? Was I trapped in some sort of horrendously distressing nightmare? Had I walked through the burning gates of hell? Had 'Orwell's pig' taken its revenge for the countless bacon butties, devoured across numerous hungover Sunday mornings? Was I in a bottomless pit? Surely not, surely it was my imagination in overdrive. Apart from upsetting life's applecart now and then, I certainly didn't deserve to be in purgatory.

"Martin, what the fuck is going on!?" I called out blindly.

My desperation was clear for all to see but alas there was no sympathetic response. "I'll be back in two days!" Martin stormed to the end of the bastille, climbed a ladder and was gone.

My eyes started adjusting to the dim light, bringing the staring strangers faces properly into focus. Being the centre of attention was not uncommon but this didn't feel right. "Alright guys, nice one, you got me. Now can someone let me out of this shithole?"

"Shush, give it a couple of minutes. Wait until he's gone."

"You have got to be kidding me." It was Sarah. As I live and breathe, I could see her through the solid metal bars! She was there, sitting in the cell next to me. Her bright blue eyes noticeably duller and her big blonde mop slightly dishevelled, but it was her alright.

In the minutes of complete silence that followed, I surveyed my surroundings. The room was long and thin. Six cells in a line, all filled with a diverse mix of scared looking individuals. A corridor ran parallel in which there were a few candles that shone no light on my predicament. A small generator hummed in the corner which powered a couple of electric spotlights. A gas stove and heater stood either side of a large red gas canister. The walls appeared to be brick and various shelving units adorned their sinister glare. Upon these, were tin solders of various edible items. Tinned beans, tinned tomatoes, tinned carrots, you name it, it was tinned! Inside each cell, there was a bucket, a water tap and a mattress. Although it was warm, there was a damp metallic taste in the air which cut through the smell of the tuna. With my senses sharpening, I stood up but it was all too much. "Now is someone going to tell me what the fuck is going on!" I snapped.

"Oh Bobby, it's been awful. We're in an old-World War II underground bunker, God knows where. He's been holding us all captive. I've been in here for a few days but some of the guys have been here for weeks!" Sarah started to cry which came across as genuine. Either she was destined to walk the wooden planks of the West End or there was more to this whole sorry saga than met the eye.

The harsh and unpleasant reality began to suffocate me with a tsunami of sadness. "Look, if this isn't some wild and wacky stunt then can someone tell me why the fuck Martin is doing this?" I could feel the red mist enveloping my anger.

Sarah continued, "I'm not going to sugar coat this. It's hard to get your head around, but the basic premise is that he feels that each one of us has wronged him in one way or another and this is his revenge."

With a growing sense of concern, I moved closer to the girl that had previously pushed me away. "I don't understand. How long is he going to keep us in this hell hole and what in the name of Jesus have YOU done to upset him?"

"You're not going to believe this, but I made the mistake of telling someone at work about the aftermath of our date Bobby. All the grim gory details. The cross dressing, the bed wetting, the disgusting magazines, the whole caboodle! The story spread-sheeted, like a Microsoft virus from the hard drives of the office gossips and Martin was put through the shredder. Lady boy became his new nickname. As you can see, he didn't react well." Sarah shrugged as she fought against a wry, unwarranted smile.

Martin had never mentioned this to me. He'd been at the same company for years and had swiftly moved through the ranks and established himself as the Company Director of Business Services. I understood that he was good at his job and well respected. It would have made sense that this kind of office tittle-tattle would have rocked his vocational world but surely a quiet word of explanation next to the photocopier would have sufficed.

She continued, almost trying to justify her defence to a grand jury. "I think he became a laughing stock. You know what guys are like, they were relentless. The little wanker blamed me, he thought I'd ruined his career, his standing in the company and turned him into the office joke."

Martin was part of a laddish friendship group who spent half their time together bantering and taking lumps out of each other. It was all good fun and no one took the ribbing too seriously. He probably took more than his fair share but I never thought he could be this sensitive. Who the hell did he think he was?

Boss Paul, one of the prison guards from the movie Cool Hand Luke? "Now I can be a nice guy, but if you trouble me, I can be a mean son of a bitch" God, that line from the film still sends a shiver down my spine. Well, he wasn't going to keep me in this box. That was for sure.

Maybe I gave the boy too much credit. If I really thought about his character, I might have come to the conclusion that he wasn't the happy go lucky, easy going friend that we knew and loved so dearly. Thinking back, he didn't take too kindly to the homosexual memorabilia that I'd placed in his room for Poppy's first visit. Also, he didn't speak to me for a week when I hid one of those shop security tags in the lining of his coat. You know the ones? The gizmos that shops place on goods, that beep if you leave without paying. This little prank kept us entertained for weeks but started to get a little taxing as we had to wait for Martin while he emptied his bags and cross checked his items each time we went shopping with him. When we gave the game away, he stormed off in a huff and told us we were immature. It didn't help when we followed this up by mocking together an official letter from our local supermarket, telling him that he was banned from the store due to being a suspected shop lifter. I could go on but I'm sure you get the idea. We never bullied him, just teased him, a lot!

I attempted to raise my right hand to tend to the cuts on my face. Not only were my wrists chained to a pully system that was locked to the cell ceiling, but I was also aghast when I realised that I was adorned with a metal waistcoat that was wrapped tightly around my chest, underneath my shirt. "What the bloody hell is this thing?" I screamed, pulling on the damn thing to indicate my frustration.

Sarah didn't pull any punches. "Mate, you won't be able to take that off! We've all tried. If you misbehave, then Martin presses a button and we all receive an electric shock that is so painful, it feels like you're being run over by a double decker bus and then pummelled by a sledgehammer."

Martin had turned into a monster! So, this was why my fellow inmates were so terrified to talk when he was in the room. "Are you actually having a laugh!" I must have shrieked my distain with far too high a pitch as the dog yelped, almost jumped out of his skin and bounded towards me.

In the Game of the Father

"So, who's this guy?" I said pointing to the creature hop skip and jumping in my direction.

A dejected murmur echoed from the other side of the room. "If you are referring to the border collie, she's mine. She's young and skinny, which allows her to slip through the bars of our cells."

I had little choice but to pat the affectionate dog on the head, "and may I ask what your name is sir? Another actor in this dull game of charades?"

Sarah jumped in, not literally of course as there were solid steel bars between us. "You need to understand that this is real Bobby. We are not part of any game. We are being held captive by your so-called friend Martin who is clearly deranged and we need you to get your shit together and help us get out of this mother fuckin hellhole!"

In answer to my question, a short, stocky chap from a few cells down, stood up and shouted, "my name's Doug and if you're wondering why I'm here then ask my bloody idiot of a son!"

Well, this was just getting more and more surreal. Martin's dad? The fellow who ruined his childhood? The chap who abandoned his beloved mother and sister to shack up with a cheap tart? So, he wasn't an urban myth, here he was, bold as brass standing right before me. "Oh, your ankle seems to have healed quickly!" I shouted.

"Eh?" He retorted.

"Oh, don't worry. Listen Doug, I live with Martin, he's talked candidly about his upbringing and I know that you two don't get on."

"Well that is the understatement of the century." Doug, who just looked like an older version of Martin with less hair, started to rant like a madman who had lost the keys to his tortured soul. "He's no son of mine, he's a wounded animal who should be put out of his misery!"

Once he'd calmed down a little, I asked him why he thought Martin had taken it upon himself to relinquish him of his freedom. Quite frankly, from what I already knew, combined with his aggressive vernacular, I was sure that the evidence was already there for all to see.

But Doug spoke with an open heart. He admitted that he'd let Martin down as a child and regretted his actions. "It all happened a long time ago! We've all made mistakes. I'm sure he's told you of my infidelities. Hey, I just went in search of happiness. I'm not the first and I won't be the last man to have his head turned. I did try to reconnect with the boy some years after realising the error of my ways but he slammed the paternal door in my face. I thought that his mother had turned him against me. I should have tried harder but well, sometimes it's just easier to move the fuck on! I hadn't seen him for many a year, until he drove past me in his fancy motor a couple of weeks back while I was taking this rapscallion for a walk." He whistled to his dog. "Come here Winston, here boy." The not so obedient canine had nestled his head on my lap and didn't move.

"He offered to take me for a drink, claiming that hatchets needed to be buried or something of the sort. I put Winnie in the back seat and clambered into the front of his car. Half a mile down the road, he pulled up and attacked me with a ruddy handkerchief. Chloroform or some shit. The next thing I know, I'm in this dump. When I get out of here, before they escort him to the electric chair, I'm going to give him a beating that he'll never forget. You know what really pisses me off, well I'll tell you lad. He doesn't know it but I funded him through college. Two bloody jobs I had. I tell thee. Two bloody jobs! What do I get in return? A bloody slap in the face and bowl of pasta once a day! Well I'm not having it."

"Well, there's the speech of a guilty man," I thought, half expecting him to recite that great line from the IRA film based on a true story, In the Name of the Father. "I'm a free man and I'm going out the front door." Daniel Day-Lewis won an Oscar for his powerful performance in that epic but I'm not sure that I'd offer Doug a wooden spoon for his efforts.

"Oh, shut up you old fool. If you hadn't messed the kid up, then none of this would be happening. It's all your fault. Why can't men keep it in their skinny jeans? Hi Bobby, I'm Susan and I've been in this rat-infested sewer for four days."

"Oh, here we go! It's all about you again Susan!" Doug retaliated.

It was starting to feel like an AA meeting with Martin being the poison running through everyone's veins. "Hi Susan." God, this was too much to take in. I'm not normally one for migraines but my head was starting to throb.

The atmosphere was tense, almost aggressive. You could hear the gentle howl of the wind over the din of the generator, its whisper offered no solace in our protest. Time management thrown out of the non-existent window and the dim haze of unnatural light cast no mercy on our fate. I gently walked around my confined space and noted that my aches hadn't subdued but my movement was restricted. The wrist and ankle shackles saw to that.

"If you need to use the loo, just shout and we'll all look away."

"I do Susan." I'd always found it difficult to urinate when standing next to well-endowed men at public conveniences but this experience was magnified and not in a good way! The bucket wasn't a bad size and once I'd got the ball rolling so to speak, the noise of my effort was so loud, it stopped me in my tracks. The wheels simply fell off and my bum cheeks rippled into life as they always did when straining the proverbial greens. It's part of the male ceremony, is it not? After a few seconds, I got going again and almost expected a round of applause when the job was complete.

"You get used to it," Sarah muttered noticing my distress. "Trust me, it gets a lot worse, if you know what I mean."

"I can imagine." I said as I poured the contents of my bucket into the drain that ran along the length at the rear of our cells. Holding on to the bars and facing my compatriots, I stretched out and felt an air of superiority. They all looked so broken and downcast. I was feeling relatively fresh and strong. These people deserved to feel the wrath of an unstable mind. Not me, I was here by accident. Surely Martin would realise this and release me if I swore my secret allegiance. I just had to survive until he returned.

I lay down on the mattress and closed my eyes. I knew that I wouldn't be able to sleep for a while but needed time to think. I cast a glance in the hope of inviting Winston but he'd gone and I didn't think it my place to call out for his warmth and the comforting beat of his heart. I could hear the muttering of cluttered voices but didn't feel part of the group. They were not my band of brothers. My mind reverted to Martin and I tried to fathom why he had become so evil. We had shared bread, laughed and joked at life's little foibles. I had his back but he had put a knife into mine. Why had he left the safe bounds of the law and become a vulgar and vicious vigilante. Had I been a part of his demise? Should I have been aware of his decline? Were there any missed signals, clues, or had I been too wrapped up in my own self-indulgence?

It was only six months ago, when Martin and I had treated ourselves to a cheap holiday in Tenerife. The Bamford twins had joined us. We'd hired some scooters on day one. Feeling fairly pleased with our new form of transport, we left the rental store and unwittingly headed the wrong way down a one-way street. After a few toots and finger wags by some local residents, we realised and began to turn around. Once we were facing the right way, three of us stopped to catch our bearings but not Martin.

"I can't control the damn thing!" he screamed as he scooted straight into a market stall, his feet trailing behind him, gripping on the dirt road as he clenched the brake while giving the accelerator more power. The incident happened in slow motion.

"Martin, what the fuck are you doing?" I shouted through uncontrollable laughter. The market stall shutter slammed down and closed him in. All you could hear was the clattering and shattering of naff pottery souvenirs over the shocked shrills of the shopkeeper. Martin handed over all of his spending money as compensation for the damage and we ripped into him for the rest of the trip.

The theme was clear, Martin had always been the butt of our jokes. His clumsiness and social awkwardness had always been a great source of entertainment to us and we loved him for that. He was our daft oaf and we would always be there for him. Had he realised this or had we been instrumental in his downfall? Were we his so-called friends and was he was too entangled in our lives to shake us off. Were we fuelling him with the hatred that he unleashed onto others?

The Indecent Disposal

I was awoken to the shouting and screaming of lunatics, escaping in the solace of my nightmare. Chains were crashing against the steel bars of the cells. A group of abandoned maniacs shouting for attention. The deafening shrill unsympathetically burdening the pain of my new-found imprisonment.

"Please help us! We are down here! Help, save us!" I bolted up from my mattress and joined the justified melee. Not questioning its seemingly outrageous display of determination. Half an hour passed and our voices began to soften, feeling weaker and weaker with every cry for freedom. "Ask and it will be given to you, seek and you will find it, knock and it will be opened to you." Our voices fizzled as our prayers went unanswered.

Once the energy levels were squeezed to insignificance, I was informed that this was the morning ritual with the hope that a passing dog walker might hear our screams. It made perfect sense. The sounds we made were desperate and our anger for Martin resonated with each gasp for breath. Even Winston barked ferociously. He was one of us, no longer a free spirit, but a barking mad symbol of our quest for justice.

As we settled down, my hunger directed my attention towards the bowl of slop that Martin had left me. Empty! I couldn't be angry with Winston, he was an animal and wasn't about to miss any opportunity to feed although the result of his misbehaviour was plain to smell. Martin had laid out some grass at one end of the bunker and Winston knew that it was for his benefit. I wasn't the only one to notice the freshly laid, off-putting stench.

"Fuck me, you dirty dog! Exclaimed Susan. "My husband's aren't even that bad after a jalfrezi and a dozen beers!"

"Leave him alone. He can't help it and let's face it, he doesn't complain about your damn snoring, does he!" Shouted Doug.

I knew that warming to Susan would be a challenge. It was clear that her outer shell would be tough to crack but as we were confined in, what the estate agents call a small but cosy space, I felt that I had to reach out to her. I took out my sympathetic harp and played her a tune. "So, Susan, you seem like such a genuine person. I really like that, you wear your heart on your sleeve. Why are you here? Please don't take this the wrong way but I've never heard Martin mention you before. No offence."

Still reeling from Doug's gentle criticism, Susan looked at me with distain, perhaps thinking that I was in some way belittling her credentials. Head bowed, her freckles darkened against her pale face as the fringe of her ginger bob hid her grimace. "Oh, nice of you to ask, but I'm not in the mood for small talk." Slightly shocked at her curt response, I looked away.

After a few seconds, she continued in her broad west country accent. "Oh, you know what, I'll tell you exactly who I am and how I know your despicable friend. I'd completely forgotten about the little shit before he rocked up at my flat the other day. Startled I was when I opened the door and saw his ugly mug. It took me a few minutes to register who the hell he even was! He claimed that we'd generated some cash from an investment that he'd made for us when we were dating. Hey, I'm a mother who's stood in line at my local food bank a couple of times. The mere mention of free cash had me hooked. I invited him in after he wittered on about some forms to sign to release it. 'Ten grand each,' he said. He sat at my kitchen table whilst I made him some tea. I even offered him my best cup and saucer, what a flaming liberty. After some polite 'how's your father' chat, he opened his briefcase. He didn't pull out any forms, just some rope, a bed sheet and a roll of duct tape. Before I could scream, he'd taped my gob shut and proceeded to tie me up. He waited until the early hours before he rolled me up in the sheet and carried me to his car. The bastard threw me into the boot and well, you know the rest."

Judging from the aggression in her tone, I was afraid to continue my line of questioning but I needed to know. "Why would he do such a thing?"

"I went to university with the flaming galah and I guess that I was his first big love. Being a bit of a loner back then, I felt that I was missing out on 'the best days of my life' so I decided to join the Student Beer Pong Society. A drinking club basically. It was mainly built up of rugby drinking buffoons. That's why I was drawn to Martin. He was pretty reserved and extremely polite, not like the other hooligans. Second night we went out, we copped off and ended up dating for a year or so. We spent all of our free time together. I wouldn't say that it was all drumrolls and fireworks but we were pretty tight."

"Cut to the chase girl, you're boring the poor lad!" I got the sense that Doug had taken a dislike to Susan.

"Alright, alright! Listen, I'm not proud of myself. The relationship ticked along, well below the speed limit and I guess I was just bored. University is supposed to be fun, right? Well, not for us, here we were, behaving like an old married couple. One Friday night, after playing a game of scrabble, yes you heard, scrabble! I told Martin that I wanted to explore my sexuality to the full and convinced him to agree to a threesome with his mate Jack. Who, by the way, I fancied the pants off. After a bit of cunning convincing, the fool agreed. Well, Jack was all that I hoped he would be. I ended up binning Martin and started dating him. Well, you can imagine Martin's reaction. After a barrage of insults every time we bumped into each other, he started stalking me. Jack beat him up a couple of times but that didn't stop him. I had to get a restraining order in the end. The Uni took a dim view of his behaviour and Martin was asked to leave his course. Listen, I knew that I'd hurt the guy but I am still with Jack. It wasn't just a mad fling, we're blissfully married and have a kid together! My relationship with Martin was borne out of boredom and loneliness. We should never have been together in the first place. I'll be quite frank, I found him as dull as ditch water. I really can't understand why he was so hung up on me. You know, someone once said, if you want something very badly, set it free. If it comes back to you, it's yours forever. If it doesn't, it was never yours to begin with."

"Didn't Demi Moore say that in Indecent Proposal?" I interrupted.

"Funny you should say that, a lot of people say I look like Demi Moore!" It was the first time I'd seen Susan crack a smile.

"More like Dudley Moore!" Doug certainly was not impressed, maybe his paternal instincts were kicking in. He had good reason to feel repulsed by someone who had not only broken his son's heart but changed the course of his life forever. His act of betrayal might have been a dig to Martin's ribs but Susan had taken a pickaxe to his face.

"Bloody hell, fair play Bobby, I remember you claiming to be a film buff on our date!" Sarah added with a gentle round of applause.

The mood in the camp turned disappointingly silent once again as I reflected on what I'd just heard. I'd spoken to three inmates. One had ruined the innocence of his childhood, one had stamped on his heart for no other reason but sexual gratification and the third had disgraced him in front of a crowd he had worked so hard to gain respect from. In a bizarre but fading loyalty towards him, I found myself sympathising with his plight.

"Do you think we'll see Martin today?" I enquired, not particularly aiming my question at anyone in particular.

"I hope so." Susan said. "I'm so hungry!"

I got the instant impression that food was a real luxury in camp. Being completely reliant on Martin, I quickly decided that I wouldn't waste any crumbs on Winston again. The dog had taken advantage of my naïve status as the camp newbie. I looked across at him curled up on the right side of freedom. Blissfully unaware of the irony of this, he wagged his tail as our eyes met.

"Anyone need to go?" shouted Doug.

"I do," replied Sarah. "Bobby, if you need to go, now's a good time. We all look at the ceiling and sing the national anthem."

The inmate code of conduct sailed over my head. "Eh? What are you talking about?"

Doug had already commenced the battle cry. "Three, two, one!" The penny soon dropped and I wasted no time in getting involved, I could hear the chorus of zippers followed by, well I'll leave that to your imagination. The moment took me back to a train station in Mumbai during my gap year. With only holes and no walls, an eclectic mix of Indian chaps staring at my lily-white bottom as we squatted in an uninterrupted line and completed our acts of uncomplicated necessity.

"God save our gracious queen, long live our noble queen…" to be fair, we didn't need to sing on and deface our national heritage any further. Everyone had completed their business.

Taps were turned on, buckets were emptied down the drain and a couple of minutes later, it was like nothing unusual had ever occurred. Even the misplaced stench that lingered drifted down the corridor as though it had been given its excremental marching orders.

I sat back down on my mattress and looked over to Sarah. She smiled at me, clearly embarrassed. Other than her metallic waistcoat, she was wearing a brightly coloured floral dress, a red cardigan and white baseball trainers. Her aqua marine eyes glowed in the dim light. She was beautiful. After our date, I didn't think I'd ever see her again but here we were, locked in a desperate situation of isolation. Were we meant to be together? Was this some sort of freak fate? Well, it would certainly be one to tell the grandchildren if we ever got together and multiplied, I wondered as I held my stare a moment or two past the stage of awkwardness. "You know, they arrested me for your disappearance Sarah. They thought that it was an act of revenge what with you giving me the brush off. After they questioned and released me, I even cried on Martin's shoulder! Can you believe that? The bugger told me not to worry. He said that you had form and were probably just on a mad bender with friends. Hey, you even made the local news. Yes, you had your fifteen minutes of fame. Well, that might be a slight exaggeration, the bulletin lasted no more than three! Not that that's any consolation."

Sarah's eyes widened. "Surely there must have been some heat on Martin?"

"No! He's managed to sidestep all of the drama. The whole shebang, nobody suspects him of anything." I replied. As I continued the conversation, I couldn't help but think, "how did I let this one get away?"

The Dead Suggs Society

Martin was right to try and set us up on a romantic journey but obviously I didn't expect it to end up in this dark web of entangled deceit. The final destination should have been down a floral church aisle and not a dark and damp disused underground World War II bunker. I nudged myself closer and asked Sarah if she thought that we'd ever get out of this mess. I wrongfully assumed that I was whispering with the intent to isolate some time together, but alas, a shout from the other side of the camp came crashing into our personal space.

"You're his mate! You tell us! Surely you can talk some sense into the creep!"

I had planned to talk to the others in the room and now was my chance to knock another one off the list. "Hey, listen, I'm in the same predicament as you. What's your name?" I asked in an attempt to swerve the initial line of questioning.

"My name's Peter Sugden but you can call me Suggs. If you're about to ask why I'm in here, then don't bother as I have no idea. I was the former headmaster at Martin's primary school. I can barely remember the boy. All I can recall is that he was a lazy little mongrel. Kept himself to himself. Never made any friends, a real loner. Was it my responsibility to see the early signs of a potential psychopath? Fuck knows. Since he left the school at the age of eleven, I thought I'd never see him again. I just can't understand why he's targeted me! I'm retired now. I should be sunning myself around a pool in the Costa del Sol, not rotting to death in this squalor!"

"If you ever laid a finger on my boy, I'll kill you." Doug stated with very little conviction although the implication of his statement was clear.

Suggs' didn't take kindly to the insinuation. "That's ridiculous and you know it! Anyway, Bobby, come on, we are relying on you to work out a plan and quickly, I'm cracking up in here. It's been over two weeks for me!"

"Fuck you Suggs, you're a dirty pervert, preying on the vulnerable, abusing a position of power. I've got my eye on you!" screamed Doug.

It was clear what was being implied and due to the heightened tension between the two alpha males locking horns, I didn't have any inclination to probe further. Suggs looked far too old and frail to be challenged. The deep lines on his seasoned face may have been hiding a sinister side, his greying comb over may have been covering more than intended, his sunken eyes may have lost their shine but now was not the time to press him further.

One thing that was for sure, it was becoming increasingly obvious that the pressure was on me. I was the odd one out, the only unconvicted inmate, I was here by default. A friend of Martin whose only indiscretion was the traditional offer of banter-based comradery. Martin's happiness, his life and career, might have been damaged by people who meant very little to him but surely I could not be tarnished with the same brush. I was his mate, his confidant, his drinking buddy, the person he shared a life and home with. Surely he would listen to me! See the error of his ways and release us. I was sure that Martin's evil alter ego was only a small percentage of a good, honest and hardworking man.

"I'll certainly try. Martin's not a bad man, I'm sure that I can talk some sense into him. I do hope he'll come today. I need to eat soon before I pass out!" There must have been a pleading nature to my voice but I certainly didn't mean to abuse my status as chief negotiator in order to satisfy my craving.

Sarah stood up sharply. "You didn't have anything to eat last night. Look, I've stashed away an apple, I was saving it just in case but your need's greater than mine."

Now, you may ask, why would you take food off a hungry girl's table? You may follow this question with, hasn't anyone taught you any basic manners and then question my gentlemanly honour but I knew what I was doing. My motive was clear. Cementing my partnership with a woman that I had cravings far beyond vitamins and minerals. This act of kindness would prove that she had my back and take us past our embarrassing initial encounter. "Thank you so much Sarah, I owe you one."

Winston had clocked the opportunity and was soon by my side. He gave me that look. You know the one. His eyes softened and glanced at mine. Just long enough to see if his animal magic was working, then away quickly, his cute face resting on his front paws. Of course, it worked. It always does, right? I traded the apple core for a cuddle before he left my cell.

Feeling slightly more energised, I continued. "Oh Sarah, I still can't believe that he pissed on my bed while wearing your clothes." I cracked a wry smile not knowing whether it would further my cause.

"Unbelievable, eh? I do feel bad that I ridiculed Martin in front of the whole office but he has got previous. It's not the first time that he's let himself down in the workplace. I bet that he's never told you about the rabbit hole he went down a few weeks ago!" Sarah now held everyone's attention and she seemed to be enjoying the moment. "Allegedly, and I say that as it's not been confirmed, but our Department Head was spending one of his hard-earned pennies in the gents when he heard a strange but familiar noise. A pop, pop, pop was coming from trap two. It took him a few seconds before he realised what was occurring. He followed up his conclusion by filling his hands with water from the tap and throwing the palm load over the cubicle door to a much-disgruntled shriek. Once back at his desk, he sent out an all staff email stating that whoever came out of the men's toilet with a wet shirt had been involved in the act of masturbation! Well, I'm sure you've guessed it, a bemused Martin walked back to his desk to a round of astonished applause. On opening the awaiting email, he vehemently denied his malpractice but the jury had already hung drawn and quartered the poor chap." The camp howled its pleasure at this story in unison. Even Martin's dad had an embarrassed smile across his face.

Once things settled and not wanting to be beaten, Susan sparked up. "I've got a funny story about Martin. On our second date, he took me to this Italian restaurant that had just opened at the end of his street. I wasn't aware at the time and bear in mind that we were freshers at Uni but Martin only had fifteen quid in his pocket. After ordering two glasses of wine and a pepperoni pizza for me, he only had a fiver left to play with. Having done the maths silently in his head, he was forced to order the cheapest dish on the menu, a starter plate of barbequed spare ribs. I was a little shocked as he'd been saying how much he was looking forward to a bowl of pasta. Through gritted teeth, he requested that everything be served together, justifying his actions by stating that the starter would be enough for him as he wasn't that hungry after all. The waiter, who had introduced himself as Luigi, wandered off having quipped that our order wouldn't be giving him writer's cramp! After a few minutes of idle chat and sips of the wine, Luigi brought over a bowl of water with a slice of lemon in it. Thinking that his ribs came with a free complimentary bowl of soup, Martin asked for a spoon. Luigi, not questioning his choice of cutlery, bought him one over. Martin then started to feast on the bowl of water to the amusement of the waiter. I didn't have the heart to tell him that the water was for the sticky fingers he'd acquire from the ribs. It wasn't until we'd left the place and he asked to borrow his bus fare home that I understood his comical behaviour."

Before we could digest this random act, Doug shouted, "God damn you, Susan, my boy only wanted to treat you like a lady! Anyway, shouldn't we be trying to work out a way of escaping as opposed to ridiculing my son!? If you lot want to exchange stories about sticky fingers, then just talk to Suggs."

"If you give me anymore of that verbal and Martin doesn't beat me to it, I'll bloody strangle you." Doug's voice echoed through the chamber.

Had Doug just stated what we were all thinking? Was that the stark reality? Was Martin planning to kill us or look after us until our natural demise? I couldn't help wondering whether my friends, family or colleagues knew that I was in trouble and a search party had been organised. I listened out, half expecting to hear a helicopter overhead but all I could absorb was the sound of Doug mumbling some profanities to himself. I stood up and wandered over to the cell bars, my chains rattling around and turning everyone's attention towards me. Firstly, tapping on them to ensure that they were indeed metal and the real McCoy, I then took in a deep breath and with all my strength tried to prize them apart. Nobody moved including the bars, Obviously, I knew that they had all attempted this ritual but I felt an internal pressure to undertake my due diligence. I shook them, pulled them, pushed them and kicked them but they were as strong as a nun's vow of chastity on Easter Sunday.

"I wonder how many prisoners around the world have walked up to their bars expecting them to effortlessly prize open?" Susan gestured mockingly.

"I paused for a second. A light bulb moment? "Hello guys, here's an idea, let's all stand in a line and on the count of three, run at the bars together and give them an almighty shove. As our cells are all connected, you never know, it might just work!"

"Yeah, why not? Worth a try." Doug strained as everyone reluctantly stood up.

It was the first time since I'd arrived that we would act as a team. A gathering of random specimens working as one to achieve a common goal in an uncommon gaol. In an attempt to muster some enthusiasm, I shouted out one of the best motivational lines from the film, Dead Poet's Society, "This is a battle, a war, and the casualties could be your hearts and souls."

"Oh, shut up Martin, you had us all at hello." I have to say, the more I heard Susan's one liners, the more I warmed to her.

Once everyone was in position, I looked down the line of misfits. "Are we ready? On your marks, set, go!" A rally cry that only resulted in the groans of agony. The only rattle was that of our aching bones. Not even a hint of any movement that would give us hope. "Fuck me, this place is like Fort Knox!" We all sat back down on our bargain basement mattresses and in the same vain, gave out a sign of resignation.

Unsurprisingly, Susan poured salt on my wounds. "Any more smart ideas Bobby?"

We had breathed in the alluring air of optimism and breathed out the cantankerous stale air of repugnance and distain for our captor. A barbarian who had single handily strategised and administered his savage and well calculated plan. Dr Jekyll would have been so proud. He might have even adopted this beast and bestowed upon him his fountain of depravity.

"God, what I wouldn't do for a plate of fish and chips with a side portion of mushy peas!" It was a random comment but my hunger dictated the direction of conversation.

Susan laughed and added, "Ok, here's one for you. Would that be the one meal you'd request to take onto a dessert island? A meal that would appear on the island every evening until your dying day?"

"I think I'd opt for a Sunday roast. Lamb would be my choice with shitloads of gravy and dollops of mint sauce. Oh, and fuck it, I know it's a little unconventional but throw in a couple of Yorkshire puddings and I'm as happy as a pig in muck!" I could feel myself salivating at the very thought.

"I'm all for playing daft games to kill time but can we avoid any discussions involving food! Trust me, it doesn't help!" Doug had a valid point but then perversely called out, "give me a chunk of fillet steak, triple cooked chips and roasted veggies any day of the week."

"Any sauce?" I asked.

Peppercorn, all day long!" Came the reply.

Sarah couldn't resist. "Come on guys, you're not using your brains! It's tapas all the way. If that's your only meal, at least you get some variety. Six dishes maketh the feast. Patatas bravas, albondigas empanadas, tortilla espanola, croquettes and some calamari. No brainer!"

Doug chortled to himself. "Not that foreign muck!"

Someone had to jump in before Susan could and so I stepped up to the oche. "Beer, wine or soft drinks?"

"God, I'd love a drink! A couple of pints of some decent craft ale would do the trick."

"Who said that?" I stupidly requested, knowing that the statement came from the cell at the far end. The last inmate. The only prisoner that remained incognito. I was yet to unmask this final hostage. Friend or foe? Man or mouse? Why was he acting so aloof?

There was no answer. "Hey mate, what's your name?" Again, no reply. I couldn't really see him across the shadowy den. Sarah shushed me and asked me to leave him alone. I nodded and smiled as I thought that eventually I'd get my chance as he wasn't exactly going anywhere.

So, six cells and six prisoners. Why six? I wasn't meant to occupy mine. Was it planned for someone else? Had I upset the chain of meticulous planning? Knowing Martin and his mild OCD, he would be infuriated with me. I'd messed up his kismet, his Feng Shuai of human absurdity. I looked around for an imaginary wall clock, my stomach was pushing my mind for answers. Why had I not satisfied its basic and only craving? I poured myself a cup of water which must have triggered an impulse as others followed.

"Don't get too excited, it's only bloody rainwater. He's rigged up a water tank, the plank!" I loved the fact that Sarah was looking after me. I took solace in the divine nature of a growing affection. How different from the first time we met. Her hair was greasy, skin dirtied and an unflattering summer dress tarnished with the grime of an unsanitary confinement but she still glowed with an outlandish beauty.

The next few hours ironically strengthened our weakness. It was becoming clear that this place wasn't an establishment famed for fine dining or in fact any culinary pleasure. As we faded through the afternoon, our energy levels suppressed our appetite for discourse. We all lay on our uncomfortable mattresses and fantasised about our escape in silence until our eyes grew heavy from the weight of waiting. We needed answers, we wanted justice, we wished for courage, we required hope but most importantly, we craved for food. It felt late. I don't know why, maybe it was the way I was brought up but I felt the urge to wish everyone a good night before I faded into a space where I could dictate my own destiny. No one replied, so I curled up into the foetal position and prepared myself for the lonely night ahead.

As I drowned in exhaustion, my thoughts once again turned to Martin. What was he doing now as his captives lay in his wait? Was he out enjoying himself? Perhaps wining and dining Poppy? Oh, hang on, he had the flat to himself. Was he eating my food, wearing my clothes, playing on my games console? I hated him. I longed for a dart board to pin his face to. He was the enemy! We had been friends for a long time but there was no going back from this. He would feel the full force of my wrath. The same vengeance that had inflicted pain on the school bully, Griffo! "No one crosses my path and gets away with it!"

Day of the Bread

Maybe I was the first to wake, maybe I wasn't, who cared? Maybe it was ten minutes after I closed my eyes, who knew? Maybe I was in the middle of a living nightmare, too true. The dim fraudulent light was consistent and unrevealing. Everyone was still confined to their barracks. I looked over at Sarah, who was present and correct and who's stare was transfixed on the ceiling. Keen to be an integral part of the morning routine, I wanted to show willing. It had to be time to alert the public to our whereabouts! Even if it wasn't, there wasn't actually much else to do.

I stood up and screamed, "help, we're down here!"

"Shut up and get some sleep you nutter, it's the middle of the night!"

Startled and somewhat confused at this response, I gesticulated a retort. "How do you know Doug?"

"Cos, I looked at my watch you der-brain! We might be perishing in a civilisation lost to man but I can still tell the time."

I reluctantly laid back down and joined Sarah in her unquestionable dedication in studying the grey monotony that the ceiling had to offer. I knew that I'd woken everyone up but what did it matter? It wasn't as though they had to get up for work, feed a crying baby or desired a lie in after a busy week of hard graft.

As I settled back down, something occurred to me. I had saved Martin's life once. Surely on the back of that he'd work out a way to bequest my freedom and release me from this salubrious situation. My mind cast back to a weekend we'd spent in Frankfurt. An event that had occurred a good few years ago and had stuck in the dark crevasse of my memory. With a cheap flight and budget hostel booked, we had two days of misdemeanour planned. We headed to a district called Sachsenhausen, an area across the river Main, filled with bars and nightclubs. That evening, it poured down with rain and a storm was clearly brewing. After a few bars and a belly full of strong continental lager, we found ourselves in a rather posh Italian restaurant. More than slightly inebriated, Martin challenged me to urinate under the table while ordering my pizza. A little bizarre I thought but none the less, I was not one to turn down a wager especially as the prize was a shot of tequila. I took on the request and as the table cloth covered my modesty, I was successful. After quickly devouring my carbonara and before the evidence leaked out across the floor, we paid and left, sniggering to ourselves as we exited. One over on the Germans or one under the radar for the Italians? We weren't that way inclined, we were simply young and foolish. To us, a childish act of facetiousness would always win the day.

We laughed so hard and as the storm was in full swing, we nipped into the nearest bar in order for me to claim my reward. After a couple more steins, we decided to walk back to the hostel. En route, we were stopped in our staggered tracks as we remembered that the main bridge was closed for reconstruction. Barriers prevented our passing. Partially dismantled with only a skeleton frame between us and the other side, we were caught in a dilemma. As the rain poured and the wind howled, we took cover, pondering our next move. I dared him to cross it. He couldn't say no, it was part two of the brotherly camaraderie. As I was leading one nil, how could he decline the offer? After a slurred debate and a little name calling, he was ready to take on the mission. I jumped in a taxi and told him I'd be waiting on the other side. After a few minutes' drive along the river and an alternative bridge, I was at the prearranged meeting place.

I could see Martin's silhouetted frame. He was only halfway across the outside of the structure. Frozen and clutching to the frame for dear life, spread-eagled across the narrow gangway, he called out for help. After branding him a yellow-bellied chicken with no response, I soon understood that he was in trouble. My first thought was to call the police but that could take time and a night in the cells. A rescue attempt was required and that was a sobering thought. I jumped across the barrier and onto the naked metallic skeleton. I clearly underestimated the severity of this challenge. The wind pulled on me, the driving rain attacked me and the angry water below called out my name but Martin needed me. Coming from the other side, I slowly dragged myself towards him. It took some time before the terror in his face was clear to see. On arrival, I enveloped his shivering body from the outside and step by step, we advanced along the framework of the bridge as we made our way to safety. We hugged, cried and called ourselves idiots. We had learnt a valuable lesson that night and generated a bond for life. Or so I thought!

Nonetheless, he owed me one! The only question was, would he pay me back?

The recluse at the far end of the chamber was the first to start the early morning alarm call. All I knew about him was that he wanted to be left alone, didn't understand why he was here and was rather rude. Everyone jumped to their feet and hollered with all their might. Today's chorus seemed weaker than yesterday's but I put that down to the low energy levels. Our calls were once again unanswered and after a short while, our demented shouts fizzled out. Breakfast consisted of a cup of water. Winston seemed the most disappointed. Not really understanding why we were being so mean. He looked wistfully at us all individually with dog distain.

A strong deep whiff of undesirable body odour forced me into action. Unannounced and therefore perhaps against the rules of the camp, I stripped down to my boxers to everyone's shock and amazement. I was sure that Sarah, whilst surveying my fine physique, gave me a wry smile or maybe I'd just wishfully imagined it.

The "nice legs, shame about the face," comment followed by a wolf whistle, unsurprisingly came from Susan. Unperturbed, I turned on my tap and gave myself a thorough scrubbing down. I was hoping the ladies might follow suit but disappointingly, they just decided to watch the free show. After I dried myself with my shirt and put back on my trousers, not before, I asked Sarah if she'd have been keen to meet again if Martin hadn't ruined our date. Before she could answer, a loud creaking sound directed our attention to the bunker hatch.

"On your toes everyone, Martin's here," Susan announced. The whole group, apart from me, proceeded to stand to a soldier's attention, each one next to the front right corner of their bunk. After Martin closed the main shutter, he strolled through with a large box, slammed it down, grabbed a stool and sat down. From a vantage point, roughly in the middle of the corridor, he just glared at us one by one with me being his final destination. Should I be afraid, petrified, who was I looking at? A friend surely, someone whom I'd bonded with along the winding road of life's ups and downs.

I felt the need to break the intimidating silence. "Martin mate, what's going on? Let us out. Whatever is troubling you, we'll sort it out together."

A short, sharp response was all he offered. "Nobody talks unless I give permission!"

I moved closer to the bars. "But Martin, this madness has to stop. I completely understand your motives but you have to release us before someone gets hurt. This behaviour doesn't become you mate. You're better than this!"

It's difficult to describe the pain that I felt. A shockwave pummelled through my body. A crippling, excruciating pain pierced its way along the length of my spine. I dropped to the floor, screaming in agony. Half embarrassed, I looked across for support, but all of us were wincing in torment. We had all been inflicted with the same unearthly torture. Still reeling from the trauma, I dusted myself off and sought composure.

"What the fuck Martin?" I looked at him in sheer disbelief and saw that he was clutching some remote-control type contraption which was loosely aimed in our direction. It didn't take me long to figure out that it was instructing our metallic chest harnesses to send an electric shock down our fragile frames. Second time around the tribulation was worse. As I sat back up and noticed that Martin had a sardonic callous grimace across his wicked face, I now knew that I despised him just as much as my fellow prisoners. He was our devil incarnate, our self-appointed enemy, the sole orchestrator of our threatened future. He had rinsed us of our optimism and was now hanging us out to dry.

Inquisitively, I watched him walk over to a handled wheel which was attached to the wall. Chains crunched as he began to rotate it into life. Linked to the ceiling and into our cells, they slowly pulled on our arms and hoisted us to our feet. Grinding to a halt just before we were lifted off the floor. Martin the inventor, who knew. Part of me felt impressed, almost proud. The other half just wanted to piss on his pathetic parade.

I didn't recognise the man he'd become. Once a trustworthy friend, a brother in arms. Someone that I could trust with my life which was now being strangled with his blood-stained hands. I wanted to plead with him for mercy but the option of pain forced me to remain reticent. We hung like carcasses in a slaughterhouse awaiting their fate. Motionless and without hope, we awaited his next move.

Martin pulled out a rather large stewing pot from his cardboard box and proceeded to dish up bowls of what Charles Dickens might have described as homemade gruel a la vegetable slop but I didn't care. Such was my hunger, I craved its culinary unsightliness. If I was honest, I knew what to expect. Martin was a lot of things but certainly not

65

a cordon bleu Michelin starred chef. If a microwave wasn't at the centre of his meal preparation then the bookies wouldn't even entertain a successful outcome.

I recalled the time he'd attempted a Christmas day feast. We'd invited over a couple of friends who were avoiding family alcohol fuelled arguments around dusty board games. Martin had given it the 'big one' and excitedly let everyone know that they were in for a festive gastronomic treat. On the big day, unbeknown to one and all, he'd thrown away the burnt turkey and replaced it with some shop bought processed chicken escalopes. He shamefully covered the disaster in cheap beef gravy. The sprouts were raw and the roast potatoes looked and tasted like lumps of coal. We congratulated him on his efforts, banned him from pulling any Christmas crackers and then ordered ourselves a turkey madras each from the local Indian takeaway.

If offered the chance, I would have chopped off my left testicle for that disastrous meal! I glanced over to Sarah and wondered whether she would prefer me emancipated or one bollocked.

"Focus lad, focus." I whispered to myself. I knew that they were all relying on me! I had to seize the day. I felt like Johnny from that low budget, high quality film, Day of the Dead. "Come on Bobby! We're countin' on ya to fly us to the promised land!"

"Martin, can I speak?" I thought that was a fair question but understood that I was now confronting a ruthless stranger. We were under this monster's roof. He made the rules and they would be uncontested. A dictatorship no less. A tyrannous, totalitarian and terrifying tirade of torture.

Luckily, no electrifying red buttons were pressed this time. "Keep it short, I'm not in the mood for any of your shite!"

I didn't allow my rage to simmer. Now was not the time. "Martin, I'm your best friend, let us go and we'll forget this ever happened. I can understand why you're doing this but it's not right."

Martin's unscrupulous tongue continued to wag. "Bobby, I'm sorry. I know that you don't deserve to be in here but you've brought it on yourself mate. You've made your bed, son. I just don't understand why the fuck you had to follow me?"

I remained calm. "Poppy thought you were having an affair. She asked me to spy on you. I did it because I care. I would never have betrayed you."

Martin's face momentarily softened but then he said something that I feared and hoped to never hear. "It doesn't matter now. You can never leave this place alive!" After delivering this contentious blow, like a prize fighter he stepped back and returned to his corner. It wasn't the punch that floored me. He lowered the chains which brought me to my knees. He didn't leave the arena to rapturous applause but just to the silence of a weary, broken and stunned opponent.

It was probably only minutes but it seemed like an eternity after he'd left before anyone spoke. "You ok Bobby?" Sarah thrust her hand through the bars which I seized to stop me drowning in self-pity.

I held on firmly to this one and only hand of friendship. "Fucking hell Sarah. I can't do this. I feel like I'm cracking up!"

Sarah pulled the plug on our connection far quicker than I'd hoped. "Come on Bobby, we are all in the same situation and we need to pull together. Let's eat before Winston steals our food. We need to keep our strength up."

I wasn't expecting much but my taste buds were still underwhelmed with the unseasoned, flavourless boiled vegetable mush. Without the option of cutlery, you could hear the slurping from every cell. We were a ravenous gathering of wild animals devouring our catch. Once feeding time at the zoo was over, we all licked our bowls clean and washed our hands. A couple of miserly scraps had been thrown in Winston's direction but even he, after a short sniff, turned his nose up at the offering.

Sitting back on my mattress, I contemplated Martin's headline statement that had felt like a knife in my back. So, this was my reality from now on? A polar opposite from the life I once moaned about on a daily basis. Why was I so ungrateful? I had it so good, a developing career, a family that never forgot my birthday and cash in the bank. Not a huge amount admittedly but enough to pay my rent, have a night out once a week and put into the holiday fund on a monthly basis. I lived in a leafy suburb of a fascinatingly cultured City, steeped in history but more importantly, nightlife. I even had a great bunch of friends, well, apart from one. One thing was for sure, I was pretty well convinced that our friendship would not survive the hot coals of forgiveness.

I could hear Doug crying to himself, just as he had the night before but I had no energy for sympathy. With an unremarkably full and unsatisfied belly, I lay back and remembered my first encounter with Martin. I used to play five a side football for a local amateur team on a Saturday morning. I joined for the exercise as my unhealthy lifestyle was fast taking its toll on my waistline. Having grown up in a small, uninspiring village, I just couldn't handle the temptation of London's bright neon takeaway lights. I knew that I had to lose weight but even though my motives were genuine, I'd actually put on poundage in the one season I played. The ground was situated right next to a decent pub that served Thai food. I don't think I need to say anymore.

One frosty Saturday matchday morning at the club, Martin rocks up and asks to join. I remember thinking at the time, "he's tall, dark but certainly not handsome," his eyes were far too close together to be given that accolade. On first appearance, he looked quite athletic and fortunately for him, we were a little shy on numbers so threw him straight into the side. In the five minutes he was on the pitch, he'd managed to score an own goal, accidentally push over the referee, stamp on our goalkeeper's hand resulting in him being substituted and then, the final straw, limped off the pitch after a crunching tackle. He was a new boy, an untalented stranger and we had little sympathy for him. After losing the game, our captain threw a bucket of water over his head and told him not to bother gracing us with his ugly mug ever again. We left him there, soaked, shivering and in agony, clutching his leg. Maybe now you can see why the football practice excuse to Poppy didn't wash with me?

Anyway, a couple of months later, I spotted him hobbling down the high street. His left leg was in a cast and he was on crutches. I felt so sorry for him. He looked so dejected and lost. I wandered over, said hello and apologised for our behaviour. The least I could do was offer him a drink, so I literally carried him to the nearest pub where we proceeded to get plastered, excuse the pun. After a few pints and a rather pleasant afternoon, I knew that this would be the start of a great and lasting friendship, especially as he allowed me to draw a massive cock on the side of his cast with a permanent marker pen. Across the subsequent years, we had cried together, joked together, laughed together, we'd stood together, walked together, ran together and now we'd fallen together. The difference was that he was free to stand back up and continue his journey and I wasn't!

As I tried to sleep, I could still hear Doug's whimpering. He was clearly struggling to contain his dismay. His cries grew louder as he became more agitated, eventually howling like a wolf but his companions gave him no comfort. We all ignored his calls for help as we fought our own miserable battles in silence. It was time to think. Think of a plan to get us out of here before we cracked up, and fast!

The Great Escapade

I dowsed my head under the tap and summoned Winston over for the sole purpose of receiving a consoling embrace. The passionate uprising of anger surged through the very bones that had been shocked into submission only a short time ago. Standing up, hands-on hips, I addressed my fellow troops. We had to treat this as a battle and in war, every successful army needs a true leader. I had failed in my first mission but that had only made me stronger and more determined or maybe my new found energy was the result of a full stomach.

"Doug, what time is it?" It was my first command as a self-appointed general.

"Who fucking cares," came back the reply. Initial subordination, surely this was fairly typical in the armed services?

"Doug, what time is it?" My repetition seemed to gain traction.

"It's ten o'clock in the damn morning!"

Success, I continued with my aggressive tone. "Right guys, I think we've all had enough of this absurd predicament we find ourselves in. It's time we had a plan! Can I ask each and every one of you to come up with a suggestion of how we can get the fuck out of here? At two o'clock, this afternoon your ideas will be presented and we'll collectively choose the best method of attack." The bullets rained in thick and fast.

"Who rattled your cage?"

"I'll have some of what he's just taken."

"Who promoted you to sergeant major?"

"A plan to escape, fuck me I wish I'd thought of that."

I was surprised that the 'man with no name,' the man that lived in the shadows with no appetite for conversation stepped up and announced himself as my comrade and brother in arms. "We can't just sit here and wait to perish. He makes a fair point. We all need to stick together. Come on, let's roll with it. You never know, we might just come up with a workable plan that can get us out of this mess."

"It's worth a try. I'm up for it." Sarah interjected.

I felt a miniscule amount of pride. "Right, great, that's settled. Doug, shout us at two. We have four hours and nothing but this job to do, let's use the time wisely." God, I hoped and prayed that they'd take this seriously, particularly Susan.

"I've got a hair appointment at one o'clock, I might have to duck out early, if that's ok?" We all laughed at Susan's wit before heads started to be clasped by hands and eyes started to stare into spaces that could unlock parts of the mind where keys to our freedom could hopefully be found.

There was a lot of pacing, head shaking and bar rattling, Suggs even started punching his mattress while shouting incoherent threats. Personally, I felt the need to engage in a handful of press-ups, star jumps and sit-ups. Exercise always focussed my mind. This was a familiar routine that I embraced before any group presentations or public speaking. I was once caught walking out of a client's office lavatory huffing and puffing. Unfortunately for me, a rather large burly bloke followed me out with a smile on his face.

He turned out to be the client's right-hand man. The presentation went exceedingly well, but I was lambasted for the whole taxi journey back to our headquarters. I have to say that when finding out that I didn't convert that particular piece of business, I was secretly pleased as my colleagues stopped saying that I was the man who would always 'take one for the team.'

After what seemed like an eternity, Susan's patience became clearly tested. "I'm finished. Surely the times up. Can't we crack on and get this damn thing underway?"

"Ten minutes and the whistle blows." Called Doug.

I waited three or four minutes and called for an early bath. "Right guys, let's get started. Who wants to get the ball rolling and commence the proceedings?"

"I'm happy to start squire." I didn't need to see his undisclosed face, the voice was familiar enough by now. It was the man with no name who lived in the shadows. I called for order after concluding the housekeeping. "Ok, let's take this seriously everyone. We need to hear each plan first and then ask questions later. Once everyone has taken their turn, we can run through each one's merits and vote on which to execute. Everyone happy with that?" Silence. "Ok, let's begin."

The faceless voice erupted. "Well, I'll keep this short."

Sugg's interrupted immediately. "There's a surprise. Here was I thinking that we'd never be able to shut you up."

"Guys please, let him speak! I took back control and asserted some authority.

He'd moved closer and I could just make out his silhouette behind his bars. "Well, Martin has placed us in here for some form of revenge. His unjustified vindictiveness has taken away our liberty. Why can't we change the definition of that reprisal? A form of compensation for the error of our ways, not that I am aware of mine. We should offer to give him everything that we own. All of our cash, our homes and our valuables for our freedom. It might take him some time to sell our properties but once he's got the funds, he could release us, buy a dodgy passport and disappear to a distant land. Surely that's a way out for him. Does he really want to be visiting us for the rest of his or our lives? That's it. That's all I got. Might sound obvious but obvious can obviously work. Nobody's going to top that. We don't really need to hear from the rest of you now, do we?"

I was impressed, he'd made a fair and balanced argument even if a little conceited. "Anyone got any questions?"

"Yes, I have." Susan threw a punch which landed slightly below the belt. "I haven't got a pot to piss in. In fact, things are so bad, I've had to steal from my son's piggybank from time to time. You lot might be high rollers but I'm just a lass who wears hair rollers."

On further fact finding and discussion, we evaluated our combined estate post mortgages and general debts to be in the region of one and a half million quid. The man with no name being the main contributor, but he wouldn't divulge how he had amassed his fortune. As the chat continued, I couldn't help but think that 'no name' might just have touched on something here. Martin was so driven by money. In fact, so much so, over the years he'd established quite the reputation of being a real tightarse. He was well known for accidentally forgetting his wallet when turning up at a pub or restaurant. If he didn't make that unsurprising statement then he'd certainly walk through the door shouting, "mines a pint whoever's buying, I'm dying to use the loo!" I could just imagine him endorsing a life consisting of lying on a beach hammock during the day and counting his ill-gotten gains at night.

The uncredited character gave his closing statement. "I'm not talking about ransom notes, hostage negotiations and all of that malarkey. All we are doing here is paying for our way out. We just need to convince him that it's just an easy and rewarding way out of this mess."

"Thanks mate. This is a great start to the debate and certainly the best option on the table so far. Now, you might think you're onto a winner but let's move on, we need to hear from everyone. Who's next?" I stared directly at Suggs if for no other reason than the domino effect and the natural order of play.

Suggs took my hint and off came his shirt, he meant business. Luckily for us, he was adorned with a vest underneath. "We cannot be soft with this mother fucker. He's an evil inbred!"

Doug was only too happy to pour water into the frying pan of hot oil. "Alright you dirty bastard, that's my son you're talking about. You're the one whose added extra sausage to his toad in the hole!"

After the troops calmed the squabbling squaddies down, Suggs took a deep breath and continued. "Listen, I'm not saying that this would be a piece of angel delight but it might just work. We tie some clothes together, lasso the generator and break the damn thing. This will turn off the power to our torture vests. When Martin returns, we say that there was an electrical surge and we all got well and truly zapped. So much so that one of us, and we have to decide who, had a heart attack and has died. The fool will open that person's cell to drag him or her out. That's the opportunity to attack. The chosen person will only get one chance so he or she better knock the fucker out. Now I'm happy to take a vote on it but, I'm assuming that you'll all agree, it has to be the strongest guy in here and that's got to be you Martin."

I puffed out my chest at the compliment although I wasn't convinced that 'no name' was a nine stone weakling.

Sarah broke the thought provoked silence. "You haven't worked this through properly Suggs. Martin always hauls us up with our chains the moment he arrives."

Sugg's returned the serve with a fair amount of top spin. "True but the darkness will nudge his routine out of kilter. He'll be disorientated and he'll make mistakes."

I sliced my shot and knew it was destined to be swallowed up by the tangential net. "Of course, I would give it my best but Martin's a strong lad. What in case I can't take him down?"

The crowd jeered, "surely, he'll use his phone torch and try and fix the generator first."

"There's no way he'll believe that load of horse manure."

"If he does pully us up he'll know we were trying to scam him."

"We'd never be able to lasso the generator anyway."

"There's far too many ifs and buts."

"Martin would beat the holy crap out of Tommy anyway."

"It's just too risky and dangerous!"

Fortunately, Susan, the match umpire, called time and thanked Suggs for his proposal but thought it time to move on to the next.

Suggs reacted to the baying audience as he left the arena. "You lily livered cowards! Not one of you has any backbone."

Match abandoned due to bad fight. As he disappeared down the proverbial tunnel, I announced the next match. "Right, Doug, what have you got for us?"

"Before I start, I just want to say sorry. I am responsible for bringing Martin into this world and I should have been a better guiding influence. If I hadn't betrayed his mother and been there for him through his childhood, none of this would be happening." Doug wiped a tear from his eye.

He made a fair point but we needed to maintain the momentum. "Come on fella, now's not the time for soul searching. There's no excuse for what he's doing. Let's just focus on the job at hand and that's getting the fuck out of here. We can have an inquest over a pint and a packet of pork scratchings on the other side."

"Thanks Bobby but I just needed to get that off my chest. I appreciate that you all want to tie my boy up and whip the living daylights out of him and I understand that it's your right to have divine retribution on his ass but please, can we not hurt him. He obviously needs to be mentally assessed and if we can, we should take pity on his soul. The men in white coats are the only ones who can put him back on the straight and narrow."

"Get on with it, you knob jockey. If I'd wanted to play a violin, I'd have joined a ruddy orchestra! Mind you, Suggs does like a fiddle, eh Suggs?" Susan began thrusting her pelvis in Suggs direction which caused Doug to roar with laughter.

After taking time out to maintain his composure, he continued. "Well look, we are all locked, chained and have the good fortune to be adorned in a ghastly and rather dangerously distressing metal waistcoat. So, you could say that our hands are tied, so to speak. While I'm on the subject, if you do try to reason with my son then we all get electrocuted. He's done it a few times now, so we've basically got no chance of talking any sense into him. We're destined to live out our days in this zero-star accommodation they call Maison de la shite-bunker."

"You're meant to be giving us hope not scaring the bejesus out of us!" Cried Sarah as she threw her dainty hands in the air.

Without reaction, Doug persevered. "The answer does not lie behind these bars or with a man's enemy. We need to put an arm around a man's best friend."

"Fuck me Doug, where are you hiding the marijuana plants?" There was anger in Sarah's voice now.

"Hear me out. Winston, here boy, good dog." Winston wagged and waddled over to him. "This little fella is our answer. All we have to do is scratch a message underneath his collar and convince Martin that he's surplus to requirement and should be released. Martin will listen, he might hate humans but he loves animals. Winston is the friendliest dog I've ever met. Once set free, he'll lick the hand of the nearest stranger, get taken to a dogs home who'll want to change his old collar and Bob's your pre op Aunt Fanny, we're out! Easy. You can all thank me later."

A gentle round of applause came from the gallows. This idea clearly had four very skinny but well-defined legs. I was the first to lay praise. "Thunderbirds are go! Nice one Doug, sounds like a winner to me. We could scribe the words, 'Help, bunker in Horsleys Green.' We should do this anyway, even if we wish to go with another option. A combo strategy would only increase our chances."

The general mood of the camp had intensified as we moved on. "Come on Susan, beat that." Doug, still basking in the glory of his contribution, couldn't help himself as he handed over the baton.

"Utilising our canine friend to good effect will be a hard one to beat but there's something about me also that will surprise you." Susan found the need to stand up to address the assemblage. "Half a dozen years ago, I represented our great nation in the fine athletic art of cross country running. I was unlucky enough to come fourth in The World Championships. There was a photo finish for the bronze medal and I'm convinced that I was only beaten due to the Slovakian runner having an oversized nose. To this day I'm convinced that it was fake. I mean, if this thing was an inch longer, it would have been a foot! I digress, the point is that I'm a fantastic runner if I don't mind saying so myself."

"So, what went wrong? A burger joint open up next door to your house?"

"Fuck off Suggs, you mug. I have had a baby you know but I'm still in good physical shape." Susan held onto the bars and began performing a pre run stretching routine.

"Well, I'm really pleased for you but I'm not sure that running around your cell is going to help us love."

"Come on Suggs, let the girl finish." I protested.

"What I'm trying to say is that if I can get Martin to take me outside then I'd easily be able to outrun the cretin and get some help."

Doug felt the need to burst Susan's bubble. "Oh, nice one. How the hell are you going to manage that? You going to give it something like, hey baby cakes, I hear the weathers really nice today. How about you and I get some fresh air? Maybe we could go for a picnic?" Doug's high-pitched impression of Susan was surprisingly accurate.

"Alright, hear me out dickhead. When I used to compete, I was a bit of a poster girl for The British Lung Foundation. It's pretty much cured now but he knows that I used to suffer from asthma and we can use this to our advantage. When he next visits, I'll start having a coughing fit, I'll plead with him that I need oxygen and implore him to take me outside for a few minutes. If he's got any heart in that demonic body of his then we'll have a chance. If he falls for it, once I'm above sea level, I'll give him an almighty shove, he'll hit the deck and I'll run like I've never run before and you reprobates will be out of this hellhole within the hour."

"But do you really think that he'll believe you and take you outside? I asked, more out of politeness as the others seemed to have switched off some time ago during her speech.

Susan turned and faced her one-man audience. "Don't underestimate my acting abilities. I once played Widow Twankey in a Christmas pantomime at our local townhall.

Smashed it I did. Cracking reviews, I tell you. Anyway, worst case scenario, I'll cough this place down and he'll go into panic mode. I'm not convinced he'd let 'the love of his life' die right in front of him."

More down to my chivalrous nature than anything else, I nodded agreeingly. "Well, I quite like the plan. It could be our last gasp attempt." No one laughed at my gag, perhaps they weren't listening but I didn't feel the need to repeat it or explain myself. "Ok, thanks Susan. We'll certainly give it some thought. It may well have legs."

All eyes were now on Sarah. She'd relocated to one of the back corners of her cell. She sat cowering with head in hands. Her fragility absorbed me into her innocence. I so wished that I could have held her at that moment and told her that everything was going to be ok. Bloody Winston beat me to it! He'd read my mind and crept over and sat right in front of her. Guarding her from my requisite destiny.

"Come on Sarah, throw the dog a bone, cat got your tongue? Feed the pony, throw the rabbit a carrot or two. What's the matter with you?" I'm sure that these words from Doug were meant only to encourage, but Sarah remained motionless.

"Sarah, are you ok?" I asked if only to endorse the fact that I was on her side and that there would be a time that we would skip into the sunset together. If only I held that small piece of the jigsaw that would reveal us holding hands on that momentous occasion in the hopefully but not too distant future.

"I think I might pass as you'll only ridicule my idea."

"Sarah, I can assure you that no one will offer any disparagement. We're in this together and anyway, I'm sure that your idea can't be any worse than Suggs contribution." I followed this with a wry smile.

Sarah took her hands away from her face. "Ok, but don't laugh. Bobby, remember on our date when you asked me my age?"

Before I could answer, Susan snapped, "What a dick, you should never ask a lady her age. How rude. If that was me, I would have chucked my champagne over you. Mind you, I bet you bought her a prosecco, you pikey."

Ignoring the pointless interruption, Sarah continued. "Well, I lied. I'm not thirty-six. It's actually my fortieth in two days' time."

I was about to hit the turbo button and go into a diatribe about always wanting to date a cougar and that she looked amazing for her age but my thoughts were side-lined as she continued with her thought-provoking plan of liberation.

"As it's a milestone birthday, why don't we plead with Martin to let us have a party. Let him think that it would lift our spirits. We could ask him if he would be kind enough to bring a load of booze and join in with our festivities."

There came a cough and splutter from the shadows at the far end of the enclave. "No offence love but I'm not sure he'll go for it. How many parties have you been to where your guests are people who you despise, want to lock up, torture and potentially murder?"

"Ignore him Sarah, please do carry on." I shouted in an overprotective manner.

Middle finger wagging, in a defensive show of protest, Sarah carried on. "Ok, I see a potential flaw in my plan but if we can appeal to his better nature and make out that we'd be so grateful, we could get him well and truly hammered. I'm sure a few of you have seen him drunk before, right? He'd be putty in our vengeful hands. Obviously, we'd have to throw our drinks into the drain which goes against the grain of a party girl but needs must. By the time we've finished with him, the bloody lightweight won't know what's hit him until he wakes up. Hopefully with a massive hangover in a police station while we're down the local spa getting our feet tickled."

"God, she's cute when she gets animated," I thought to myself. "Well, what an amazing birthday present that would be if it worked, eh? And just so you know, Martin told me your age before the date." I winked at her but quickly turned away when I realised how creepy this made me look.

Before my cheeks reddened, Susan barged in. "I don't really get it. So, we get the boy drunk, then what? He's hardly going to unlock the cell doors, release us from our chains and allow us to have a dance on the roof terrace of this sham of a party."

I had so many tales of Martin's drunken debauchery and wanting to support my newly crowned princess, I quickly sieved through them and offered up a 'glass slipper' that would strengthen Sarah's argument. "Guys, she's right. Martin loves the world and everyone in it when he's drunk. I remember one night when he was at least half a dozen sheets to the wind. Admittedly this was our fault. We were at the Coach and Three-legged Pony in Ealing when the landlady rang the bell and called time. We'd been out since lunchtime and were well on our way. With time and the licensing laws against us, someone bet Martin a fiver that he couldn't polish off the seven half consumed drinks on our table. A mix of rum colas, lager, cider and wine. Up for the challenge, he downed each and every one of them. Half an hour later, in the kebab shop across the street, we sat his unsteady frame down and proceeded to convince him that there was a global lamb shortage and after tomorrow, no one in the country would be able to afford it. Martin, in his drunken stupor was so mortified, he went straight up to the counter and ordered twenty dirty doners and proceeded to give them out for free to anyone who would accept one. Two days later, he was found still unconscious in his bed, cuddling one of the damn things. Slices of tomato covering his eyes and stinking of chilli sauce."

"What a twat," announced Susan. "Ok Sarah, you might have a fairly decent idea. We'll stick it on the pile. Come on then Bobby you dickweed, this whole thing was your idea. Enlighten us."

I felt the need to test the steely nature of my contingent. Tread on their toes and verify the controversial direction of my thoughts. I stood, hands on hips and announced myself to the stage. After taking a deep breath, I began. "Don't ever talk to me like that! I'm not one of you! I'm not the scum who've made Martin's life miserable and meaningless. You lot deserve to be in here. You aren't even fit to wipe my mate Martin's arse. Fuck the lot of you. I hope you all rot in here for the rest of your repugnant lives!"

My passionate tirade was purposely directed over Sarah's head but she was the first to react. "How can you say these things Bobby? I thought you were on our side."

She was caught in the crossfire but I had to persist. "Your side? How can I be on the side of bullies, a group who condemn and persecute a perfectly good-natured pillar of our community. You lot are worthless. You're sewer rats of society. You should all be ashamed of yourselves. You don't even deserve to walk in Martin's shadow, let alone eat at his table!"

"You're lucky that these bloody bars are in the way or I'd give you a good hiding, you little prick!" Sugg's rubber stamped his manifesto with some fist waving.

Raising my voice even further, I delivered my final flourish. "I stand here tall and proud, together with my emotionally scarred friend, against the tyranny of your terror. Your war against my innocent, vulnerable friend is futile and must end now!" Mouth's lay aghast and if the exit doors were open, I'm sure the audience would have left but they were not and silence fell. "Guys, I'm truly sorry. You know I don't mean a word of what I've just said. Of course, I'm on your side. I'm just as angry with Martin as you lot are. Forgive me but that was just a taste of my plan."

After the initial shock, Susan appeared to back me up. "Oh, I'm on it like a racing car's bonnet. You're a devious bastard, Bobby!"

I wasn't convinced that everyone was onboard the escape vehicle so I continued my argument. "Look, I've never done anything to Martin that would warrant my presence here. If I hadn't thought that the randy bugger was having an affair then I wouldn't be here with you now. I'm

Martin's closest mate. He must be missing our friendship. We do everything together apart from the obvious. I'll make out that I understand why he's done this and throw my towel into the ring to acknowledge his victory. I'll slag you lot off to high heaven and persuade him to release me on the promise that I'll help him. Help him to administer his punishment. You'll have to react to my performance but please believe me when I say that I'm only doing it for the greater good and once I'm out, I'll get help. What do you think? You'd all have to be one hundred percent onboard if it's going to work. Hands in the air if you think that my acting skills warrant an Oscar."

I was unable to make out the silhouette of the caped crusader in the far corner but everyone else raised their proverbials.

I felt drained. Maybe because I had just upset the people who held my future in their hands or maybe because my energy levels were low due to the strenuous circumstances combined with the lack of calories in my system. I heaved a sigh of relief that we had developed some form of strategy and therefore hope. "Ok, great. So, everyone has offered up a sensible game plan.

We have in effect put all our rotten eggs in one basket and we intend to watch this basket carefully. Before you ask, that's a quote from The Great Escape."

"Oh, fuck off with your film quotes. I'm bored of them!" Shouted Doug.

"Let's all take some time to digest the ideas," I said. "We can discuss their merits tomorrow morning. I think we've got some workable plans guys. I just wish that we had some champagne to toast our upcoming success."

"Here, here, I'll second that," gestured Sarah. I smiled warmly at her and for some reason wondered what she'd look like holding that alcoholic mirage while sitting opposite me in a classy restaurant. I filled my plastic cup with the only lubricant available, sat down, took a long slow sip with my eyes firmly shut, then collapsed on my mattress. It suddenly dawned on me why Martin had signed up to a handyman course a few months ago. The bunker plumbing was a fairly decent standard. The taps and drainage worked a treat. The pulley system was cleverly designed and the electronics behind the torture vests was admirable. The cells were sturdy and the space was efficiently managed but he clearly didn't give much attention to the painting and decorating part of the syllabus. Personally, I would have added some mood lighting and a state-of-the-art sound system. Also, a few pictures and indoor plantation would have helped to transform the gaff but credit where it's due, Martin had created a functioning prison. "Who was the first to check into this hotel?" I randomly asked.

"It was me. I didn't book it online but actually just took the gamble. I will not be giving it a five-star review and certainly won't be recommending it to anyone else." Replied Suggs. "When I first arrived, there was only one large cell. A week later, it had been split into six."

"God, I wonder how long he's been planning this charade. Seems like it was just meant for Suggs and then things got out of control." Muttered Sarah.

Winston, after barking his confirmation, wandered over to me and snuggled by my side. My mind focussed on the six carefully thought out plans. They all had their own particular plus points and for the first time since my arrival, I felt a slither of optimism.

Midnight Redress

With plans to discuss and excitement in the toxic air, we rushed through our early morning routine. Once the final tap had been turned off, we all sat down in anticipation and prepared ourselves to work through our escape strategy. Seeing that everybody was awaiting my lead, I rallied the troops. "Right, I'm happy to start the proceedings." I announced. "Although, I'd be gutted to see the little fellow go, the Winston idea has got to be a goer, irrelevant of what other options we plump for. Anyone disagree?" Only nods of approval followed. "No? Ok, that's decided. Doug, it's your idea and your pet, surely you're best placed to take full ownership of this one?"

"Ok, leave it with me. I'm on it." Confirmed Doug enthusiastically.

What followed, generated multiple lines of questioning, huge debate, a pick and mix of emotions but most importantly, well-constructed reasoning for the choices we made. Some were enamoured, some went with the flow, some passionately defended their offering with blinkered defiance but eventually we got there. A course of favourable action had been agreed.

"Great guys, so just to confirm, we'll focus on Sarah's birthday plan to get Martin drunk and convince him to release us. We'll promise not to say anything on the back of us learning our lessons in his quest for revenge. If the idea of a party sends him barking mad and he won't play ball then at least he might let Winston go as some form of compensation. Let's really try hard with this one but if it fails and falls flat on its head then we will consider the next option on the list. All in favour say Aye!"

"Aye…"

"The ayes have it, the ayes have it. A resounding success. Motion carried, now all we have to do is await the halfwits arrival." I said, stating the obvious.

"I'm not going to lie, I'm a little scared but tingling with excitement at the prospect of getting one over on this mug. I can't wait for him to turn up and get a slice of 'quod erat demonstrandum' thrust up his arse." Everyone laughed at Susan's choice of words but you could sense a feverish spark of anticipation within the collective.

Doug called over Winston, petted him enthusiastically and then proceeded to take off his collar. Using his belt buckle pin, he started to scratch the agreed statement on the inside of the band and placed it back on the unlikely potential saviour. Stage one of the plan was complete. It was now a waiting game.

"I'm nervous. Anyone fancy another dump?" Assuming that Suggs was court jestering, no one responded but that didn't stop him. We all knew that he was struggling the most and as a result, behaving extremely erratically. In some ways, knowing that helped us in our own battle to control our mental state.

I was nominated to request the birthday soiree. Being the last in line for the electric chair offered little comfort. Twiddling my thumbs and pacing the boards, I gathered my composure and thoughts. How should I play it? Come straight out with the request? Start a random conversation and risk the groups scorn if he became annoyed and decided to send an electric pulse through our bones? This would be a challenge, the stakes were high. I was used to high pressured situations due to the work experience I had gained within my role as a manager, but this felt different. Failure wasn't an option, I had to succeed.

In that moment, an image of my mother appeared. Her face startled as she opened the front door and witnessed the return of her parodical son. I could hear her fragile voice. "Where in the name of Dick Wittington have you bloody been? Now take your shoes off and sit down while I make you a brew and you can tell me all about it." I knew that she would be so worried for my safety.

Listen, I'm not saying that I hadn't disappeared before. Once I went missing for four days. On finishing my last A Level exam, a group of us hit a club in Manchester. In celebration, we'd mixed a good few cheap cocktails. Once the desired effect had kicked in, I staggered out and for no good and apparent reason, followed a group of protesters straight onto a coach which happened to be parked opposite. I fell asleep on the back seats and the following morning, awoke in Glasgow. My fellow passengers were laden with global warming and climate change banners. After I'd recovered from the initial shock, I decided not to join their worthy quests. As it was my first time in Scotland, I enjoyed a tourist trek through the beautiful city. As my phone and wallet were missing, the casualties of a good night out, I was unable to let anyone know of my whereabouts. With only a little change to my name, I had no other option but to hitch home. Looking rather dishevelled, it took me two park benches and three days to get back. Not my finest hour and with good reason, my mother lectured me on the dangers of alcohol until the cows came home. Obviously, her preaching went in one ear and out the other. Bless her, what must she be thinking now?

We didn't have to wait long before we heard the rumbling of someone's heavy hooves bursting through the hatch door. Everyone looked at me, their faith in my abilities as a leader would be tested but I had no intention of letting them down.

"Martin, is that you mate?" Cor blimey governor, why oh why did I did I say that? Not a great start to the proceedings I thought. Of course, it was Martin. It was hardly going to be the Queen of Sheba. I put my initial foible down to nerves and carried on.

"Yes, only me. How's it all going down here?" Martin appeared to be in a fairly upbeat mood. Surely it was time to strike.

"All the better for seeing you buddy." I said stroking his misguided ego. "Do you have any food with you? I'm bloody starving."

"I come bearing gifts. Pasta bake and a truck load of fruit. I've even got some fizzy pop for you all."

"Oh amazing. Sounds great. That's very kind of you." Enough of the pleasantries before I sound too disingenuous. "Hey, Martin, it's Sarah's fortieth birthday tomorrow. I hope you don't mind but we were wondering if you could bring some booze and join us for a party to celebrate her big day?" I confidently requested, biting down hard on my lip.

Martin didn't respond straight away. He focussed on winching us up and dishing out the meal into our bowls that we had kindly cleaned and left outside our cells. Two apples, one orange, one banana and a packet of prawn cocktail crisps were then neatly placed next to the servings. He was clearly deep in thought, perhaps digesting my question, perhaps admiring his handy work but one thing was for sure, he was certainly not giving anything away.

Once the unconventional feast was laid bare, Martin sat down, perched forward on his chair and stared into my hopeful eyes.

"Are you having a bubble? A Steffi Graf, a fucking laugh? Why should I care if one of you has a birthday? You lot don't deserve anything that remotely resembles any form of entertainment. Why would I want to celebrate any of you fuckers reaching another milestone? Are you forgetting why you're in here?"

"Please Martin, it would lift our spirits." I could no longer maintain eye contact but I would be damned if I gave up at the first hurdle.

Martin sat back and scratched his head in deep thought. "Ok, here's the deal. Sarah, give us a flash of your tits and I'll bring you some drinks tomorrow night."

"My God, what the hell had I just heard?" I thought. "Who was this monster before me?"

"Don't do it Sarah!" pleaded Susan. The rest of us stayed silent. Was it a step too far or just another value exchange? A small stepping stone across the treacherous river to freedom? Sarah looked over at me, perhaps for some form of confirmation or guidance. I gave her a gentle glum nod. Did I cave in order to satisfy my own sexual craving? Before I had time to consider this thought, she lifted her dress and unleashed one of the finest pair of mammary glands I've ever had the great fortune of witnessing. That mesmerising moment was over in an instant but I knew that it would be etched in my memory for a while.

"Fair play. I'll even throw in a box of smokes for that performance." On that note and after a sarcastic slow hand clap, Martin stood up and left.

For the next ten minutes, all you could hear was the slurping of flavourless cold pasta which lay drowning in a tomato sauce mixed with some peas and carrots. It didn't matter, I was so hungry that I found myself thoroughly enjoying the feed. Although, this time I left some for my four-legged friend. On reflection, the mornings events had given me a small sense of achievement. We had won the first battle, taken control of a mole hill in a long-forgotten field in the middle of nowhere.

"Well, the Winston idea was a huge success, eh Bobby?" It was Suggs who broke the euphoria of my accomplishment.

"Oh damn. Of course. Silly me. Come on Suggs, forgive us our trespasses. I'm not a professional jail breaker you know and you're not watching the film Midnight Express." I snapped.

"Oh, here he goes again. Showing off with his movie knowledge." Mocked Susan.

Sarah cupped her breast. "Did that really just happen? I can't believe that I got my girls out. I feel really dirty. Can you all please do me a favour and just forget that ever happened."

"I'm so sorry that I put you in that position but it was the right thing to do Sarah. The end will justify the means. We've got to play this deviant at his own game." I replied, lying down, almost in a food coma. "Oh, and Sarah, I never even looked."

Perhaps, feeling guilty that I'd forgotten about him, I spent most of the afternoon playing fetch with Winston. My only prop being a malnourished apple core. Sarah joined my churlish game with the friendly dog who amazingly always returned our makeshift toy to its rightful master. After a while, the game became a sideshow and I took the opportunity to talk properly with the only person in the bunker that stimulated the affectionate side of my soul. Sarah soon opened up and talked about her childhood and her experiences of living on a farm. She'd certainly come a long way from the wellie wearing chicken feeder who liked making dens out of hay bales. We whiled away the hours discussing the favourite games we used to play as children. Sneaking up on unsuspecting friends and pouring frog spawn down their pants generated a mutual high five. She was certainly a tomboy when she was young. One who loved rolling around in the mud with a homemade wooden sword while planning her next attack on the resident rooster. Being a village kid myself, I could relate to her carefree escapades. Life was so different back then. Parents were happy for us to roam free after school as long as we were back by nightfall. As we chatted about our childhood memories, I felt a closeness to Sarah. We'd both initially resisted the golden path to the City but now found ourselves flourishing in its chaotic but colourful nature. We agreed that the thing we liked the most about London was its cosmopolitan feel and the fact that you had no excuse to be bored. We talked about the places we loved the most, home and abroad. Sandy beaches, rugged coastlines, gentle green rolling hills, 'old skool' piers and quirky rooftop bars. We'd both been lucky enough to visit Cuba and we discussed opening up a decent steak and rum bar in Havana when we finally got out of our underground lair. I loved the fact that plans together were being made. Maybe, just maybe, there was hope for a fulfilling life as a couple on the outside world. Cuba might have become the dream but would West London become the reality? Who cared, we were bonding in the most unusual of places.

I was really enjoying the moment before Suggs burst its bubble. "You idiots do know that Cuba is a communist country and you'd have to give all of your profits to the government, don't you?"

Realising that everyone was listening to our innocent flirting, we pulled apart and for some unexplainable reason, we both started scratching the back of our necks and looking in opposite directions.

"You two should get a room. One without bloody big bars in the middle of it." Doug smiled, acknowledging his own humour.

Not surprisingly Susan got involved. "Eh Doug, God, if they started dating in here, imagine what it would be like if they broke up."

"How are they going to break up? It's not like one of them is going to move out after catching the other one in bed with their best friend." Now doubled up in hysterics, Doug roared with laughter.

I saw that Sarah was feeling uncomfortable with the banter. "Alright guys, let's start to focus on tomorrow night's plan of attack!"

"I don't think we can plan too much. It all depends on his mood. We'll just have to play it by ear." Sarah noted my diversion and once again offered the voice of reason.

The night fell and we all took to our beds. I was not convinced that anyone apart from the habitual snorer at the far end slept adequately that night but that was hardly surprising. The justified weight of the angst smothered our slumber. We pushed through our broken sleep and as I lay awake, awaiting the general coughing and spluttering that signalled the official arrival of the day, I couldn't help but wonder how Martin would cope if the roles were reversed. He was a massive foody. If he didn't eat at his allocated time slots, he would become extremely irritable and moody. Also, much to my annoyance, the boy couldn't sit still for more than half an hour. Every time we sat down to watch one of my favourite films, he would leave the room half way through. It used to agitate the hell out of me but I just considered it to be one of his many loving characteristics. Added to these traits, was the fact that he hated confined spaces. How would be manage living in a small cage? I once told him that I'd found a bag of money stashed in the loft. Embracing the prank, I told him that I couldn't bring it down as it was too heavy. We all love the idea of free money and Martin was certainly no different. I followed him to the bottom of the ladder and watched his body disappear into the upper storey. Locking the hatch door behind him gave me great amusement especially as I knew that the light bulb had blown. At that moment, the doorbell went. It was my downstairs neighbour. I invited him in for a coffee. We sat and chewed the cud for an hour or so until I heard the doorbell ring once again. It was some random chap pointing to the roof. Martin had broken through some tiles and sat hugging the chimney stack, crying like a baby. The following few days were pretty quiet in the flat. I didn't mind paying for the repairs as the petrified look on his face was worth every penny.

God, when I really thought about it, there were so many times we had teased the cotton socks off the poor fellow. I promised myself there and then, that if I didn't get too badly burnt from this experience, I'd march the fellow down to the nearest charity shop and buy him a second hand backbone!

Sarah was the first to stir. "Bobby, if we are successful and get out of here tonight, I'll let you have another go at wining and dining me."

"I'd be well up for that. With Martin banged up, at least your clothes will be safe!" I was never one to miss a golden opportunity when it presented itself on a silver platter. I sidled over to her and held her hand. Looking adoringly into her deep blue eyes, I assured her that whether it was today, tomorrow or the next decade, I'd get her out of this living nightmare, take her to the finest restaurant and treat her like a Disney princess.

"You guys make me sick!" Surely Susan wasn't jealous? "Do you mind if we concentrate on the challenges of today?" She ranted.

The objective was clear but there were differing opinions on how to mastermind the plan. Everyone threw different ingredients into the recipe that was designed to fry up our freedom.

"Let's start by being super nice to the freak." Suggs poached the eggs.

"No one is allowed to drink so there's more for him!" Susan chopped up the mushrooms.

"He liked us all once, we need to make him warm to us again. Everyone has to apologise to him and show some full-blown remorse." Doug threw bacon under the grill.

"We have to convince him that we deserved his wrath, we have taken our rightful punishment and we will never again throw him under the bus of misery." Someone began frying the sausages.

"I'll tell him that I would have done exactly the same and I completely understand his behaviour." I said, placing the bread into the toaster.

"Let's explain to him that he has done us a massive favour, we have seen the light and the path to becoming better people." Sarah sprinkled the salt and pepper.

The full English breakfast of redemption was prepared, we had the appetite for freedom and we were ready to dine out on our diet of desire.

There's Something About Sarah

It seemed an age before Doug announced that it was seven o'clock and that his paternal instinct sensed Martin's imminent arrival. He wasn't wrong, within half an hour we heard the rummaging sound of a lost soul heaving and weaving his way through to our domain. He entered, carrying his large cardboard box, packed to the rafters with what looked like the contents fit for a children's party. Crisps, packets of peanuts, boxes of various cakes and bucket loads of booze spilled out from the treasure chest of goodies. Hey presto, we were in business. We were about to receive exactly what we had requested. May the lord make us truly grateful, not!

"Hi Martin, we've been counting down the hours mate. So good to see you." I'm not sure why but I opened my arms through the bars expecting a hug and a pat on the back. Back when life was less complicated, this would have been our traditional greeting. We'd once mastered a rather complex 'rapper style' handshake but after being ridiculed a couple of times, converted back to the more conventional method of address.

But times were very different and I was completely blanked by Martin who on arrival, simply wished Sarah many happy returns. I literally could not believe what I was hearing. Not the fact that Martin was being reasonably civil but the fact that all of us hadn't congratulated the birthday girl on her special day. To make up for our absentmindedness, I burst into song and everyone, including the devil worshiper, joined in.

"Happy birthday to you, happy birthday to you, happy birthday dear Sarah, happy birthday to you!"

Sarah appeared genuinely grateful. "Aww thanks guys, I didn't realise you cared so much." I was about to extend the official opening ceremony with a chorus of 'for she's a jolly good fellow,' but my appetite was quickly squashed.

"Right, get stuck into these tasty treats guys." Martin began tossing his donations through the cage bars. We all thanked and praised him for his outstanding generosity. Basking in his glory, he grabbed some plastic cups out of the box and poured cheap brandy into them. My eye caught sight of the label. He'd bought this particular brand before and I knew from experience that it would be pretty unremarkable, perhaps that's why his measures appeared generous.

"Oh amazing, this is great. You're a star Martin!" exclaimed Sarah.

"Pour yourself a cup and let's have a toast." Called out Suggs.

"So far so good," I thought as Martin followed the instruction.

We all raised our fraudulent glasses and ironically wished Sarah a happy life filled with much joy and success.

"So, Martin, how was your day buddy?" I asked while taking a huge slug of the brandy. As expected, it tasted vile but took the edge off. At that moment I could sense Sarah's eyes burning through the back of my head. I quietly and astutely poured the rest of it into the drain.

"Yeah, not bad Bobby. How.." Martin stopped in his tracks, he must have realised that there was no real point returning the ill-fitting question back to the retailer.

"Come on Martin lad, get it down you son. You drink like a camel that's got the hump. I'm already gasping for another one."

"Here, here Doug. I'm with you on that one." Agreed Susan.

I'd told the group that Martin hated being called a lightweight and he didn't let me down. The more we egged him on, the more he cracked on. Things could not have been going any better and before we knew it, we found ourselves with our fifth cup in hand. Much to Sarah's annoyance, with each cup, I took a couple of large slugs of the battle juice before discarding the rest and if I'm honest, I could feel a slight twinge of merriment

"Hey Martin, how's about sticking some beats on? What about some eighties classics?" Sarah purred with a childlike smile that ran across her red cheeked face. Clearly, as the evidence proved, she had been following the same drinking rule of thumb.

"Ok, but I'm not turning the volume up too high."

"Right you are, Martin." I said before anyone had the chance to complain. The mission was progressing far too well for it to be jeopardised by some mindless carelessness. This rather unconventional party was now in full swing. Music playing, drinks flowing and surprisingly, some half decent chat.

Martin was clearly loving his position of power. He was holding court. All eyes of the guilty, caressed his ego. All ears of the sentenced hung on his every word. All questions from the convicted were taken and addressed on their merits. The dictator still had control. We had to ramp up our game while the momentum was still on our side.

Sarah must have sensed this. "It's tradition to play drinking games on my birthday. Anyone for a game of yee haw? Martin, can we?"

Not even a suspecting flinch from our captor. "Ok, just a quick game. Let me top up your goblets before we start."

Well, every drinking game is tactical and has its own rules but not this one. Game after game, the cowboys fired round after round into the Indian. The Yee Ha's, the Hoe downs, the hey barns and all bucking horses were ridden in Martin's direction. He was clumsy, maybe slightly complacent but that didn't deflect from the fact that he was getting driven down a hole that we had cleverly prepared. Losing round after round, Martin took his punishment and drank shot after shot. In his increasingly inebriated state, his volume levels went up a notch, his pitch higher, his words slurred and his movement slowed.

With a momentary lapse in the game, Susan struck first. "I always regretted leaving you Martin. You were such a great boyfriend. The love of my life. The one that got away. I've often wondered why we broke up. On my part, an error of epic proportions. I've regretted it for many a year. I guess, it was just a timing thing. We were just too young. God, if only we'd met years later." With no response and a shocked look on his face, Martin just stared at her. Had Susan just chipped away a little of the pain from his intestinal fortitude?

Sarah slipstreamed past the silence and expressed how sorry she was for making fun of him at work. She called herself stupid and naive and claimed that she had the upmost respect for him. Again, nothing from Martin. Did he suspect that he had become an extra in the screen play that we had written or was he just taken aback by the turn of events?

"I should have been a better father. The fact that I fell out of love with your mother should never have made me abandon you. A day hasn't gone by that I haven't regretted my actions. I was wrong and I'd like to make amends. Can't we look to the future? It will take time and I'm sure that it will cost me dearly in devotion and dosh but I'd like to try son."

I'm sure that Doug had more to give but the voice from the dark and fiery corner of hell cut him short. "Martin, I am truly sorry. You know what I'm talking about. I beat myself up every day for what I did. Trust me, the events of that fateful day haunt me a lot more that you, I'll make a promise to you that I'll do everything in my power to rectify my mistake if you let me out of here."

Only Martin knew the meaning of this apology and now wasn't the time to investigate its warmth. The intervention moved to its final stages and all eyes relocated to Suggs who could only look down at the floor for redemption. Perhaps he realised that he was in a no-win situation. A confession at best would mean him moving from one hellhole to another. The unwelcoming and isolated second option could perhaps result in his demise.

"Martin, what can I say that would give me the right to ask for your forgiveness. I'm not even sure why you've targeted me. What am I even doing here? My crime is what? Trying to do my best as an educator. Well, I've got news for you. I'm a man of honour and decency. One whose only passion was to prepare children for the challenges that life has to offer. I'm not perfect, I'm sure I've made mistakes but my intentions were always pure. I realise what these people think of me." Suggs gestured a sweeping hand across the listening gallery. "But you know that I'm not that despicable person. I have never touched anybody inappropriately nor would I. Martin, whatever I've done to upset you, please, I have a wife that's in a wheelchair. I implore you to release me if only for her sake."

The subpoenaed witnesses had given their statements and I felt the need to sum up the underground court proceedings. "Martin, in your eyes, everyone here deserves to be punished. That is clear and cannot be argued or debated. I would not try to defend any of these transgressors but I would say that they have learnt their lessons. They have shown remorse, paid their dues and should be allowed their freedom. If everyone promises on their lives that they will not implicate you regarding their disappearance, will you let them go?"

Martin looked to the sky for guidance only it was not there. It was our sky that he stared at for instruction. A substitute sky that bore no resemblance to reality and the privileges that defined a man's immunity. There were no translucent clouds empowering the blue background of opportunity and freedom. No pots of gold pointing out the richness of our existence. No rainbows to show the beauty of our emotions. No bright light to shine on our souls. No glistening stars to guide us through our transgressions. No swallows and sparrows to share our bounty with. Just the dark grey to encompass our misery. With hopeful ambition we awaited our acquittal but Martin stood up, threw his drink to the ground in distain and began his walk to the exit.

"Martin mate, where are you going? We are offering you a way out. Quid pro quo, my friend, quid pro quo!" I called out, canvassing my last-ditch attempt of support.

"You idiots think I was born yesterday. Fuck off the lot of you. I hate you all with a passion!"

The trapdoor slammed shut. We slumped and wiped our brows until the ten minutes of customary silence was broken by Sarah. "We've only bloody done it again and forgotten about Winston!"

"Oh God, damn it! Don't make me open up a can of whoop-ass!" I said with a huge sigh. "That's from the movie, There's Something About Mary, before you ask!"

"We weren't!" Suggs proceeded to scream so loudly, causing some plaster to fall off the bunker ceiling.

"If I hear one more movie quote, I'm going to save Martin a job and strangle you myself!" Susan barked once Suggs' shrill had concluded.

Martin had left two bottles of brandy which I could just about reach. I hauled them both in to my cage and topped up my cup. An alcohol fuelled production line was soon established and before long everyone was drowning their sorrows with the hard stuff.

I knew that it was little compensation for our defeat and it was time to rally the troops. "Listen guys, I think we should raise our cups and toast our performance. It might not have been a waste of time. You lot sounded so sincere and genuine, whether you meant it or not. He may well sleep on it, gather his thoughts and release us tomorrow.

He's a proud man and he was never going to take our bait straight away. I think that you might have just given him the very thing he's been craving. The opportunity to forgive and move on with his life. Let the little fucker stew in his own poison. If he's got any heart he might just realise that he's taken this thing way too far."

"Don't talk rubbish Bobby. It's been said before. You know as well as I do that he could never release us. The risk for him would be too substantial." Doug's words cut through our drunken stupor and brought us back down to earth with the heavy weight of our burden.

We all sat back and drank but we were just too exhausted to radiate our merriment. The frivolity had disappeared and we only consumed the rest of the alcohol because it was there and we were bored. We drank to drown out the realisation of our impasse. We drank to blot out the memories of a former life and the loved ones who embraced our self-worth. We drank to disguise the defeatism of our circumstance. We drank, not because we needed to but because it helped. We drank until our consciousness was engulfed by the flames of delirium that were overtaken by sheer tiredness. We drank until the alcohol dried out, the lights dimmed and our eyes no longer had to witness the insipidness of our presence.

The next morning, the banging of hard plastic cups against metal bars did nothing to assist in the clearance of my severe headache but it had to be done. The shouting and screaming for help did nothing to fix my dehydration but I knew that it was required. The domino effect of defecation did not ease my nausea but it was the routine. The running of cold water over my head was the only thing that did benefit that morning. We all knew that Martin would not make his daily appearance. He'd left enough food for survival even though the treats lacked any substance. As we all tidied our cells, God only knew why but Sarah started to sing. She had a lovely voice but her song choice could have been better. 'It's Raining Men' is a sure-fire lady's night out classic but it didn't work for me for three reasons. One, I'm not female, two, I hated the rain and three, I really wouldn't have wanted any more testosterone in the bunker. I wanted to be the only male interest for Sarah but as the others joined in the chorus, I guessed the upbeat track was welcomed.

The Secret Life of Martin Bunratty

Unbeknownst to us, Martin did dwell on the confessions and pleads of forgiveness that night. A wave of guilt did flow through his veins but his unperturbed dedication and stubbornness did not waiver. The predictability of his sleepless night did not dilute the compassion of his conviction. These people had committed sins against him and they deserved to be punished. He'd made his decision and he was way too far down the road of retribution to turn back. Why should he show any remorse for these scoundrels? They had bet against him and lost. Lost in a world of dark art, armed with a blank canvas but without any possibility to paint a brighter future.

After a quick shower and shave, Martin prepared himself a sausage sandwich. A fair treat for yesterday's good deed. Sitting at the breakfast table, he pondered the events of the previous night. He sensed their desperation but again concluded that they had made their immoral beds. "The fools have enough supplies so I'll take a day off from the deviants," he thought as he dialled Poppy's number. It was the long-awaited weekend and they'd planned to meet up for some lunch.

"Hey darling, how are you? I'm really looking forward to catching up. Fancy meeting in the park opposite mine at eleven? We could have a nice walk and work up an appetite. I quite fancy that Greek place for lunch, if you're up for it? The weather's lovely and they have outside tables. What do you reckon?"

Poppy's reply caught him a little off guard. "Listen, I'll come but make it twelve thirty, I can't stay out long but I do need to speak to you. I'll meet you on the bench next to the big oak tree. Got to go. See you soon. Bye."

Why was she so cold-blooded, almost apathetic? It was usually so difficult to get her off the phone. While the new generation liked to converse via text message, she was one of the old breed who could pick up the phone and talk the hind legs off a drove of donkeys. So why was she being such an ass and why couldn't she stay out long? It was a Sunday and she never planned anything on what she called 'the day for the language of leisure.' So, what did she mean when she said that she couldn't stay out long? Where was she going? Was she meeting anyone else later? Martin didn't want to ponder on these questions. He needed to make himself presentable and still find time to buy a simple but profoundly beautiful bouquet of flowers. As he dashed out of the flat still combing his hair, he smiled to himself. "She loves a good bunch! If I turn up with roses, she won't be going anywhere."

It would be fair to say, Poppy wasn't blown away with the bunch of twelve red roses. In fact, she asked Martin to hold them as she sat down on the park bench and rummaged through her handbag for her sunglasses. There was little to suggest that the initial conversation wasn't awkward and clumsy but it didn't take long before she got straight to the point.

"Martin, I'm just not really feeling it. You've become very distant and I just don't think that you're committed to our relationship. You've clearly got a lot on and I just feel like I'm a distraction for you. I'm not prepared to play second fiddle and waste my time any longer. I think that it would be sensible to end it before one of us gets hurt. I'm sorry, there's no one else involved, it's just how I feel."

Martin felt a heavy weight plunge through his slouching frame. He squeezed the rose stems to relieve the emotional pain. Petals fell to the floor. It was happening again. More undeserved betrayal and with little or no genuine justification. He tried to reason with her, offering more of his time and attention. He told her how much he needed her and what she meant to him especially as he had lost his best friend. With a tear in his eye, he implored her to give him another chance, suggesting that things would be different but it was too late. A solemn glaze appeared across Poppy's face. Her mind was made up and the lady was not for turning.

After patting his knee with her hand, she took off her necklace and placed it next to her on the bench. An unwanted gift returned to sender. "I'm so sorry Martin. You're a good person with a generous heart and I wish you all the best in the future but this is goodbye. I'm sure that one day, you'll make someone very happy but unfortunatcly that's not going to be me."

With that she upped and left him to deal with the grief of another lost relationship. En route back to his flat, Martin saw an elderly lady struggling to push a shopping trolley across the cobbled stones to the entrance of the park. Without saying a word, he handed the flowers to her and walked on with his head bowed to the resignation of his further failings. By the time he was sat back down at the kitchen table, opening a can of lager, an eruption of anger was pumping through his battered heart. His thoughts manifested into hatred, the message was loud and clear.

"She has to pay. I will not let anyone walk all over me again. She can join the others in the pit. She needs to be taught a lesson of respect."

By the time Martin had finished his can of anger management and was opening the second, he had wrestled with his demons enough to realise that if his flatmate and his girlfriend both went missing then the long arm of the law, perhaps with the aid of a basic torch would surely shine on his parade. He had to let this one go, at least for the moment. As he took a deep breath of frustration, there came a loud and rather exaggerated knock at the door. Martin ignored it at first but the knocking continued. This time a rather obnoxious voice came bellowing through the letterbox.

"Answer this bloody door, I know you're in there!"

Assuming that it was some desperate window salesman or perhaps someone flogging a weekly subscription for a far too healthy weekly food box, Martin opened the door and was about to give the disturbance a piece of his mind, when he realised much to his surprise that it was the landlord. A man he had not seen since renewing the tenancy contract at least six months ago.

"Oh, hi Mr Bullock. Good to see you." Martin said holding out a greeting hand which was ignored.

The large burly figure wasted no time in expressing his feelings. "You've only paid half this month's rent. I really haven't got the time or inclination for this. I want the other half now please."

Almost nonchalantly, Martin offered his excuse. "Oh right, there's a good reason for that. Simon Dingle aka Bobby, my flatmate has disappeared. The police are trying to track him down. Surely you've seen something on the news."

"Listen, with all due respect, I don't give a fuck. I just want my money." Shouted Mr Bullock as he pushed past Martin and into the flat. He scowled and scoured his valuable possession with great scrutiny, entering and inspecting each room in turn until he arrived in the kitchen. His timing couldn't have been worse. Martin's anger was already over revved and his creditor's demands tipped him over the edge, resulting in a march straight to the cupboard under the stairs and the selection of a claw hammer as his weapon of choice from the tool box. With his implement concealed behind his back, he entered the kitchen and stood facing his menacing adversary.

"I'm not paying you Bobby's half of the rent. I'll try and get a replacement flatmate and once I do you'll be paid the full amount from that point onwards."

Not noticing that Martin was armed, Mr Bullock continued with his rant. "No, that's not acceptable. I'll be back at the same time tomorrow and you'll pay it then. If you're not in, you'll find your belongings out on the street. You understand what I'm saying?"

Martin grimaced. "Ok, you can have your God damn rent now." He strode forward and unleashed the hammer over the unwelcome visitor's head. Mr Bullock, reeled back and collapsed in a heap. A faint drop of blood being the only witness to the shocking act of aggression.

"You can thank my ex-girlfriend for that, you arsehole!" Martin shrieked, bending over the unconscious bundle of a body that littered the galley floor. It obviously wasn't the first time Martin had bound and gagged an arched enemy. In fact, he was a dab hand and a self-proclaimed master of this fine art. Within five minutes, the wild beast had been tamed and lay awaiting his fate, handcuffed to the bathroom radiator.

As he sat back at the kitchen table, Martin felt flustered. Had Mr Bullock told anyone his whereabouts? Had he acted in haste and irrationally? He hadn't planned on adding anyone else to his community of betrayal and there wasn't any room for this particular traitor. "When in doubt, brew up." Martin added a little whiskey into his tea and stood by the window, staring into the abyss of the abnormality he had created in his once uncomplicated life. "I wish I could undo this one. He's not part of the plan." Martin mumbled under his bated breath. "Fuck it, it will be a tight squeeze but where there's a will…"

Feeling uncomfortable with his actions, Martin got to work cleaning and polishing the flat from top to toe. All evidence had to be eradicated. He knew that he had at least twenty-four hours to tidy up his mess. The irony of the whole situation was not lost. "The place has never looked so tidy, the landlord will be pleased!" He smirked to himself. "I'll take the body to the den of delinquents in the dark of night," he concluded before grabbing his coat and taking to the street.

Martin walked and smoked then smoked and walked until he found himself in unfamiliar surroundings. He found a bench, sat down and pulled out another cigarette.

Since beginning this adventure, Martin had not for one minute questioned his own behaviour. He realised that he needed to quench his thirst for revenge. The pint-sized devils needed to be devoured, the barrels of bemusement needed to be stored away but why did he have to take down Bobby. He needed him now more than ever. He missed him. His one true friend. A wave of loneliness clouded his thoughts. Now he was left with no real friends, a family by name only and was the source of bemusement at work. At that moment, he longed for the company of his prisoners. "At least they're compelled to be nice to me," he thought.

By the time Martin had returned to the flat, checked on his now awake but confused hostage, he felt that he was drowning in his own debauched thoughts. He set his alarm for three in the morning, switched on the television and lay on the settee. Before he made sense of what he was watching, he was spark out.

The alarm caused him to sit bolt upright and before long, he was soon swinging into action. Martin manoeuvred his car so the boot faced his front door. He soon realised that due to his constant squirming, Mr Bullock would have to be put to sleep. Out came the opened bottle of chloroform and once he was away with the fairies of circumstance, it didn't take Martin long to heave his lifeless body into the boot and knock together a pick and mix of prison scran.

There weren't many cars on the road at this time of the night so not wanting to create any suspicion, Martin drove carefully and well within all speed restrictions, a feat that was completely foreign to him. He found a late-night debate on the radio entitled, 'is feminism away with the birds?' Some bloke was explaining why he was confused with the whole subject matter. His example consisted of how the other day he got told off by a woman for not giving up his seat on the underground and the next minute, for offering to carry the same woman's suitcase down the platform stairs. He talked about the good old days when you could tell a perfect stranger that she looked beautiful and not get slapped. Laura from Chepstow followed his call and asked the host for the gentleman's phone number stating that chivalry was not dead but hidden under a cloud of effeminateness. Apart from the heated discussion, the journey was fairly quiet and untroubled.

Martin enjoyed his newly acclaimed power and the control he had over his renegades but hated facing Bobby. He couldn't work out a way to justify taking his freedom. He was collateral damage. A blot on his new landscape, a bump in the road of his new life. The chippings of his new carving, the memories of an old existence. All he knew was that he was surplus to requirements, but there was nothing that he could do to reverse his imbroglio.

But Martin was a man who needed a best friend. Someone that he could lean on, who would support him in his convictions and someone who he could confide in. Maybe that was it, he thought, Bobby had let him down. If he had been a true best friend then he would have trusted him and wouldn't have opened this Pandora's box. "Eureka, QED, so, there you have it!" He said, adjusting the rear-view mirror and gesturing to himself.

He then considered carefully who would make a suitable replacement. The only person that sprung to mind was good old Jeff Spacey. "Spacey by name, spacey by nature. Yeah he likes the ganja a little too much but he's a sound chap." He thought. "He's got finely tuned morals although he is a little monotonous and monosyllabic." Martin cast his mind back to his favourite memory of Jeff. A confirmed urban myth that happened in his first week of his new job as an International Recruitment Manager. Jeff and a colleague of his were asked to fly to Berlin to present at the Institute of Technology. They had arrived the night before the big day and enjoyed an evening of drinking around the Alexander Platz area of the city centre. Feeling extremely drunk on the fine kraft beers that the German city had to offer, Jeff, once back in his hotel room, felt the need to celebrate his crapulence by using the hotel's free Wi-Fi and enjoy some decent knechtschaft porn. After falling asleep with his trousers around his ankles, he woke up late the next morning, dashed to his presentation in the University lecture hall, where his colleague was already waiting. Apologising for his unprofessionalism, he quickly linked up his laptop to the big screen on offer. The wolf whistles and shrieks of dismay gave the game away. Well, I'm sure that you can guess the rest but suffice as to say, the company didn't do their reputation any favours that day, which as you can imagine, was Jeff's last.

"Perhaps he's not a suitable replacement. I'll revisit this dilemma later." Martin giggled to himself which was short lived due to the heavy thudding sound coming from the boot. "Fuck, he's awake." They were only about three miles from their destination and the village offered no late-night party strollers so all was safe. On arrival into the quiet layby, Martin got out of his vehicle and looked around.

Once he was happy that the coast was clear, he opened the boot, told Mr Bullock to remain calm and proceeded to drag him down towards his new home. As Martin struggled with his large frame, he thought that his victim would appreciate some good news. "I'm not going to charge you any rent for this place." His well-positioned car headlights uncovered the path through the forested maze. On arrival, Martin removed the leaves from the disguised hatch door, opened it and thrust Mr Bullock through the hole.

"Life is about courage and going into the unknown!" Martin shouted this more for the benefit of his old flatmate. He knew that Bobby would be impressed with his The Secret Life of Walter Mitty quote.

The Bemused

"Fuck, he's coming." I whispered, holding my gaze firmly on Susan. She took my hint and started to cough and splutter in the loudest way possible. Martin, clearly not amused at the commotion, reacted quickly and we felt the full force of his anger. The electricity ran through our veins thick and fast. Our metal vests rattled a painful protest. We had suspected that this might happen and were mentally prepared for the electrical beating.

"Please Martin, please stop." I begged. "It's Susan, she's been having an asthma attack for a couple of hours. She needs help."

Susan dramatically played up to the cameras, theatrically lying in the recovery position, gulping for air, wheezing and maintaining a constant hacking sound. Martin ignored my pleas and to our shock and amazement, was not alone. It took a few moments for my eyes to unveil our new acquaintance.

"Mr Bullock, is that you?" I asked in a startled wonderment. Exactly what was I witnessing?

"Shut up Bobby and do me a favour, give that drama queen some water!" Martin momentarily stopped what he was doing, pointed at Susan for a fraction of a second before continuing to drag Mr Bullock into the centre of the bunker.

"This dickhead will be moving in with you Bobby." I'd only just managed to pass Susan a cup of water moments before I could hear the cast iron wheel turning and my arms raising, positioning me in the middle of my cell.

Martin pulled out a comically large key from his trouser pocket, opened my cell door and proceeded to manacle Mr Bullock to the inside bars before locking up and releasing my strain. Could I have kicked the blighter and knocked him out? It was too late and what good would it have done? I doubted if I could have managed more than a surface wound. Perhaps a dead leg and then what? Now was not the moment for bravery nor the opportunity.

"Martin, I need some air, I feel like I'm going to die. Please, take me outside just for five minutes," supplicated Susan. Martin sat down on his throne, which looked more like an antique milk maid's stool and surveyed his kingdom. It was clear that he was digesting the question. Surely, he was not capable of allowing someone, even his fiercest enemy to suffer in front of him.

Grabbing a pair of handcuffs from the shelf, Martin demanded that Susan remain completely still. He used the same giant key to open her cell door and another smaller one to remove her shackles. Positioning her arms behind her back, he secured them with the handcuffs. Grabbing her midriff, he elevated her to an upright position and forcefully pushed her from behind, his hands gripping her waist. She shuffled out of her cage, through the corridor and towards the ladder that we'd all longed to climb.

"If you make a sound then I'll kill you myself and that ugly kid of yours! I'm giving you five minutes so don't get too excited." With that, the trap door slammed shut.

"I really could do without this," thought Martin. He'd never intended any of his victims to see the natural light of the day ever again but he could not let Susan suffer. He'd witnessed her attacks before and knew exactly how dreadful they could be. On a number of occasions throughout their relationship he'd been forced to drive her to the hospital due to the condition.

Once outside, Susan took a deep breath of fresh air and surveyed her surroundings. As she resurfaced from her hibernation, her sensitive eyes took a few moments to acclimatise. She felt the cool breeze caress her malnourished body. As the blurred images sharpened, she noticed that the night sky was resplendent against the back drop of an impressive lunar flambeau. But she wasn't there to take in the view and immediately focussed on searching for a clear path to escape. The wooded area was thick with umbrage but Susan could see an opening which would guide her into an expanse of open farmland. She was aware that the restrictions forced upon her would hinder her breakout but she could feel the adrenalin pumping through her veins and a wave of oncoming excitement.

"Enjoy it while you can," snorted Martin. She took his insensitive comment as her starter gun and bolted out of her blocks, running like a woman possessed. Raising her legs higher than she was accustomed to, avoiding tripping over the lost leaves and hazardous roots. She moved swiftly between the topiary, not looking back for a second. Taking risks had never come naturally but she loved the thrill of the danger. As the wind howled around her uncertainty, the flap of a birds wings gave her inspiration. She moved with stealth and grace, speed and precision. She felt strong and as she picked up pace, she couldn't help but think that Martin would be no match for her. As she neared the gateway to her sanctuary, she could make out a farmhouse in the far distance. A downstairs light gave her all the hope she required. With a slight change in direction, her finishing line was clear. She could almost hear the underground crowd clapping her home!

"No, you don't. Come here you bitch!" The voice of condemnation resonated and echoed through the undergrowth.

There was no rational conclusion to where this sound had come from. "Surely that's the wind playing a trick on me," she thought. "There's no way a two left footed hippopotamus could ever catch me, even if I am hindered." She had to fuel her speculation with a quick glance behind, which realised her fears.

"No, fuck you, help, help!" She screamed.

It was a tug on the chain between her hands that she acknowledged first. Then, the full weight of his frame as he rugby tackled Susan to the ground. She was down, beaten, her adventure was over and not even a wooden spoon would be presented. Martin pushed her head into the soil with one hand as he reached into his pocket to grab a handkerchief with the other, which was quickly stuffed into her mouth. "Surely Martin would respect her valiant attempt," she presumed. The smell of his cologne struck her immediately. It was the same scent that he'd used all those years ago to disguise the smell of his rancid body odour. She'd tried to change this unpleasant perfume by gifting alternatives for birthdays and Christmases but to no avail. "That was Martin all over," she thought. "He hasn't changed. Still tasteless, boring and interminably predictable."

Martin dragged her back towards the hatch, kicking and attempting to scream with only a muffled non-descript reverberation highlighting her defeat.

"You fucking whore. You need to be taught a lesson." Martin's face had convulsed into a snarling grimace. There was anger in his tone and further revenge on his mind. Susan became aware of his hate filled manner and softened her appearance. She had a 'look' in her arsenal, it had been noticed before by several men that had crossed her path. One that, in the past, had helped her to get away with many an audacious misdemeanour. One, that nine times out of ten gave her an extra strike. Martin had seen it before but this time he would not be fooled. He freed one of her handcuffed wrists, stood her up, pushed her face firmly against a sturdy tree and relocked the cuffs around its solid trunk.

Susan tried to voice the words, "what the hell do you think you're doing?" But the question was lost in a sea of denial. She knew damn well what was about to happen. She'd feared the worst having considered the potential situation whilst killing time in her cell. She was the ex-girlfriend. The love of his life. He wanted to punish her for breaking his heart. He was the strong villain with a key to her freedom while she was the weak damsel in desperate distress. This literally would be the nail in her coffin of punishment. He still found her desirable and now he didn't need permission to take what he wanted. At that moment she thought about her son. How pure and innocent he was. How much she worshipped the earth he walked on, how his smile lit up the whole residential estate, never mind the room. His eyes shone so bright like a beacon of eternal hope. Nobody could compete with him. He simply gave the best hugs ever. She could feel his arms around her neck only it wasn't the soft skin of a child but the hairy brawn of a monster.

She felt her jogging pants being pulled down as she looked up at the stars and focussed on the one that shone the brightest. Her life on earth was about to irreversibly change forever and all she could think of was the missed dentist appointment which she'd scheduled the day before she was kidnapped. Would she be charged a cancellation fee? Susan hated the dentist but even more so, having needles thrust into her gums. She recognised the feeling of unpleasant anticipation at that moment. Maybe that's why she thought of her appointment. The needle would go in any time soon and it would hurt but not as much as she'd bargained for. She braced herself and continued to stare at the star but no pain was endured by a needle. Astonishingly, it was a hand that caused her to writhe in agony. A hand that continued to slap her backside.

"Never try anything like that again, you naughty girl."

Susan felt like crying, but not due to the stinging affliction but more the relief that her suffering was not due to the punishment that she feared the most. After at least ten whips of the hand that fed her, she was pushed back down into the sanctuary of her cell and rechained much to the disappointment of those around her. Martin opened his backpack and threw apples, sandwiches, chocolate and coke cans through the bars and into the animal pits. Nobody else moved as he muttered some profanities before he once again abandoned them.

I knew that Mr Bullock would be the first to address his new companions. Why would he wait the now customary ten minutes? "Simon, Bobby or whatever they call you, what the fuck is going on? That bloody prick needs a good kicking!"

"Shush mate, wait until he's long gone." I said, feeling déjà vu.

Martin must have been listening outside. He burst back in, unlocked my cell and pulled out a knife. Pointing it at the newcomer, he placed the empty rucksack over his head. He then moved Sarah from her cell into mine and attached my right shackled arm to her left wrist. Mr Bullock was shoved, kicking and screaming into her old cell. My electric vest was removed and placed onto the new inmate. The bolts and locks where checked over twice before Martin began walking to the exit.

"Do you want money? We will give you everything we own. Houses, jewellery, cars, savings the lot." Suggs shouted his plea with genuine sincerity.

"This is not about money you old fool." Martin slammed the trapdoor shut with more passion than ever.

I held Sarah's hand, comforting her with the knowledge that I couldn't be refused. I was wrong. She unclipped my digits and to my amazement she put her arm around my neck and placed her head on my shoulder. Was this coincidence, had Mr Bullock given me a shot at some happiness in a place where none existed? Or was this Martin's way of saying sorry? A gift to a wrongly convicted man. I was free from the torture garment and I was inextricably linked to the girl who I was developing strong romantic feelings for. Could this be a sting in the tale or a twist in my recent fortunes?

Our attention soon turned to Susan who was languishing in the corner of her cell, whimpering with Winston snuggled up next to her.

"Susan, are you ok? What happened out there?" Doug asked with an uncharacteristic friend like compassion.

"I don't want to talk about it." She snapped, her head now buried in Winston's torso.

"We need to know Susan, good or bad, we have to be informed of everything." A confirmatory acknowledgement accompanied my reasoning.

"Well if you must know, I ran, I got caught, I got hauled back and was given a spanked bottom. Just like a naughty teenager who had been caught smoking by her parents behind the shed in the garden." She began a full-blown woeful wail. "I thought that he was going to do something else. I was petrified."

"My son might be a kidnapper, a torturer, a liar and a modern-day arsehole but he is certainly not a rapist."

There was a slight irony in Doug's judgement of Martin but he was right. Martin was no sexual deviant. He told me that at the ripe old age of eighteen, he'd been dating a West Indian girl. Someone had told him that her family were quite religious and presumptuously added that he'd be lucky to 'get any' before marriage. As a virgin and one that was keen to pop his cherry, he went straight round to her house and asked her mother whether it would be ok to have sexual relations with her daughter. Her mother was a little taken aback but replied with, "of course my darling but if you do, it will be the last time you see your God damn testicles." Martin has never really changed. He worships the local kebab house and respects its opening hours. He would never break in and steal the forbidden shish or be tempted to take the delicious Baba Ganoush without permission.

"No, you're right Doug, he's a conniving evil bastard but he's not capable of that type of depredation. I'm not Jodie Foster and he's not being accused. With that, Susan wiped her eyes and calmed herself down. "I'm ok, just a little disappointed that I failed you all. I felt so close to breaking away. If it wasn't for the handcuffs then we'd be watching Netflix and chilling by now."

"Err, don't you mean eating popcorn and watching movies? Anyway, The Accused is a bloody good film." I laughed.

"Ha ha, fair point." Susan was back in the room and everyone joined in with the much needed and healthy diversion.

It was the voice from beyond that halted the merry go round. "You forgot about Winston again!"

Suggs stomped his feet and then tried to squeeze his face through the bars while singing 'The Doggie in the Window' by Patti Page.

Gone in Over a Minute

The shrill of the phone awakened him with a jolt. He turned over and put the duvet over his head. "Who could this be at this unearthly hour?" He turned to look at the time on his alarm clock. Ten o'clock. With sudden panic, he answered.

"Martin, where are you? You're late. Everything ok?" It was Mike Smalls, his line manager.

"I'm so sorry, I should have called. I'm err sick, yes, sick. I haven't slept a wink. Been tossing and turning all night. It's coming out from both ends. I think it's the man flu mate. I've already booked an appointment to see the doctor. Apologies, I should have let you know."

"Martin, this is the third time in the last two weeks. I know you've got your head in the cement mixer, what with your friend disappearing and all the drama, but you need to get a grip. Make sure you're in tomorrow. I'll schedule a 'catch up' with you first thing. Don't let me down." Mike ended the call without awaiting any response.

"Did he suspect something? Did he acknowledge my double life? Surely he should have cut me some slack! Had I not been convincing enough? Had anyone been talking or gossiping about me in the office?" Martin rolled out of his bed and put on the kettle. He had one important job to do today and that certainly did not involve worrying what his boss thought of him. He'd taken Mr Bullock's car keys from his pocket and he had to move it well away from the crime scene. His wallet had already been discarded after he'd checked to see if any cash was buried inside. The solitary twenty-pound note would see him right for the journey home once he'd ditched the vehicle. "It should be an easy mission." He thought. A Mercedes logo was imbedded into the key fob and the motor in question would surely be on his street. Martin showered and changed, keen to get on with the task at hand. Before leaving the flat, he peered out of the window, half expecting to see the car parked right outside but to his disappointment, it was not there. He then walked up and down the street twice but his search came to no avail. It didn't take Martin long to locate the evidence that could potentially point the finger in his direction. A finger that in turn would allow the media and the criminal justice system to turn the tide and force him to face his demons. The car was parked on double yellow lines outside the library on the busy road at the top of his street. A press on the key fob and a beep beep confirmed his find. To his shock and distain, a traffic warden appeared to be circling with intent. Martin's arrival was timely but he needed to move quickly.

"Hey buddy, sorry about this. I was just dropping off some flowers for my sick aunty. Please don't give me a ticket, I'll move the car now."

"Sir, the vehicle has been on these double yellow lines for over thirty minutes. You've left me no choice. I've already started to type out a penalty notice. It's in the system and therefore too late to cancel."

Martin panicked, he knew that this 'jobsworth' would be placing the car in the vicinity of his address. "Please mate. I've had a bad morning and you're making it worse."

Martin protested in vain as the heavy rimmed spectacled man in uniform continued to tap in the details that any court of law would acknowledge. "How about we settle this, man to man?" Martin pulled out the appropriated twenty-pound note from his wallet.

The official glanced at the note, considered its royal definition and after a few obligatory seconds, continued to process the ticket. "Look, that's not going to work with me. I'll have to add a record that you tried to bribe me. It's part of our procedure sir."

With that, Martin snapped. He grabbed the warden's ticket machine and threw it with all his might to the ground, then proceeded to kick one of the broken fragments onto the road, which in turn, found itself under the wheels of a trundling postal lorry. As the warden took to his walkie talkie, Martin pushed him hard. He stumbled backwards, banged his head on a lamppost and was knocked out cold. Martin didn't waste any time, he jumped into the high-performance car, adjusted the driver's seat and slammed the door shut faster than you can say "Jack Robinson stole my wheels." Quickly familiarising himself with his new surroundings, he pushed the start button and drove off, aimlessly taking left then right turns for no reason other than he'd seen this happen in his favourite car chase movie, Gone in Sixty Seconds.

"Fuck, what have I done?" He screamed into the driving wheel of misfortune. Shaking his head vehemently, his cage was severely rattled. "You idiot, you've fucked up this time. What is wrong with you?" It took him a few minutes to calm down as he made peace with the fact that there was nothing he could do about the altercation, but just hoped that Mr Bullock's car details had not been logged. "Had the idiot hit the process button before I smashed up the machine?" He prayed that the incident hadn't been picked up on CCTV. "I'll check for cameras later," he thought as he headed well away from the area. Martin had never driven a car this expensive before. In fact, he had never driven a car weighing in with so much vanity in his life. He loved the raised feeling of power on the road. "Maybe I should treat myself to one. It would suit my new outlaw lifestyle!" Martin grinned as he looked at himself in the mirror above the steering wheel. It didn't take long to find his bearings as he proceeded to drive north, away from London in order to find a suitable tube station to dump the evidence and return home. Martin meandered his way through the chaotic maze of suburban mayhem until he stumbled on a quiet side street which housed an underground station. After parking up, he wiped down the steering wheel, gearstick and door handles before heading through the barriers and onto the platform. "I'm sure that Nicolas Cage must have done that after nicking the 1967 Shelby?" Feeling more relaxed, he entered the tube station, trotted down the stairs and sat down on a plastic seat covered in graffiti. Seven minutes until the next tube. In ten it arrived and with a mischievous wink to the platforms security camera, he boarded the busy tube and upgraded his seat to one more padded. His comfort was broken at the second stop when a pretty woman with a 'baby on board' badge pinned to her oversized cardigan stood over him and stared with a hopeful ambition.

"Would you like my seat?" He enquired.

"Oh, thank you so much. You are such a kind soul." Little did she know but she was praising a man that was beyond redemption. A man that a few minutes later would walk past the ticket warden that he'd assaulted and laugh in his face.

Once in the safety of his own abode, Martin looked at himself in the full-length mirror that dominated Bobby's old room. It was abundantly clear that he had lost weight. Looking a tad gaunt, his face strained with the pressures of his new life and although the mirror didn't give it away, he bloody stunk. In order to alleviate his angst, Martin pulled out his phone and ordered a takeaway. Then ran himself a hot bath with enough bubbles to recreate the Himalayan mountain range. After scrubbing his bits, his attention returned to his family of misfits. "God, they must hate me." He thought. "Do they really deserve this punishment? Of course, they do! An eye for an eye!" Anyway, it was too late. He was too far into his journey of reprisal. In actual fact, the reality was, he was over a dozen kilometres past the point of no return. "It is what it is!" He surmised as the doorbell rang.

Winston, a Dog Bails

The next morning, Martin took the beating that he deserved. His manager reiterated the five core values behind the success of the company. Hard work, product knowledge, understanding a client's business, fairness but most importantly, trust. Mike Smalls, ironically, was a large gentle man. He was everyone's friend and everyone wanted to work for him. Calmly reprimanding a subordinate who had lost his way was his forte. By the end of the chat, Martin found himself apologising profusely and promising to make more effort to focus his mind on the busy financial period ahead. He walked straight from the meeting room into the bathroom, where he sat on the pan and checked his social media for over an hour. When he returned back to his desk, there was a holiday form awaiting his signature. Mike stormed straight over.

"Martin, where have you been? Wait, it doesn't matter, just listen. You've just not been yourself lately, something's amiss. You've plenty of annual leave available. Take a week off. Get your head straight and come back fresh. You're no good to me like this. This is not me as your boss speaking, it's me as your friend and confidant. Understand? Now go on, get yourself off and buy a bloody TV boxset on your way home. Take your mind off whatever is troubling you!"

Martin didn't even look at him. Once the paperwork was autographed, he was out the door. He needed to see his underground friends and family. They needed him, even if it was for no other reason than sheer hunger. Once home, he grabbed everything he required and jumped into his car. An impromptu visit would be just what the doctor would have prescribed. A tonic of torment and an injection of injustice.

The journey was dull but without incident. Sure, there was traffic, a bumbling bee hive of motorised madness. Everyone on a mission, each one more important that the others. Martin didn't mind that his driving ability was being scrutinised and judged. He prided himself on being a master of the road. This journey felt different though. A builders van beeped at him, a mother, off to collect her kids cut him up. A delivery van followed him as he weaved through the slower more cautious drivers. An overtaking motorcyclist turned and glanced at him. A beggar ignored him at the traffic lights. A helicopter hung over him, sirens caused him to turn down the radio three times. As he turned into the village of vengeance, a church sign caught his attention. 'It's never too late for redemption.' He stopped for a moment. He wasn't sure exactly why. Maybe on the off chance that salvation would come and save his soul. He sat there for ten minutes but nobody came to take him away. He felt a ripple of sorrow. Being arrested would have meant the end of the winding road. Being pulled off the track would have given him at least some certainty. After wiping away the paranoia, he continued his drive to the bunker. He felt indestructible, almost untouchable. On arrival, he parked, took out his bags and stood looking around for a few minutes before continuing his self-serving plight. He jumped through the trap door, half expecting his entrance to be accompanied by cheers and whoops of joy but there was only silence. The room smelt of hopelessness and despair. There was no fanfare. In fact, his appearance was barely acknowledged.

"Guys, I ordered pizza last night and guess what, I got one for each of you." Martin slipped the various boxes underneath the bars.

"Pepperoni for you Bobby boy, your favourite. I even got them to chuck on a few jalapenos for you lad. Sarah, I took a gamble on a Hawaiian. Suze, chicken and sweetcorn, for you my sweet. Yes, I remembered. Dad, I've got you spicy chicken wings as well as a margarita. Got to be happy with that eh? Suggs, there's an extra-large calzone for you but you've got to share it with Dennis. Big bad Bullock, I've got you a large bag of chips you fat bastard. Now, everyone happy? Who said that I don't look after you?" Nothing! No thank you, no pleasantries, not even a nod of acknowledgement. None of the starving, weakened and weary animals moved. "Come on guys, I thought you'd all be excited. Bobby, talk to me. What's up?" Nothing. "Dad, has something happened? Sorry about not coming yesterday but I had things to do." Nothing. "Mr Bullock, how was your first day? Everyone looking after you? Starting to get to know one and all?" Nothing. "Dennis, you keeping your fitness levels up?" Nothing. Martin felt awkward. This was not what he'd anticipated. He just wanted to sit on his pretend throne and pamper his peasants. All hail the almighty! There was no rule book, no idiots guide to kidnapping but if there was, this behaviour would surely not be on the back cover. "Has anyone got anything to say?" implored Martin.

"I have."

"Ok, go on Bobby mate."

"Please take Winston with you. He doesn't deserve this. The poor creature is suffering. Please let him go. Let him smell the unfathomable freshness of nature, let him taste the freedom of life, let him hear the birds sing his name. Please Martin."

Martin looked across at the dog and felt a wave of sadness as their eyes met.

"Dad, is this what you want?"

"Yes son. I love this mutt with all my heart but I can't bear to see him in this state. Of course, I'd miss him but he loves the outdoors and I can feel his free spirit withering in front of me. He's not done anything to hurt you. Why not just let him go?"

"Come here Winnie. Come here boy." Martin grabbed the mutts collar, picked him up with little protest and carried him out of the gloom.

"Hey. You know we love you Winston. We want you to stay here with us. If you have to go...that's okay too. Goodbye, Winston."

"Don't be a smart aleck Bobby, I know that's a quote from the film "A Dogs Tale!""

As soon as the trap door shut, the pack of wolves picked off their prey. "What a twat, I hate chicken on pizza! Remembered, my arse!?" Susan protested as she stared down at the takeaway. Drumsticks and slices were passed amongst the rabble until they were no more.

"Fuck me, I'm so stuffed." I said as I handed my last slice to Sarah. Once she'd delicately devoured it, I held her hand and kissed her on the lips. Our relationship had developed over the last couple of days. The intimacy of our confined space had magnified our feelings and brought us closer. I'd only known her for a few days but I had nothing else to do but stare into her deep blue eyes. I felt that I'd known her for years. Privacy was the main obstacle to pushing our familiarity to the next level. I'd managed a couple of cheeky squeezes but the future surrounding this particular area of our romance looked pretty bleak.

"I bloody told you lot that playing the sympathy card would work!" Susan said with a smugness that we all revelled in.

"Yes, fair play, you little brainbox you." Continued Mr Suggs. "Now it's all down to our four-legged friend. Doug, you know him best. We know he's more intelligent than you but how do you think he will get on?"

"Stop being a dick. Mind you, I bet you'd love to be a giant cock so you could play with yourself all day long, you bellend. Winston is a dog. He behaves like a dog. He likes walkies, having a poo and the occasional bone, not the young boners that you like but big fuck off T-bones. What will be will be. He's hardly going to nip to the local police station and report our whereabouts. What we need is a fair wind and some good old-fashioned luck!"

"Come on Doug. No need for that. Suggs is only questioning whether Winston recognises Martin as the enemy and will run away at the first possible opportunity or whether he'll see him as his new master." I'd thought that their animosity might have diluted as the team spirit increased but I guess that the 'honour amongst thieves' nonsense didn't translate to homewreckers and kiddie fiddlers.

Doug soon realised his temper was mistimed and loosened up. "I really don't know Bobby. He is generally obedient with everyone. Fingers crossed eh? We just need someone somewhere to take that damn collar off."

"Only time will tell my friend. Hey, on another note, we learned something new today, didn't we Dennis? Anything to add dear boy?" I said, remembering the hot gossip of the day.

Dennis, of course, didn't answer my question and I don't think anyone else really cared that I had uncovered one of the oldest and most whispered mysteries that the bunker had to offer. Well, in the modern era anyway. Not wishing to prod his stubbornness any further, I patted down my mattress and ushered Sarah to lie with me so we could feel its softness together. We lay back and she rested her head on my chest.

I whispered into her ear. "Well, at least we know his name now but am I the only one who wants to know why he's in here?"

"I think so sweetheart." She replied. I smiled back at her and rewarded her affection. It had been a while since cupid's arrow had wounded me and its resulting pain filled me with joy.

"I know this might sound ludicrous but I'm glad you're in here with me." You would be forgiven in thinking that to be an outrageous statement but I knew exactly what Sarah meant.

"I want you to know that I fancied you the very first moment I clapped eyes on you." I also need you to know that those naughty magazines were not mine." I digressed.

Sarah giggled. "I believe you, thousands wouldn't. Anyway, it doesn't matter, I quite like a bit of 'Frankie Vaughan.'

"Oh please, you guys are gross. I'm happy for you both but can you remember that we are in this bloody bunker too!"

Sarah looked slightly sheepish as she turned to face her mocker. "Sorry Susan, we'll try to keep it down. Um, I mean, keep a lid on it."

At that affable moment, the trap door was prised open much to the group's astonishment and confusion. There was a scurry of little feet before Winston came bounding towards us and into his true masters arms. There was no sign of Martin, just his echo of anger. "The little fucker bit me and ran back here. I bet you trained him to do that!"

Apart from me, the rest of the bewildered group doubled up with the pain. It had been a little while since Martin had used the shock treatment and it certainly caught everyone off guard.

"You deserve that and another thing, the next time I return, you lot better be more welcoming or I shan't be coming back ever again." With that, the hatch was slammed firmly shut.

After honouring the now customary ten minutes of silence. Filling in the time by stroking Sarah's hair, I mustered up the courage to state what we were all thinking. "I don't know about you lot but I think he meant that!"

When I first became friends with Martin, it wasn't long before I'd introduced him to the gang. Not many of them took to him, mainly due to the fact he was always skint, especially towards the back end of the month. Begging and borrowing, scrounging and whinging are never popular traits. On one particular night out down the pub, Martin was masterminding his usual drinking blag. "I'll get the next one, I promise." We were all quickly on to his roguery and to every last man, we had reached the end of our tether. My pal Bugsy, aptly named due to his bulging fly-like eyes, called time on his antics. "No Martin, if you can't afford to be here then you should go home. We are not paying for a friendship that isn't worth tuppence." Martin, looking rather tearful, started to put on his jacket with the clear and obvious intention of leaving.

"You can't say that mate." I remonstrated with little conviction.

Bugsy, who had a mischievous private school boy mentality, sighed and threw Martin a vulgar 'get out of jail' card. "Ok, I'll get you a beer if you stand on a table, point at me and shout, what's your name? When I give you my made-up name, you've then got to shout at the top of your voice, I love and the name that I declare, three times. Get it?"

Martin, wanting to return to the fold, agreed far too quickly so Bugsy added to his misery. "Then you've got to down a pint of whatever I give you while still standing on the table." To the group's amazement, Martin accepted the full challenge and Bugsy disappeared to the toilet with his empty pint glass. When he returned, Martin was already creating attention from his elevated position.

"What's your name!" He shouted pointing at my devilish friend.

"Mike Hunt!" The whole pub was now focussed on the commotion. "I love Mike Hunt, I love Mike Hunt, I love Mike Hunt. Bugsy then handed him his prize. We all cheered as he downed the warm beverage. Of course, much to Martin's dismay, we all got thrown out of the bar and decided to call it a night but the one thing we learnt from our folly was that Martin was a man of his word.

It was the newly crowned Dennis who disturbed my moment of reminisce. "No shit Einstein. So, what's our next move?"

Before I could answer, Sarah squeezed my hand. "Sweetheart, I feel weak. I can't do this much longer. You have to get us out of here. Beg, plead, borrow, steal, fight, love, I don't care but all I know is that I need to get out of this dump before I crack up or give up."

As Sarah's voice lacked any resilience, I knew that it was time to put my plan into action. It would be my final go on the roller-coaster of desperation, my final bungee jump of optimism and the last time I would parachute out of an aeroplane for freedom. I'd been considering the blue print of my game plan for a couple of days. I just couldn't discuss it with anyone as I knew that they'd be against my controversial tactics. They had to be kept in the dark for their own sake. It just had to work or we'd be doomed. It was time for the hunted to become the hunter.

Midday Address

Martin felt a strange haunting feeling on the drive home. Ever since he'd sentenced his first victim, there wasn't a day that had gone by where he hadn't felt that feeling of someone walking over his grave. He knew that they would be all huddled around discussing how much they despised him. That was ok, the feeling was replicated. But today was different, he felt a sense of self-loathing. Not because of what he'd done or the man he'd become but because he hadn't realised how hard it would be to look after them and maintain a balanced life for himself. They had added an extra strain on his already fragile relationship with Poppy, tipping it over the precipice and into the failed romance section of his past. His work had suffered, his network of friends lay threadbare, leaving an almost non-existent social life. "A prisoner is not just for Christmas but for the time of his or her sentence." He thought. "God, that's my whole damn life!" He pondered the question. Could he just walk away now and get on with the life that they had all tried to destroy? On his return to his roost of respite and by the time he had found a parking spot on his street, he'd worked through the answer. "Yes, but I would need to go back one last time to apologise to Bobby."

Martin wrestled with his decision the whole night. Getting up every hour on the hour to smoke a cigarette. He'd forgotten to switch off his early morning work alarm but that didn't matter, he was awake and it was time. He felt pumped, nervous but with an untapped excitement as he forced a bowl of cereal into his tank followed by a shot of tequila. He sat and waited until the rush hour traffic died a city death and then headed to the supermarket.

"Are you having a party?" The check-out girl asked as he paid for the three trolley loads of food he'd carefully selected, a leaving gift for his 'out of contract' tenants.

"My friend has just had some bad news. I'm hoping that this will cheer him up!"

"Oh, that's kind. The world needs more people like you." She said as she handed over the receipt. With that thought in his head, Martin set off on his final mission which he hoped would ironically set him free from the terrible burden he'd bequeathed on himself.

Back at the bunker, a masterplan was starting to take shape. "Bobby, you seem a little distracted. Are you ok?" Sarah asked, caressing my face. I felt blinded by the mist of apprehension, sensing that Martin was on his way and the next passage of peril would redefine my very existence. I was confident in my approach. I knew my perpetrator well and was convinced that he would accept my deal of atonement. The majority of the time that we had lived together, was conducted in perfect harmony. Our friendship was successful mainly due to me always getting my way. That's not to say that Martin could be played like a fiddle, it was the very science behind one needing a friend more than the other. I feared Sarah's reaction more than anything else and knew that I had to speak to her before the planned event took place. Now was the time. I held her close and whispered into her ear.

"My darling, when Martin arrives, I'm going to offer him a deal. You might not like the sound of it but please just play along. What I'm about to do, I do for us and the sake of our future. Just trust me. Ok?"

"Of course honey, I believe in you. Do what you have to do to get us out of here. I trust you one million percent."

"Thank you Sarah. I knew that you'd have my back."

Susan stirred in her pit. "If you two don't stop whispering, you'll be witnessing the camp's first dirty protest. You guys are the only soap opera that we have in here. Don't deny us that, for God's sake."

I couldn't help but think. "When and if we do get out of this dump, I'm going to miss her."

Bags came flying in through the trap door. The time had arrived. It was the moment I was born for, the juncture that would define me. My race for a medal, my charge to win the war, it was my opportunity to be a hero.

"Brace yourselves guys, you might encounter a couple of shocks here." I whispered loudly.

One being received in response to my current plan and the other, perhaps more painful, for its shocking impact. The atmosphere was electric and highly charged. The temperature was about to rise, short tempers needed to be managed. This wasn't a light bulb moment, it was well planned. My finger had to be on the pulse as I knew Martin wasn't wired correctly and I needed ample power to diffuse any sparks that might fly. I was about to sock it to him in an unplugged manner, causing a chain reaction of events, moving heaven and earth to feel the sun's heat on my face once more.

"Martin, mate. I need to speak with you. I have an interesting proposition. One that I think will give you solace." My first dart was thrown.

"Mate, sounds good. I need to speak to you too. Just give me a minute to get these bags of food sorted."

"Ok buddy." I wasn't expecting him to fire his arrow in the same half of the board, clearly he was intrigued.

Martin placed a bulging sack next to each of the cells and then grabbed the milkmaids stool and placed it in front of me. He looked shattered, almost broken as he wiped the sweat off his brow, sat down and took off his antiquated oversized aviators. "Can I go first?" This didn't sound like a question but I didn't feel either capable or in a position to protest. I simply nodded. "Bobby lad, for what I am about to say, let the lord forgive me one day for I have trespassed on my one true friend's precious land and stolen his forbidden fruit. I'm sorry but this will be the last time I see you. Thank you for being the one person in my life that truly believed in me. I've let you down in the worst way possible. It's time for me to say goodbye and if we ever meet again on the other side, I hope that you can release me from my guilt which I'm sure will burden me with every step I continue to take on this earth."

"No Martin, no!" Susan began to wail and whimper like a demented animal.

"You can't be serious." Shouted Doug like a deluded tennis pro.

"Please Martin, don't do this!" Screamed Suggs as he adopted the nightly prayer position. Kneeling and rocking from side to side.

Doug took a more reasonable approach. "Come on son, I know you're hurting but this is not the way. You're no killer! I'm sure that we can find a way through this."

Mr Bullock decided that it was time to model for Edvard Munch's follow up painting. Even Dennis let out a gasp of bewildered distress.

I remained calm. It was time for the big reveal. "Martin, I hear you loud and clear. I understand what these people have done to you but what I can't accept is your reasoning for throwing me in this snake pit. These bastards deserve to be punished. What they've all done to you is unforgivable. They are scum and the world will be a better place without them. I get it. Let me help you to serve the divine retribution that warrants their evil crimes. Allow me to assist you in carrying out your mission of justice. I am your friend and can be your comrade in arms. Release me and I will continue your obligation to keep them alive. You can trust me, I will tell no one of our mandate. I will continue to deliver them food parcels and you can get on with the pursuit of happiness. You can clean the landscape that tarnishes your very existence. You can purify the polluted air that sits stale in your lungs. You don't desire or need these demons to haunt you anymore. Let me take that pressure off you. Let me free Martin and we'll do this together. We are and always will be two peas in a pod. You must know that you can trust me! I've always been there for you. Even saved your life once, remember? Now, let me out of here. Let me catch the midnight express!"

"You piece of shit. You'll both burn in hell." Screamed Susan.

The electric shock brought everyone to their knees apart from me. My vest of torment had been removed and I was free from its pain. I didn't feel the others contempt as I held my scare and continued to search for a glimmer of hope in Martin's soul.

After a few seconds, Martin's finger released them from their torture. "God, Bobby! You and your bloody film quotes! Well, let me tell you now, the midnight express doesn't stop here. I just can't take the risk. How do I know that you won't turn me in? I might be naive but I'm not stupid."

I expected this reaction from Martin and was undeterred in my ambition. "Martin wait! I understand and I do not underestimate your resolution and determination to this great and justified cause. I do realise that to guarantee my silence, I need to become part of your plight. Let me take one of these perpetrators penance to the next level. Allow me to serve the ultimate punishment and end their life. An eye for an eye Martin. You choose and I will extinguish the fire in their eyes. Pick one Martin and witness them take their last breath on this earth. I will do this for you and we will become one. I will have committed a more severe crime in the eyes of the law and therefore, you will have my silence. Come on, who deserves it the most Martin?"

Sugg's immediately started to remonstrate, perhaps fearing himself as the bookies favourite. "Murder? Are you actually saying that you will sacrifice one of us to save yourself? Have you lost your marbles and gone stark raving mad?"

"Shut the fuck up you lot! The adults are talking." Martin was up and running but was he about to handover the baton and leave me to finish his race?

"Wow Bobby. I wasn't expecting that! I don't know what to say. Let me get this straight to ensure clarity and take away any element of confusion. You are offering to kill one of these dickheads to save your own foreskin. You will then take over my role as camp guardian and allow me to crack on with my own business. You are saying that once I hand over the keys, I will never have to come here again? Have I understood you properly?"

I confirmed my well-rehearsed statement. "Correct. I'll be completely complicit and the new caretaker. You will still hold all of the cards."

"And you'll still be my flatmate and friend?"

"Of course. If that's what you want." I replied.

"You do realise that there will be witnesses and to guarantee my safety, I would have to film the execution?"

"I would expect nothing less." Did I have him on the line? Was it time to reel him in?

"For fuck sake. Spanner in the works or what! Let me think about it. If I don't return tomorrow, you'll know my answer." With that, he stood up, surveyed the surroundings, perhaps for the last time and stormed off.

For the first time since my arrival in the bunker, I was relieved that my fellow prisoners were segregated and their movements restricted. Otherwise, I'm pretty sure I would have been lynched by a mob that felt I'd betrayed their mantra of unity. Their leader had abandoned them and a coup d'état would not have been surprising. I understood that an explanation was required and that the friends I'd never chosen to bond with, deserved one. Surely Sarah, my cell mate, my companion through these menacing times would understand. Afterall, I had warned her.

She shuffled away from me until the chains would take her no further. "Fuck me Martin!" I knew that she didn't mean this literally but how I longed for her to say those words under different circumstances. Perhaps I'd blown it. Not my load but the respect and admiration that I'd managed to build between the two of us.

I began my justification. "Sarah, one of us dies or we all die. The maths is simple. There are no quadratic equations, no algebraic fractions not even a hint of long multiplication, if I get out then we all get out. Even if that means sacrificing my liberty for you. Hopefully the courts will take pity and understand my reasoning. I'm doing this for us all. If he doesn't validate my proposal then we are all doomed anyway. Surely you understand?"

I looked around for support but my fellow inmates were too busy trying to apprehend the depths of my sanity. "Come on guys, you heard what he said." I remonstrated, "He's done with us, finito, the games up. He came to say his final farewell, to sign our death warrants. I had to throw one final pair of dice. It's better to save six of us than none at all. Look, I'm the one who will have to commit the murder. Do you think I want to? When I was a kid, knee high to a grasshopper and my parents asked me what I wanted to become when I grew up, do you think that I replied with…. a killer?"

The first sign of understanding came from the softening voice of Doug. "Alright, alright. I get it. You can calm yourself down now. You're not bloody Martin Luther King."

"More like Martin Luther Queen!" Cried Susan.

Doug, the elder statesman, the wiser and most empathetic of the group continued. "I think what you've just done deserves some respect. You could potentially be making a great sacrifice for our freedom. If it doesn't work then hey ho, at least you've tried. Let's just hope and pray that he returns tomorrow."

Sarah's demeanour had changed completely. She didn't even look me in the eye when she delivered the question that was on everyone's lips. "Let's just say, for the sake of argument that he does come back tomorrow, who do you think he'll choose?"

"It will be Suggs and I'll help you strangle the mother fucker myself." Shouted Doug.

Suggs had no retort. He sat down on his mattress, head in hands and began to sob.

I felt the need to show support, not because he deserved it but because I sensed that Doug might be right. "Come on fella, let's not jump to any conclusions. We don't even know why Dennis is in here. Dennis, care to elaborate?"

"Nothing ventured, nothing gained. Now bog off and leave me alone!"

"Anything else Dennis? I like your profound words but you didn't exactly answer the question."

Dennis left us with bated breath and revealed nothing. An admission of fear or confidence in his resolve? "The hangman will decide," I thought to myself.

Martin's journey home was fairly upbeat and uneventful. He felt a weight had lifted from his shoulders. There were decisions to be made which would call for thoughtful deliberation but the door to the next chapter of his life was slightly ajar. He made the decision to wait until he was in the comfortable surroundings of his homestead, with a glass of chardonnay in his hand before he'd go about contemplating the answers which would unlock the dark caverns in his heart and allow his tainted spirit to be cleansed. His demons needed exercising before he could allow them to hide away in his distant memory.

On his return he made the call to the local Chinese and ordered a chicken chow mien to compliment his choice of wine. "A well-deserved treat," he thought to himself as he turned the radio on and laid the table, for one.

"Police are asking witnesses to come forward. An assault on a traffic warden took place on Ealing High Street on Monday at ten am and they believe the perpetrator may be involved in the disappearance of a local businessman. A reward will be given to anyone with information that leads to his arrest. CCTV in the area was able to capture a photo of the assailant and we have placed it on our website. If you've seen anything or recognise the photo, please do not hesitate to contact the local police. Thanks for your assistance and now back to our resident disk jockey, Bizzy Boy Barry!"

At first the words did not sink in. Martin's initial thought was, "I hope they find the thug." Then it dawned on him like a float bobbing in a rippling pond, he was the fish they wanted to catch. He downed his glass of wine, grabbed his laptop and logged onto the radio station's home page. There it was, as large as a cold sore on a super model's lip. The picture was slightly grainy but it was him alright. He could tell but could anyone else? He trawled through the internet to see if there were any other news stories on the incident. Nothing, and by the time the alcohol began working its charm, Martin decided that the picture was unrecognisable but for safety, he'd keep his head down for a while until the story made its way to the local chip shop. The doorbell interrupted his dark thoughts but Martin took no chances and answered it donning his baseball cap and sunglasses. The food tasted lovely but Martin had lost his appetite. "I'll have it tomorrow before I leave." He lay on the settee, staring aimlessly through the window at the night sky. His mind was made up. "I've had enough!" I'll take Bobby's offer but I not going to fall into his trap. He can select the victim to be slaughtered." After taking a pain killer and finishing off the bottle, he decided to retire to bed. As he closed his eyes, all he could see was the grainy website photo of himself. "When this is over, I must get back to the gym," he breathed as he slipped into the night.

Internal Haze of the Freckled Soul

When Martin awoke, he only had one thought on his mind. "It's my way or the slip road that will force them into a motorway pile-up." He knew that he had to remain in control of the situation and wanted today to be over so he could move on with repairing the damage to his disrupted life. He sat on the sofa, carefully forking his reheated takeaway into his mouth to avoid any stains on his new white shirt. A shirt that symbolised the purity that he craved. It was crystal clear in his troubled soul that a decision had to be made and its consequence would have severe repercussions. It weighed heavy on his mind and he knew that any potential risk would be drowned in his guilt. "If I choose the sacrificial lamb then I'll be an accomplice to the assassination." He carefully considered his options. "No way, I will not be fooled again. Bobby's not hoodwinking me into this crime. I'm the one doing him the favour! It's his idea so he can choose his victim."

Martin felt comfort in his judgement as he grabbed his largest and sharpest kitchen knife before leaving the flat. He collected some blankets and a spade at a DIY store en route. He was no expert in the art of planning the perfect murder but one thing he knew for sure was that the evidence had to disappear. "Does it really matter, is it really my problem? Who cares, I'll offer the demonic 'starter pack' as a present anyway." Doffing his baseball cap, he paid cash and hurried to his vehicle.

This would be his final journey to the carefully selected crime scene. It had taken many months to find a suitable location. He'd stumbled on the remote bunker idea which was listed in a World War II manuscript covering the High Wycombe area. When he'd first clapped eyes on it, he knew that it would be perfect. It was suitably hidden and intentionally forgotten about. He set to work on converting it to suit his mission of vengeance. Discreetly and in the depths of the nights, he set about masterminding his creation. So proud, he was on completion. So much so, he bought two bottles of Champagne, smashed one by the entrance and consumed the other with an air of satisfaction in his work. Martin asked himself, "will I miss the old place?" His mindful, carefully thought out answer came back negative. He knew that it was built to last and, if necessary, would outlive every one of those sorry, good for nothing miserable beings.

It suddenly dawned on Martin that if everything went to plan he would be outside in the fresh air with Bobby in a couple of meaningful hours. "God, how will he act? What will we talk about? I will have to stay close, very close to him for a few days to ensure that he is dedicated and committed to his new role. He has to take our secret to his grave or his grave will find him sooner than expected!" Martin felt like turning around the car. "Am I doing the right thing? Is it just too precarious? Do I have any other choice if I want to pass on my burden?" Before Martin had the chance to reconcile any other verdict, he found himself pulling off the A40 and into Horsleys Green.

The funeral march to the bunker left him shaking as he took a deep breath and entered the lair. The one place he was the master, the only setting where he was shown respect, his only dream that had become a reality. Was this all about to change?

His audience was waiting. Apprehension and sheer bewilderment adorned their strained faces. They were hungry. This time, it wasn't food that they craved but information. Information dictating their future happiness or lack of it.

Martin stood before them, arms placed on hips. "Right, there's no point wasting any time. I'll get straight to the point. No reason to beat about the bush. Bobby, I've considered your offer and I'd like to take you up on it but on one condition, you will have to decide who to kill."

I sat there, gripping Sarah's hand, shocked, trying to digest the grim words that I had just heard. "Surely, he couldn't mean it. Why was he turning the tables of doom?"

"What! You can't be serious! Absolutely no chance, I won't do it. That's not what we agreed." I protested. "This is not 'The Last Supper' where you pass me the poisoned chalice! This is a circus and you are the ringmaster! You have to make this decision!"

Martin turned his back on me. "We agreed nothing. Take this deal, agree terms with the devil and sign away your innocence. If you want your freedom Bobby, then you'll do as I say. If not, I'll understand and with a heavy heart, I'll say my final goodbye and leave you to it."

"Bobby, you have to agree to his ridiculous offer or we're all doomed." Implored Sarah as she began to choke up in a blaze of bewildered bemusement.

"I can't do it. I'm not qualified to be the judge. Taking instruction and allowing someone's blood to drip though my fingers is the only part I'm prepared to play in this dark web of betrayal." I declared my objection but was only wasting my time. It was clear that Martin's mind was made up of all the broken fragments of a damaged life.

"Fine, ok, if you don't want to take my offer, I'll leave you to drown in your own righteousness." Martin turned to leave, knowing full well that his tracks would be halted.

"Ok, ok. I'll do it but you need to give me time to make a decision." My outburst came as no surprise to Martin who beckoned Winston over and attached a lead to his collar."

His camera phone was then placed on a shelf and strategically positioned. The moment would be captured and stored in the archives of history forever. "I'll take this mutt for a walk. I'll be gone for fifteen minutes."

"Wait Martin, before you go, I need to understand why Dennis is here. He won't speak and I need all the facts to make my judgement."

"Bobby, this is your idea and you need to own it. You've got a quarter of an hour. Use the time wisely." With that, he left.

I immediately set to work. "Right Doug. You're in charge of the countdown. Give me a minutes warning before the bell tolls. I will allow each of you a maximum of two minutes to explain to me why your life should be spared. I know this is not ideal but I can't think of any other way. Mr Bullock, I'm going to pass on you. We are brothers from another mother. We simply picked out the joker from the deck of cards. You have left no scars on Martin's heart, only a flesh wound. You will live another day. Sarah, can you begin?"

"Ok, I'll keep this short. Look, I'm not going to lie, I made a couple of gags too many at work. I took the piss out of Martin for wearing my clothes and pissing on your bed. Shoot me now! We've all enjoyed a bit of banter in the office haven't we? Anyone would have done the same in my boat. Also, I know this sounds corny but I'm falling for you and really want to be with you on the outside?"

I ignored her inappropriate wink. "Ok, cool. Susan, you next."

"Mate, seriously? I'm not the first person to break up with someone and I won't be the last. Hey, I feel bad for the way I treated the poor sod but I was young and naive. It's not like I set out to hurt the bloke. We were happy for eighteen months. I gave him my heart and my bed. You know what he's like. Surely you can understand how and why someone better came along. Anyway, it wasn't just a sexual experiment or even a fling. I'm married with a kid to the fella I left him for. Surely that doesn't deserve a silver bullet?"

Susan would have rabbled on for hours if I'd let her. I already knew that she was in no danger so I called a halt to her diatribe.

"Constantly talking isn't necessarily communicating. Sorry, probably not the right time for a movie quote but if anyone's interested, that's from Eternal Sunshine of the Spotless Mind."

The stunned looks of their faces forced me to move on quickly. "No? Ok, over to you Doug."

"Oh, very good Bobby, very good. Now, I know you look at me and think that I'm to blame for creating this monster. I'm his dad, he has my toxic blood running through his evil veins. I get that but I want you to know that I tried so hard to stay part of his life when I left his mother. I called and called. I wrote and wrote. All my efforts were knocked out of the park. I know that I should never have given up but it's hard. I'll never forgive myself for behaving the way I did. I'd lost my family, even my affair failed. I'm the perfect cliché, I found solace in the bottle. It numbed my pain. The one positive thing about being in here is that my head is clear now. The mist has thinned. I can focus without my bifocals. If I ever get the chance, I'll make it up to my boy and live out my days correcting the error of my ways. Please allow Martin that chance, if you don't, he'll never forgive you, especially if one day he has kids of his own. I'm his father not his enemy. I've never done anything willingly to hurt him. I need him to realise that. I know that I haven't got many years left anyway but please don't let me die without him forgiving me."

I'd heard enough. "I understand Doug. Suggs, cut the shit and give me the whole truth and nothing but the truth so help me God or you will feel my divine retribution on your scrawny ass."

Suggs cleared his voice and looked into space. "I know I'm the odds-on favourite to walk the plank. I know what you all think of me. You believe the reason I'm here is because I'm a paedophile but your assumptions are based on unfounded presumptions! You've hung drawn and quartered me as a kiddie fiddler. That just couldn't be further from the truth! I'm a happily married man, a school teacher from a day gone by, one that just believes in old-fashioned discipline. I'll hold my hand up. I've used a cane or two in my time but that's all!"

"Absolute bollocks. You're nothing but a dirty sexual predator. Preying on the vulnerable. You're the scum of the earth. You deserve to die, you pervert. You're a stain on society."

"Ok Doug, that's enough. Let the man continue. There is no time for debate." I shouted impatiently.

Suggs, unperturbed, carried on, "listen, I've taken my belt to Martin on a number of occasions but trust me, only if he deserved it. I knew that it was illegal but some of the other teachers did it and it was hard to change my ways. In hindsight, I now know that corporal punishment was wrong but it was a hidden secret at the time and sanctioned in the shadows of the classroom. I understand that I might have embarrassed him in front of his class. That was the idea but ask yourself this? Have I beaten the wickedness out of him? Well, obviously not, but you can't condemn a man for trying. I'm not the anomalous person you think I am. Look, I'm just an old retired headmaster who went about his business the best way he knew how. At worst, I was wrong and too harsh to give him a bruise or two but there's people in here who have disfigured him for life."

Doug had heard enough and made his feelings clear. "Bobby, he's offering you a main course of verbal diarrhoea. Surely, you're not washing that shit down with a glass of his vile piss! Do me a favour and ask Martin when he returns. He'll put you straight. This guy is a heinous abomination, a man who enjoys playing with young innocent boys. Surely he's the one to be sacrificed!"

"Dennis, help me out mate. I'm sure that you don't want to listen to these two men squabble as much as me. Now's the time. Tell us your story." I said, looking into the darkness that cloaked a man whose life lay in my hands.

His voice boomed through the corridor of death row. "You've got your man. Just leave me out of the whole abominable mess."

I just couldn't let this go. Not through personal intrigue but for the greater good and fairness. It was the most important decision that I would ever make and one that would stick a knife in the heart of a mother, a father, a son, a daughter or even a long lost distant second cousin twice removed. "No Dennis. I will pick you unless you convince me otherwise. I mean it. It's up to you but your silence will cost you. It's time you stopped believing that you're better than us. You've clearly judged us, now it's time to judge you. Come on, last chance, time is running out!"

"Harsh but fair." Interjected Susan.

"Leave him, he's obviously done something far worse than any of us!" Shouted Suggs.

"Who the fuck do you think you are? Chief prosecutor and executioner my arse. I'm Den Folks. Yes, you heard me. I play cricket for England. Fifty-two test matches and eighty-six one day internationals. Like all sporting stars, I've had good days and bad days. If you must know, that's why I'm in here. The lowest point of my career was when I got hit for four consecutive sixes in the last over of the T-20 final against the West Indies last April. We lost the game and it was all my fault."

"Fuck off you prankster. You're a not a wicket taker, you're either a faker or a porkie pie maker." Doug cried out almost choking at this own ridiculous riddle.

Shocked at what I'd just heard, I implored him to back up his claims. "What, are you serious? Ok, prove it and reveal yourself."

Dennis pushed his face up against the bars. "Well, I'll be damned. It's only Den Folks." Announced Suggs.

"Yes, it's definitely him." Followed up Doug.

I couldn't quite make out his facial detail but as his status had been confirmed, I had no choice but to believe that he was genuine. "Bloody hell. This whole thing is a mind fuck. Look, I still don't understand. You were shocking in the last over, I remember it well. You gave the game away on a roasting dish. But I still don't get it, why are you in here?" I continued to search for the answers I required.

"You're not going to believe this, but Martin told me after the event, he'd placed a rather large bet on us winning that game. He placed it with a couple of overs to go. Well, I've just told you how it ended. It's written in the sporting history books. They needed twenty-four off the last over. Impossible you say. Well, I bowled that last over and bloody well rolled over, had my belly tickled and gave them the runs. Four balls, four huge sixes. He reckons that he lost thousands. His life savings, a deposit for a house he said, God knows the exact amount."

I was in shock. Being a huge fan of the gentleman's game, I felt a sense of excitement that we had cricketing royalty in our presence. Slightly star struck, I didn't know whether to ask Dennis for his autograph, berate him on his poor performance in that final or begin working through the extreme and fatal quandary that was forced upon me. I don't know why I said it but I did. "I'll give you a free pass

Den if you promise you'll invite me for drinks with the rest of the England team when we get out of here."

"You have my word Bobby lad."

Susan took this to heart. "Fuck me Bobby, I told you that I've represented my country in the wonderful sport of cross country and you didn't even blink a glass eye. Talk about an old boys club!"

"Bobby, sorry to interrupt your celebrity love fest but you only have five minutes to make your fatal decision."

"Oh yes, thanks Doug. Ok, can everyone please be quiet while I gather my thoughts and consider your statements."

The silence was eerie. There had been long spells of serenity during my time in the bunker but this was different. You could cut through it with a rolling pin. I had made my decision but felt compelled to go through the motions for the sake of my apprehensive inmates. My mind turned to the actual act of murder. Would I be able to go through with it? What qualifications does one need to fulfil such a horrific crime? In the past, I'd stamped on a few creepy crawlies, pulled apart a few dozen worms and run over a pigeon, by accident, I might add. Hardly a great CV for a hitman.

I looked over at Sarah and whispered to my conscience. "I'll do it for her, for our future, we'll replace the lost life with a couple of children. That will be my redemption. That will readdress the balance. Two for the price of one. A haunted, tarnished soul for two pure ones. I might not be able to forgive myself but God will understand." I felt myself shake as I heard the magnified creek of the trap door and the heavy panting of an excited dog.

"Ok, Bobby. It's now or never. Have you made your choice?"

"I have Martin."

"Good. Who have you chosen?" Martin's request sounded so sincere. I was sure that he pitied my plight. He knew me as well as anyone. I clocked him once, pulling a limb off a daddy long legs. He wasn't shocked when I super glued it back on and released it back into the wild.

I spoke clearly and without emotion. "I choose Suggs. Now tell me, have I made the right call?" I looked closely at Martin's reaction.

"Oh, ok. I wasn't expecting that. This is your decision, Bobby. I refuse to sway you in any direction. Right, here's how it's going to play out. I'll place him in your cell, turn on the video camera and then disappear for ten minutes while you do the deed. It will all be on tape for my own protection."

The candy bar had been ripped out of Suggs' hand's and he began to blubber like a child with the weight of the world on his shoulders. "No Martin, you can't let this happen. I have children. How can you take their father away from them? And what about my poor wife. She's ill. She needs me for God's sake. No, please. All I tried to do is make you a better person. What about Susan, she ripped out your heart. What about your dad, he abandoned you in your hour of need, what about Dennis, he cost you dearly, what about Sarah, she humiliated you, what about you let us all go!"

"Nothing to do with me Suggs." Martin had to raise his voice to be heard over the loud sobbing that filled the sullenness of the dimly lit space. He began to wrench up the chains as Suggs' howls continued and increased in their intensity.

Once he entered his cell, it didn't take long to attach extra shackles to his feet and wrists, then lead him into the makeshift execution chamber that was my cell. He reattached him to my front bars and carefully relocked my cage. After tossing in the knife and blankets, he lowered us from our 'Christ on the cross' like positions and set up his video phone in order to capture the whole heart wrenching episode. Ensuring that he would not be in the footage, he raised ten digits to me and quietly left the bunker.

"Fuck, is this really happening?" I was transfixed on this senior citizen who was weeping into his hands. Frozen in time, all I could think of was facing this man's family and telling them that I killed their loved one so I could get my end away with a pretty girl.

"I can't do it." I breathed the words that I knew everyone was thinking.

"You have to. It's him or us." Doug shouted in an attempt to reassure me that I was doing the right thing. "The world will be a better place without him anyway."

I picked up the knife and felt its acuminous edge to the point of drawing my own blood. I looked directly at the camera, maybe for some displaced guidance or maybe because I was the star actor in the movie and deserved some credit. I then placed the knife on his throat and held my breath. The good in me shouted out to stop this burning injustice but the bad in me began to beat the death drum. "Come on, you know it makes sense. Just do it, just do it." One minute passed, then two, then three. "Just do it, just do it." Some in the room were now joining in with the mantra.

"Just do it, just do it." Four minutes passed, then five then six. Suggs continued to weep. "Please don't kill me. Please let me live." Eight minutes passed then nine.

"You have to do it now, Martin. The clock's ticking down mate. He'll be here in any second." Coaxed Doug.

"Shut up Doug, you're not calling last orders. This is fucking hard." I expostulated with all my might. At that moment, I felt Sarah's presence. She was behind me, one hand wrapping itself around my armed knuckles. It happened so quickly, with a sudden swipe the blade moved across our victim's throat with all the stealth of a paint brush stroking its final path of a masterpiece. We both rolled back in unison and fell to the ground while the blood left the body of our prey and channelled its way towards our feet. Suggs, slumped forward but the light in his eyes refused to let go of his stare. His eyes transfixed on me. The shock, the fear of the unknown, his life unravelling in those final few moments. He didn't need to say any final words. We felt his hatred, his animosity towards us was clear. We knew that our lives would never be the same again, but the deed was done. I held him as the final breath left his tortured soul. "I'm so sorry Suggs. Please forgive me and may you rest in peace." Tears rolled down my face as I rocked him back and forth like a newborn baby.

"Careful Bobby, if he's still got any lead in his pencil, he might stick a finger in."

Momentarily interrupted in my final ritual, I felt the anger rise. "Go fuck yourself Doug!"

Enemy of the Mate

The drive back to the flat was awkward to say the least. It felt surreal to leave my new-found family but the tide had turned and the torrid undercurrent would not take me away for long. We'd heaved Suggs out of one coffin and into another. Martin had used his ten minutes effectively and dug a suitable hole in the heart of the woods. After burying God's new angel or perhaps, Satan's new servant, I gave my sincerest rendition of the lord's prayer before we left. It was unceremonious, cold and heartless but it had to be done. Unbeknown to Martin, I'd slipped off his wedding ring, a symbol of eternal love. Sending it back to the person who had placed so much hope and ambition in its circle of trust, was surely the right thing to do. It was strange seeing ordinary people going about their business on the side of the road. Little did they know what had just occurred in their tranquil back garden. As we hit the motorway, Martin turned off the radio and put on his sunglasses. Was he shading his eyes from the sun or hiding his face from the guilty act of self-deprecation?

"Right, we need to discuss where you've been for the last few days." He began. "I have thought long and hard about an explanation but all I can come up with is this. You were out and about in central London, were attacked, robbed and pushed to the ground by mindless thugs. You banged your head badly, causing concussion and memory loss. You've been wandering the streets, effectively homeless, not even knowing who you were. Begging and sleeping rough has been your only focus until now. You are still massively confused but your memory is returning. Whatever they say, just stick to this damn story but be vague about exact locations. They will never be able to prove otherwise. Once we're home and half way through a brew, you can call the police. Tell them that you've heard they've been looking for you and let them know you're ok. Once they're off your back, you can start ringing around friends and family. Your final call will be to your office, ask for a couple of days grace to clear your head but that's all. We need to get back to normal as soon as possible. Understand?"

I was still in shock after the events of the day and showed no resilience to his plan, apart from a confirmatory grunt, so he continued.

"Ok, good. Right, I'm handing over the proverbial keys. Those goons are your responsibility from now on. I don't want you to even mention their dirty good for nothing names in my presence. Don't get any ideas. I have your murder on camera. It's locked, loaded and the film barrel is full. The evidence will be transferred to a USB stick. I've already bought a coded security box. Don't worry, it will be looked after and left with someone we can trust. Be sure though, they will be left instructions to hand it over to the police if I give them the nod or if anything happens to me. Understand?"

This time, I felt the need to interject. "I do and you have my word, but only if I can ask you one last question on the matter."

"Ok, fire away and I'll give you an honest answer but afterwards, that's it! No more! That will be my final involvement. Agreed?"

I granted his wish and nodded. "Why did you kidnap Suggs?" I asked.

"I knew that you were going to ask me that! Well, don't laugh but he was my old primary school headmaster who had it in for me from the very first day I arrived. The jumped-up fool always picked on me at school. Back then I was weak and a bit of a softy. I'd never look for or cause any trouble but I'd be they first boy accused if there was any. He used the slipper on me a few times, just as a show of force against the tougher kids who he was scared of. He made my early school days a bloody misery. I was a kid, all I wanted to do was paint, sing and play in the fields. At that age, what I certainly shouldn't have been doing was crying in dark corners and hiding bruises from my mother. If you play with fire then you are going to get burnt my friend, and that arsehole was a pyromaniac! Fuck him, he deserved what he got!"

"So, he never touched you inappropriately?"

"Of course not. Why would you ever think that?"

I slumped back in my seat. "Oh fuck, I'm going to burn in hell." I turned the radio back on to drown out the noise of his irritating small talk and began to wrestle with my conscience. "I have to give myself up." I thought, realising my error of judgement. "The courts will understand. The guys will collectively support me and defend my position. They may go easy on me. Even if they throw the kitchen sink and a couple of dozen legal books at me, I deserve everything I get. No, wait, what am I saying? I can't and will not turn myself in! What about Sarah? She was involved, she's as guilty as I am. Surely, she will help me through this. Help me to get my life back on track. It's our time now. Our time to hold the candle of happiness together." My mind was made up and as we walked through our front door, I had made the decision to go along with Martin's clumsy plan.

The police passed me from pillar to post until Inspector Mary Whatdoyoucallher, said that she was happy that I had returned home safely. As her questioning relented, she offered her best wishes but not before requesting my attendance at the local station to give an official statement, before the week was out.

"Oh, thank the Lord," cried my mother. She had booked into a local bed and breakfast and had spent the last few days walking aimlessly around the city, calling out my name and showing anyone who would listen to the ramblings of a mad woman, a photo of me at my graduation. "I'm on my way over. I love you son. I'm just so relieved that your safe and sound." My brother, on the other hand, reminded me that I still owed him forty quid. "You ain't getting away with it that easily!"

I posted a message and a photo on Facebook. "Don't worry one and all. I'm safe and back at home. Just had a knock on the head and a touch of memory loss." 123 likes out of 650 friends. I sensed that I'd have to be content with that, it was my new record after all. Although, it was only two more likes than a photo of me with my trousers around my ankles, sitting on a toilet with a can of cider in my hand. My mobile, which Martin returned, began ringing off the hook but I was far too apprehensive to answer any of these concerns. "Probably people just being nosey." My boss sounded a little relieved, more than likely due to him not having access to my inbox which would have been filled with potential business. After giving him my passwords, he allowed me the rest of the week off, non-gratis.

I was back in the land of the living and it felt surreal but intoxicating. After I'd unblocked my bank cards, I ordered a chicken tikka masala from the local takeaway. The curry of choice would offer no compensation for my misfortune but would at least take my mind off the horrendous shortcomings of my tailor-made fate. The spices exploded in my mouth, as I turned on the television and straight to the news channel, half expecting to see a breaking story regarding my reappearance, with reporters setting up tents outside my home. It was not to be. Only a piece on how a bride charged her guests fifty pounds to attend her wedding, and one such invitee exclaiming that she was disappointed having only been offered cheese and sausages on sticks at the reception. "Not even a glass of fizz!" I almost felt a sense of relief that the topical first world problems of the modern era appeared to remain unsolved during my absence.

"You've missed some really nice sunshine while you've been away, you know." My mother's generation was only three sentences removed from discussing the weather. On arrival, she asked how I was and before listening to the answer, told me that I'd put on weight. After a cup of tea and half the cookie jar, she left. Content that her mission was complete and she could return home, safely in the knowledge that I had learnt another valuable life lesson.

Her parting gift resonated her concern. "Do not go out alone late at night. It's not safe."

"Fancy a couple of cheeky beers?"

I didn't even respond to Martin. I simply entered my room and closed the door in his face. Not my finest protest but my energy levels were low and the takeaway was beginning to place me in a food coma. I lay on the bed, stared at my prized possession, a poster of a tennis player with her back to the camera and her arse cheek on display. Then imagined what Sarah might be doing right at this moment in time. "I do hope that Mr Bullock is not trying to take my seat at the table of romance," I thought as I felt the weight of my eyes.

I awoke to the smell of bacon. This was going to be so hard but I felt the need to embrace the olive branch.

"Mushrooms on the side or in the sandwich?" The words reverberating through the thin walls of the flat. Music to my ears. Some form of normality or an indirect comparison to my previous morning's routine? It was not a time for debate. I opted for out, devoured my peace offering, told Martin that I was off for a walk alone and left the flat.

It was the city noise of hustle and bustle that hit me before the sunshine. The cars revved, the commuters shouted, the dogs growled and the wind screamed the words, "murderer, murderer!" I walked and walked, constantly looking around to see if anyone was following me. Surely, they knew. Surely, they had worked out the reason for my sudden appearance. I had to go to the police station to confess my sins, to offer up my co-conspirator. I walked around the official building four times before I entered. "Hello, my name is Simon Dingle and I have murdered an innocent man." The words pumped around my head as I neared the counter.

"Hello, my name is Simon Dingle. I had been reported missing. I'd just like to confirm that I'm safe. I called yesterday to let you know and was asked to sign an official statement."

They didn't hold me for long. Just a few formalities they said. After half an hour of scribbling down my rhetoric, I signed away my lies and was told that I was free to leave, unless I had anything else to add. Shaking my head, I bolted for the door. "What did they mean anything else? Did they know something? Were they toying with me? Perhaps they were busy gathering more evidence?" I hurried down the high street and burst into the nearest cafe with an ever-increasing torrent of sweat pouring off my forehead.

The barista or perhaps the academic, reluctantly trying to reduce her student debts, looked concerned. "You ok Sir?"

Being called a name that wasn't offensive, made me feel slightly more refreshed. "I'm fine. A double espresso please and before you ask, I'll have it here."

"As you wish. Take a pew and I'll bring it right over."

I grabbed the free newspaper which rested on an abandoned plate of half eaten omelette and took a seat by the window. The headline hit me hard and almost caused me to fall backwards off my stool. "Den Folks Still Missing and Presumed Dead. All Star Ashes Tribute Match Announced at Lords in Two Weeks."

"If only they knew." All I could think of was that I'd absolutely love to attend the match. What a cracking spectacle it would be. Could I wait a couple of weeks before releasing the poor sods and go to the game? No, that would be far too selfish. Could I release them at all? If they dobbed me in, missing a cricket match would be the last thing on my mind. Although, maybe a stint in prison would allow me time to wash the blood off my hands. As I sipped on my espresso, I considered my options once again. I knew that I couldn't handle a 'site visit' today and was convinced that they would understand. I'd promised them liberty but how could they believe a person capable of murder? Was it I who was responsible for the death of a hardworking man? One of educational cloth and substantial standing or was it the girl that I had fallen for, hook line and stinker? Was she the real prize draw? It was her after all that had forced the blade across Suggs' throat. The real murderer in sheep's clothing? Had I been used and abused? Was my release even a victory? Should a loser celebrate the win if he steals the trophy? My head was pounding with the unanswered questions. Ones that I could never discuss with anyone.

"Would you like anything else?" I took this as an indication that I had outstayed my welcome.

"No, I'm ok, thanks." I paid my bill and left. Walking aimlessly through the town of Ealing. Not wanting to find any particular destination to offload my sins. I continued until my purpose waned, my feet tired and my head hurt, then reluctantly ambled back to the flat.

"Where have you been mate?" Martin met me as I entered the lair.

"I had to report to the cop shop. Don't worry. They seemed to believe my story. Everything is fine."

Head down, I made a run across 'no man's land' towards my bedroom and threw on the nearest bit of vinyl to hand. The music caressed my eardrums and stroked my emotions. I cried, not because Den Folks would miss the game of the century but because I had become a different person. A living embodiment of a deceased soul, tarnished through the actions of an abused being. I felt anger but I could not fathom the value of revenge. An eye for an eyeful of destruction and heartache?

Using my undeserved free time wisely, I rang back a handful of my nearest and dearest. They were not characters of detail, they we're all just happy that I would still be around to buy them beer, offer them cigarettes and laugh at their jokes. Not one of them asked to see me. "Catch up soon." "Later dude." "Drink soon." "Cheerio fella." "Adios amigo." What did I expect? Nothing, but that's why I loved them.

I offered the final call to my friend Josh. We hadn't spoken for a few months due to a minor falling out but he had left eight messages so I felt that it was time to draw a line under our feud which seemed more than insignificant due to my present circumstances. He was a chap that I'd been on vacation with a few times. A travelling buddy, one who liked a couple of days on the beach, sipping fancy cocktails but also embraced the opportunity to explore the various sights that the destination had to offer. The perfect companion some might say. It was for that reason, I'd once offered him a place to stay for a few nights when he was in-between tenancy agreements.

On the first evening of his residential busman's holiday, he invited his girlfriend around for the evening. The lack of permission was a minor misdemeanour, after all I had told him to make himself at home. It was the loud banging in the kitchen that alerted me to the culinary activity and as I was hungry, I found myself walking into its aromatic embrace. His partner scolded me for not having a measuring jug and a garlic crusher but I took the beating after witnessing a large bird entering the oven. I left the room with anticipation. The succulent flavours soon filled the flat with an essence worthy of a fine restaurant. The louder the banging, the better the smell and the hungrier I became. I found myself salivating with impatience. The clinking of glass jars called out, "all the trimmings!" I waited for my table number to be called. Then I waited some more. I held onto my hat or rather my knife and fork for an hour or so until I heard the front door slammed shut. I dashed into the palatable epicentre only to discover the greatest kitchen mess of all time. Every pot, pan, baking tray, cooking utensil known to man was out on display and each one dirtier than the other. There were miniscule bits of food everywhere but no sign of a plate with my name on it. Two hours it took me to clean that kitchen before I was able to make myself beans on toast. What did I get for dessert, only the line, "I didn't think you'd want any!"

"Fancy a drink at the local?" Martin interrupted my favourite Jimi Hendrix guitar riff.

"No, but I wouldn't mind a can if you've got any." It was far too soon to be chewing any form of cud with him in public.

"Coming right up. Then maybe we could watch a film together like the good old days? Which one do you fancy?"

"We could watch Enemy of the State?" I called out.

"Planning a quick getaway?"

I couldn't believe that we were on the same wavelength. "Yeah. Ever since I met you!"

"I'll let you have that quote. He said as my fake laughter filled the void."

As he disappeared into the kitchen, I couldn't help but think of that famous Peter Cook sketch from the days gone by. Out for a gentle stroll, he walked through his home town and bumped into a fellow that he'd not seen for many a moon. I couldn't remember the exact script but he said something like: "Oh, hi there. How are you doing? I haven't seen you in years. You're looking well. So good to see you. Big hi to the family. Ok then. Bye then. Hope to see you soon." As he wanders off into the distance, he mutters to himself, "What a wanker."

A stretched arm appeared through my slightly ajar bedroom door. Its contents, a can of lemonade. "Wanker!" I mumbled.

Bliss Family Reunion

I turned up at the exam unprepared. What had I been doing? God, I was useless! I knew that this day would arrive. Why had I not done any revision? My misguided dalliance with the summer had left me without a chance of success. My father, a stickler for academic accomplishment would surely disown me. All of the other students strode to their desks with fulfilled confidence while I sauntered to my inevitable fate. I'd literally done no work for it and I entered the room with justified resignation. I'd let myself down. "No, I can't do it. I just can't! The humiliation will turn me into a laughing stock!" I ran out of the lecture theatre with the might of a gazelle staring down the scowl of a hungry tiger. My teacher ran after me, shouting my name but I was too fast. I would have been home free if it wasn't for the metal bin. Crashing into it caused it to tumble along the college entrance, making quite the racket. I sat bolt upright. The crashing noise continued. I looked around the room. There was no college, no wailing teacher and certainly no missed exam. It was that reoccurring dream again but this time the noise continued and turned into a repetitive banging sound.

It was someone hammering at the front door. "Ok, ok, I'm coming. At least allow a man to put his trousers on!" Martin called out with distain in his voice.

I looked at the alarm clock, positioned precariously on my bedside table. "Six thirty. Who would knock at the door at this ungodly hour?" I wrapped my modesty into a dressing gown and entered the confusion only to see Martin, naked apart from his under crackers, opening the front door. To my shock and amazement, there stood Officer Mary Thingymabob with some small and stocky uniformed policeman.

"Martin Bunratty, we are arresting you in connection with the disappearance of Anthony Egbert Bullock." She followed up this spine-chilling traffic stopper with the usual. "You have the right to remain silent and all that nonsense that no one really understands. "PC Mick Dibley will accompany you to your room in order for you to put some clothes on."

I'm not sure whether it was a direct result of my guilty conscience or self-preservation but I cowered back into my room and stuck my mental gearshift into auto. Quickly getting dressed, I snuck out of my bedroom window and dashed up the street. Pretty convinced that she'd clocked me when she read Martin his rights, I was taking no chances. Surely it wouldn't take them too long to realise that the man they were arresting for the kidnap of his landlord was also rather upset at his father, work colleague, old headmaster, first love and sporting hero who had also gone bloody missing. Oh, and I wasn't convinced that they'd believe that his best friend, who had disappeared for a few days, suddenly returned and moved back in, to console him. If you've ever seen the face of a solutionist who places the final piece of his or her one-thousand-piece jigsaw, you'd realise why I had to run. Well, I was convinced I had just seen that very same expression on Mary's face.

There was only one place that I was drawn, the same place that I'd handed over thirty pieces of silver in exchange for a life of guilt but a place that housed the answers to my prayers. Sarah would advise me on the way forward. She was the six to my two threes, the hard place to my rock but more importantly, she was just as deep in the proverbial shit as I was. If nothing else, she'd give me a comforting hug, a shoulder to cry on and a smile that could light up my way out of this mess. A long journey for my cry of mercy, it was one that had to be done. What was I thinking? I was making my way there to release all of those who had been wronged, surely. As I entered the delayed train to High Wycombe, I was still none the wiser. Do I free all of the wild spirits as promised and risk one of them offering me up on a supermarket conveyer belt or should I only gift Sarah her freedom in order to keep me warm at night? All I could conclude was that the answer would be awaiting me in that damp, dispiriting, dungeon that I used to call home and if all else failed, at least I'd be returning in my beloved car if it hadn't been stolen.

A taxi to the venue from the train station was the only option although if felt a little mischievous. My destination was hardly a late-night drinking establishment. There wouldn't be a pint on the table awaiting my arrival but the similarity would be apparent on the faces of my awaiting guests. They would be overjoyed to see me. The crowd would cheer as I walked towards them but would they be disappointed with my company? There was no doubt that Sarah would succumb to my charms but what about the others? The cabbie dropped me in the heart of the hamlet and I gave him a small tip. One not too large, so he would remember my generosity but also one not too small to draw any unwanted attention. My whole life, I wanted to be someone special but that would have to wait. Today, I needed to be John Doe! A chap merely meeting a relative for tea, a friend for advice or a prospective buyer of an old farm house. It didn't matter to the minicab driver, with a decent fare, he went on his merry way.

I wandered over to my rusting vehicle, half surprised to see its presence. It looked lonely, unloved, hardly the carriage of desire but when I turned the key, it sprang into life and announced its pleasure. I didn't let it tick over for long, I had places to be. Meetings in my calendar, announcements to be made and unprecedented verdicts to declare. My fanatics awaited, overzealous creatures awaiting their fate but how long could my dictatorship last? I had taken over the bejewelled crown of an unpopular ruler. I didn't want its dazzle nor needed its glory. Its virtue felt awkward and its forced status, uncomfortable.

Finding the trap door was not easy. It was well hidden and concealed by a variety of woodland bric-a-brac. Happy to find myself in the right place, I opened the black hole with caution, half hoping to see it empty. But the familiar cackle of hyenas was all too apparent as I lowered my head below ground in an attempt to embrace their desperate mutterings.

"I really can't see him freeing us all. If I was him, I wouldn't. Why would he jeopardise his safety for no apparent gain? We are purely an unwanted inconvenience. He didn't know us before and he doesn't need to know us now! No wait, hang on a minute! He did know Sarah and he has feelings for you, if anyone has a chance, it's you."

"Don't worry guys. I'm confident that he'll let me out. I'll play the dippy sod like a finely tuned fiddle. Once I'm outta here, I'll bring in the rescue team. You'll be in a hot tub before you can say where's the bubble bath!"

Did Sarah and Susan's conversation ring true? Would Sarah stab me in the back with the weapon that still had blood on the blade? Had I been substituted from the first team and Sarah taken the captain's armband. I couldn't listen any more. It was time to reveal myself and get to the bottom of this complex web of deceit.

"Bobby, you're back. How long have you been there?" Welcomed a startled Susan. There was a couple of cheery screams and nervous shouts of joy until they all saw the serious look on my face.

I stood there in a frozen state of astonishment. "Long enough to hear enough. I'm on your side and all you can do is sharpen your knives. Don't treat me for a fool, tell me what's going on? Sarah, talk to me babe. What melancholic tune are you going to play on my violin?"

"Bobby, don't be like that, it doesn't suit you. We were just chewing the cud, or what's left of it. Passing the time of day. Yes, I was giving it the big one but I didn't mean anything by it. I've missed you. Now, can we please stop this nonsense and let me out?"

"Hang on. You've just said and correct me if I'm wrong, that you'll happily sacrifice me to free everyone?"

"Don't be so sensitive Bobby. We're all a little stressed. Unchain me, I'm so happy to see you, let me give you a hug. Then you can take me back to London, I'll tidy myself up and then we can go to the pub and forget this ever happened. How does that sound, my love?"

Was I being unfairly lambasted? "Why did you call me a dippy sod?" There was clear disappointment in my voice but why wouldn't there be, I was wounded. My partner in crime, the bow to my arrow, the snake to my ladder and the crutch to my limp was literally throwing me under a bus!

"Come on my darling. I was only playing to the crowd. You and I are lucky that we've found each other. What have these guys got? Well, let me tell you, they've got fuck all. I was only trying to cheer them up. Listen, come on, lead the way, I know that you've got my back and I'm confident that the safety rope that connects us, is strong and secure. Let me out Bobby!"

Susan, in an attempt to diffuse my anger, jumped in. "Right now, being alive is more important than being found."

She knew that I'd be impressed with her film knowledge. "That's an easy one. Swiss family Robinson?"

"Bullseye." Replied Susan with a smug smile as my mood softened.

I knew that I had zero choice in the matter. Being completely isolated and having to deal with my traumatic situation on my own was not an option. I was vulnerable and the sweet talk of a siren was all it took for me to drop my draws and take my medicine the old-fashioned way. I grabbed the bunch of keys, such an important pawn in the game of chess that hung so clumsily by a rusty nail. Without a word or protest from anyone, I released her from her heavy burden and escorted her out and into the fresh air of her God given right. She breathed it in, almost choking on its purity.

"Jesus, son of Mary that feels good. Thank you Bobby. Now, please, can we let the others go free?"

"No, not yet Sarah. We need time to work out what to do. You know that one of them will squeal like a pig."

"Then can we just go home?"

"Of course." I added without purpose. "Let's get you back to the land of the living."

Happy to enter the familiar confines of my car, I wasted no time in setting off. The trip back was smothered in holiday blues. The return journey of a loving couple that had been away for a couple of weeks. Back to normality. Back to face the music and questions that had been left unanswered. What did that famous Greek philosopher once say? 'Music gives a soul to the universe, wings to the mind, flight to the imagination and life to everything.' So why should we fear facing it?

"Sarah, Martin's been arrested. They have evidence that he was involved in the disappearance of Mr Bullock. I might be just being paranoid but it was the same inspector who came to my office to question me about you. When she came to our flat, I'm sure that she clocked me. She must have made a connection. She's a trained professional, so can't be that stupid. Do you think that she's cracked the code and submitted her findings? I didn't hang around to find out. God, this is just awful. I feel like we're trapped in some murder mystery play and I've left the stage, straight through the fire escape. We need to know what's going on. Shall I call him?"

"No, you can't. Just in case she didn't see you or make any connection. Let's not jump to an unnecessary conclusions. Let's just let Martin stew in his own juices. They're probably checking through his phone as we speak to see if Mr Bullock and Martin had arranged to meet."

We both took our eyes off the road and stared at each other like two rabbits startled in the full beam of the situation. In unison, we screamed. "Oh fuck. The video!" The severity of our entanglement immediately dawned on us. I swung the car off the main road and into an empty truckers bypass.

"Oh, God! What shall we do? I couldn't handle being locked up again! I'd rather eat my own eyeballs."

Sarah held my trembling hand. "Let's stay calm. I thought that we had agreed not to make any assumptions. We're going to have to call Martin. If he doesn't pick up then we'll reset the compass and head north to find an alternative solution." I dialled his number, Placing the phone on loud speaker. It rang and rang. Our gaze transfixed on the screen. Our hope slowly slipping away. The riptide of emotion dragging us deeper and deeper into the dire straits of suffering.

"You have reached the voicemail of Martin Bunratty. I'm not around to take your call right now. Please leave a message and I'll call you back at my earliest convenience.

The Scorpion Sting

Officer Mary Blackthorn was well respected at Ealing Police station. After starting a family, her general outlook on the world changed. Wanting to make the streets of London safer for her young daughter became her ambition as she paused her bookkeeping career to serve in the Met. Life to that point, had been far too comfortable. She felt the desire to be challenged and prove her self worth.

In hindsight, joining the Force might have been one step too far. Maybe a little voluntary charity work would have sufficed. The long and stressful hours put a strain on her relationship which ended within a year after she'd enrolled. With a supportive set of parents, juggling childcare became second nature and she embraced her new life with the gusto and guile of a seasoned old war horse. She prided herself on the attention to detail and fairness she offered each and every testing situation that she found herself engaged. Having pounded the beat for three years, taking selfies with tourists, taming drunken revellers and moving on the homeless from street doors, she'd been offered her first interesting and high-profile case. Assisting with the recent spate of disappearances would offer her the gravitas to achieve the promotion that she felt was long overdue. Having cuffed and escorted Martin Bunratty to the Station, she led him to an interview room and offered him some liquid refreshments.

"I'll take a coffee with three sugars, please."

"Ok Sir, my colleague will bring one to you. I'll be back in around ten minutes. Would you like me to invite the duty solicitor?"

"No, that won't be necessary, I've got nothing to hide." Martin instantly regretted his decision but it was too late. The door banged shut and he found himself alone in the steely, unwelcoming room.

Mary knocked on Sergeant Parry's office door and entered without official consent. She rested the palms of her hands on his desk, allowing the hint of cleavage to support her argument. "I've brought in our key suspect, Martin Bunratty. I'd like to lead the interview. I'll feedback once I'm done. Ok with you boss?"

"Without the need or willingness for eye contact, Sergeant Parry simply nodded. He had a soft spot for Mary. He admired her tenaciousness and ambition against the male chauvinistic odds that he knew the police stood for. He had her back and the more time he spent with her, the more he warmed to her. He often wondered what a romantic connection would be like but he was happily married. A man punching above his weight with a thumb sized indent on the top of his head. Three children and the burden of keeping them in the very silk of the life that they had become accustomed. Three grains of guilt would put pay to the harmonious balance that he'd created. As his door closed, he continued with his game of online solitaire and opened his homemade packed lunch.

Mary, accompanied by her junior, stepped into the interview room with purpose. After taking their seats and starting the cassette recorder, she began.

Names, dates and locations were all documented before she commenced her well-rehearsed castigation. "We have witnesses and CCTV footage of you attacking a traffic warden and driving away in Tony Bullock's car, the day after his disappearance. Am I right in saying that this man is your landlord and you owed him a large sum of money? Is it also true that he came to collect and no one has seen or heard from him since? I put it to you Martin, that you have killed this man! We have a motive and substantive evidence. Make life easier for yourself and tell us how you did it and where you've left the body."

Martin sat forward. Shaking slightly and muttering something in the direction of the tape recorder.

Mary interrupted his weak diatribe. "Please speak louder and more clearly."

"I cannot believe what you're saying. Accusing me of murder, preposterous?! Yes, you are correct about one thing. Mr Bullock did come to my flat asking for some rent money. I quite like Tony so I invited him in and offered him a drink. One turned into six. As the clock ticked, he became more and more drunk and eventually crashed out on the sofa. The next morning, suffering from a massive hangover, he asked me to move his car before it got ticketed. I was a little concerned about being over the limit myself but agreed, nonetheless. If I'm honest, that's probably the reason I had an altercation with the traffic warden and I'm sorry for that. I realise now that I owe him an apology. Anyway, I moved the car to a side road without any controlled parking, walked back via the cash machine, paid the money I owed before Tony left. That's it. I'm not sure what happened to him after that." Martin had worked through his story in the patrol car on the way to the station. He knew that it had more pot holes than the main Cambodian drag from Phnom Penh to Siem Reap but it was the best he could do in the time allocated.

Mary was caught a little off guard. Her first ever interrogation was not quite going to plan. "You are lying. Something untoward happened in your flat with Tony Bullock and we want to know what."

Martin stuck to his story. "What, is it a crime now to have a few drinks with a mate and put the world to rights?" Mary left the room three times in order to seek guidance. The third time would be her last.

"I'm sorry but you just don't have enough evidence to hold him." Sergeant Parry said confirming her fears. "Let him go but let's get a search warrant for his flat. Check the CCTV, if it's available, to see if we can confirm that Tony Bullock did indeed leave his flat the next morning. Ask Mr Bunratty where he left the vehicle. We need to find inconsistencies in his story. If you think he's guilty, then let's focus our minds. Oh, and one other thing, organise a surveillance team to trail him. Don't give up at the first hurdle Mary. You've taken a fall, maybe sprained your ankle but get up and win the race like the champion I know you can be."

Mary reluctantly walked with Martin to the Station front door. "Don't go too far, I'm sure we'll need to see you again for further questioning." Martin hightailed it out of there as quickly as his guilty feet could take him. Holding onto the phone that had been returned to him. A device that held the digital testimony they required. One that would corroborate his involvement and expose his heinous crimes. It had been untouched.

"Thank fuck for that." He sighed as he turned it back on. "A message from Bobby." What should he say about the mornings events? Was Bobby even aware that he'd been hauled away by the suspicious arm of the law? There was only one way to find out.

"Bobby hello, is that you? What, no, listen, don't panic. Slow down, you're not making any sense. Where are you? Where? Ok, stay there, I'm on my way."

Mary sat down in the station canteen with her predictable subsidised ham salad and looked out of the window, just catching Martin disappearing out of sight. "Bollocks, I forgot to ask him where he'd parked the damn car." As she aggressively speared a cherry tomato with her plastic fork, a bolt of unearthing clarity stuck her. As fast as she could say "Mary you fool," she ran through the corridor, knocking into a shocked cleaning lady and straight into Parry's office.

"We've got to bring him back in. It's him, this is huge, they are in it together. I'm telling you, it's a bloody conspiracy!" She barked like a demented dog.

Parry closed his laptop, grabbed his glasses off the desk and stood up. "Mary, you need to calm down. I take it that you're talking about the Bullock case. Take a deep breath and tell me calmly why we need to bring back your suspect."

"Sergeant, when we went to pick up Martin Bunratty, I'm sure that I saw Simon Dingle at the flat. He's the guy that I questioned over the disappearance of Sarah McKay. Bit of a coincidence don't you think?"

Parry, digested the announcement for a moment. "Wait, Simon Dingle you say? I recall reading the report on him. He's the chap who turned up out of the blue after being reported missing for over a week. Ok, sounds like you might be onto something here. Gather all of the information that we have on these two. Check the missing persons list, is he linked to any others? Be sharp about it."

Mary walked out of his office with a giddy excitement. "At last, something to get my teeth into." She thought as she called for her team to assemble in the main meeting room. The whiteboard was scrubbed clean and soon became the hub of criminal dexterity. Photos were positioned, names were scribbled, paths were intertwined, missing people were crossed off lists and conclusions were drawn. Within an hour, Sergeant Parry was summoned into the epicentre of the developing investigation.

Mary proudly stood next to the whiteboard, admiring her artistry. She had given a virtuoso performance of unconstitutional entanglement. Each brush stroke, symbolising a step forward in the fight against crime. Each photo representing a giant leap forward in the success of the Force that she was so proud to serve but most importantly, each arrow pointing to the same man, Martin Bunratty.

Mary rolled up her sleeves and cleared her throat. "Sir, I'll cut to the chase, this is what we have so far. Martin's flatmate, Simon Dingle aka Bobby was reported missing but has since turned up claiming memory loss. Martin's work colleague Sarah McKay, who is also an ex-girlfriend of Bobby's, reported missing. Martin's father Doug Bunratty, reported missing and finally, Martin's landlord,

Tony Bullock, reported missing. We are still working through the missing persons list from last month but you have to agree, we have a pattern building here Sarge."

"Well, fuck me sideways. This is a sting in the tail." Parry cried out, alerting the group to his satisfaction. "Great work guys. Keep this well away from the press for God's sake. We have a serial kidnapper and a potential killer on the loose. Bring him in immediately and his halfwit sidekick, Simon Dingle. I want them found, their flat searched, phone records and bank cards statements analysed."

It had been a good few years since Mary had felt this type of emotional high. It was her time to shine and she knew it.

"And one other thing, take that fork with the cherry tomato out of your top pocket!" Parry grabbed his mobile as he left the meeting room. "Now, what's that press office number?" He thought. "They'll have my name up in lights before the night is out."

Day of the Misfits

They sat nervously in the stationary car, listening intently to the news on the radio. The blustering mantra of a self-serving politician filled the void until they were served the exposé they were dreading to hear. "A top London Met Police spokesperson, today announced that the spate of recent disappearances in the Greater London area could be connected." He also said that they were following a number of lines of inquiry but have turned their attention to one key suspect. "More to follow on this news story." There was no surprised look on their apprehensive faces. Martin had to be the key suspect but they were now inextricably linked. Fearing the worst, it was now time to contemplate their fate. The crime bomb was ticking and they lay in its path of potential destruction.

"I hope Martin gets here soon. We need to know exactly what he's said to the coppers." I said playing with the gear stick of inevitability.

Sarah nodded, "Do you think he's thrown us under a fuck off massive red double decker bus filled with Japanese tourists taking photos of our decapitated bodies?"

I attempted a reassuring smile but judging from her ever increasing frown, failed miserably. "I wonder what they've got on him. Knowing Martin, if he was grilled, he would have served me up like an unexpected amuse bouche in a greasy cafe. Blamed everything on me. Cried like a baby who's had his comfort blanket taken away and burnt right in front of him. Nothing would surprise me anymore. He's a diabolical disgrace of a human. Why would they let him go? It's going to be so hard to contain my anger. I feel like ripping out his eyeballs and serving them to him with a side order of cock and balls!"

"Come on Bobby. Where's your devil may care attitude? Let's not be over hasty in our prognosis. Let's just wait to hear what the tosser wants to mix in with his salad. Maybe, just maybe, he has some good news for us. Anyway, we need to take our minds off this for a minute or two before it gives me a headache." Sarah then looked across at me and winked. At first, her intentions were not clear to me. The cobwebs still spread-eagled the branch, the rust still lay heavy on the nail and the mould still discoloured the bread. She winked again and this time, the wind blew through my sails.

"Fuck, yes." I flung off my jumper and dived into the back seat before the starting gun had shot its load. Sarah followed, albeit, slightly more gracefully. We kissed as I fumbled for buttons that did not exist. She felt my frustration, pushing me to one side before entrancingly exposing herself. The present was unwrapped, the one on top of my Christmas list and I was ready to play. Batteries included or not. The Garden of Eden was unkept and overgrown but its fruit still tasted fresh. Sarah couldn't contain her pleasure as I drank from her well of desire. She moaned and writhed as her legs clamped me in a position of extreme self-indulgent passion. My left hand clasped her bosom for balance, while my right caressed her leg for pleasure. She screamed as the windows steamed. My head momentarily held in a vice until the bubble was burst. She glowed as we kissed once more before she tickled my flag to full mast. Her tiffany blue eyes lit up my soul as she bathed my tower of titillation with her succulent gateway of adulation. The blowjob made me feel alive. It had been a while and I had been devoid of any affection. With a willingness to impress, I discarded my own immediate ambition and focussed on the stale smell of a woman who had not seen soap for a while. It was too late. No point fighting against it. More joy and intensity would be available if I embraced it. My fingers gripped the cloth of the seat as I looked out to the heavens only to see a face staring in. Were my eyes deceiving me in my moment of intense blissfulness? I stared hard, wiping the dizziness from my eyes. The voyeur had ended my stage performance. I quickly pulled up my wears, almost knocking Sarah out cold.

"Stop, there's someone watching us!" I squealed as the windows demisted. "You've got to be kidding me. Martin, fuck off you pervert!"

Martin didn't avert his gaze. His eyes blazed like an excited puppy, his mouth agape with the eager promise of unsolicited carnal knowledge. "Any chance I could join in?"

Sarah looked disgusted, the distain on her face clear to see. Grabbing at her clothes, the moment was over. My first sexual step on the ladder of my new blossoming relationship was slipping away. Was it a comedy heckle or did Martin really believe that he had us in his back pocket? I opened the car door and with an almighty push, Martin hit the deck, his pinkie still visible through his flies.

"Martin, what do you think you're doing? We are not fucking doggers. You didn't see any headlights flashing, did you? Sod off and come back in five minutes while we get ourselves together. Oh, and put your little bloody Johnson away." Was I right to castigate his presence, I was hardly as white as the driven snow.

Martin looked slightly embarrassed. "Sorry Bobby, you're right. I might have stepped over the line somewhat. But, what the bloody hell is Sarah doing out of the bunker!"

Sarah, now fully clothed with butter melting at the side of her mouth, stepped out of the car and looked down at Martin. "Stepped over the line? You turbo boosted that line a while ago. If I had my way, I'd grab that line, wrap it around your neck and throttle you with it. How the fuck did you get here so quickly anyway?"

After a good, proper and well justified lambasting, Martin opened the carrier bag that accompanied him and offered up a bottle of wine. "Peace offering? Can we just forget about it and move on? We have a lot to discuss."

It was a fair point on the map of our worriment. Plotting our journey to absolution was clearly far more pressing than me getting my end away. "Ok, Martin. Just to be clear, Sarah is now part of the deal. That's just how it is! Now, tell us what happened. Take your time. The devil will be in the detail." I requested with a more relaxed and sincere tone.

We sat on the grass verge, I opened the bottle of wine and took a man-sized slug. Martin regaled his experience, moment by nail biting moment. Each episode accentuated with a long pause. Each dramatic verse followed up by a deep breath or a slow wipe of his forehead. We hung from the gallows of his every word. No eye contact but plenty of gesticulation, he delivered his version of events. With every dot, the wine was passed. With every cross the wine was gulped. I consumed the last drop with his final punchline. "So, one thing is for sure, they're on to me big time."

"Martin, take a moment, this is really important! Where have you put the incriminating video? Please tell me it's somewhere safe and not still on your phone or on some USB stick in the flat." I wasn't trying to be facetious but Martin was the clumsiest person I knew.

With an uncomfortable relationship with the truth, Martin stumbled through his response. "I'm not stupid Bobby. I've deleted it from my mobile and yes it is on a USB stick and in the flat but it's safe. I've hidden it inside one of my gym socks and placed it in the Alibaba basket. No fucker will find it there." Martin raised his hand aloft for a customary high five but his celebration was not only ignored but short lived. Once the verbal battering had ceased, Martin got himself up from the proverbial canvass within the count and took another bottle of wine out of his bag.

"Jesus, how could you be so stupid? No, don't answer that. So, what are we going to do now?" Sarah shouted with clear frustration in her voice. "There's only three straws in the haystack and the needle is the size of a combine harvester!"

After looking to the skies for inspiration, I grabbed Martin's shoulder. "I'll tell you what we're going to do. We are going to the bunker to release everyone. Then, we are going to see Mary Blackthorn together. Martin, you will tell her the truth, the whole truth and nothing but. Tell her that you made us kill Suggs. That if we didn't, you were going to leave us to our fatal destiny. Then sit back and take the consequences like a man. They'll pick the bones off your worthless carcass but hopefully they'll go easy on Sarah and me. This is your mess and you need to clear it up. You must know that it's the only fair and just option. You owe us that Martin."

"Ain't happening bro. If I go down, I'm taking you both with me. We are talking the full Thelma and Louise cliff edge experience. We are in this together now. The three amigos, the three musketeers but more importantly, the three blind mice. We are lost in a sea of peril and we will swim together against the tide of torment or sink and get swallowed by the blood thirsty sharks."

It was the tale of the expected. I was fuming and it clearly showed. "Alright, if that's the game you want to play. But do me a favour and keep your fucking wig on so we don't have to see that giant cock that seems to be growing on the top of your head!"

I put my arm around my newly crowned princess. Sure, in the fact that her new title was little consolation in her increasingly complicated life. We needed a moment to re-evaluate the new chemical formula of our destiny. We just needed to gather our thoughts, we needed a plan. "Wait here Martin. Sarah and I need five minutes. We're going for a walk." Before he could answer, I grabbed Sarah's hand and we began our stroll but his reply followed us like a bad smell.

"Oh yeah, off to finish what you started? Go on my son, give her one from me. Eh, Bobby lad? Oh, ignoring me are you? Fine, you just go ahead and spear the bearded clam but don't forget, if it wasn't for me, you'd have no bush to hide your one-eyed snake. It was me who brought you together. You owe me and never forget that!" We ignored his vociferous comments as we walked around a bend in the country lane and out of ear shot.

We stopped by a gate and I closed in on Sarah's right ear and whispered gently. "I've got a monkey wrench in the boot of my car. Let's knock the ignoramus out and throw him in the bunker. Let the dogs have their bone."

"No, we can't. That would make us as guilty as him. What we've done is despicable but we did it to save the group. We have to release them and accept our punishment. Whatever or whoever breaks us will only make us stronger."

"I can't take the chance Sarah. I'm a good-looking rooster with perfect gluts. Just imagine me in prison, they'll make hay on my ass while the sun shines through it. There must be another way."

"Well, I'll have to take your word for that. I haven't seen it yet due to that plumb fairy. There is one other option. We let them go and make a run for it. My Aunt has a place in Spain, she only uses it once a year, outside of that, it's empty. Not sure how we'll get there but where there's a will there's a pill, eh Bobby?"

"Run towards the sun? I like it Sarah. We could learn Spanish, have a couple of pequeños and lie around the pool watching them grow up. What are we going to say to Martin?"

Sarah didn't have to think twice before she fired the friendly shot across my bow. "We are going to have to invite him to join us. We simply have no choice. You heard what he said. He'll throw us to the lions. Anyway, he knows about the villa. I mentioned it at work, showed him photos. He knows exactly where it is and it won't take him long to realise that we've gone there. Look, trust me, we have no choice. It this is to work, we'll need to plead to the others to stay quiet about Suggs. At least until we get away."

At that moment, I placed a hand on Sarah's shoulder. "About Suggs. I've spoken to Martin about him. Turns out, he's nothing more than a strict teacher."

"OMG! Are you serious? Fuck Bobby, what have we done?" After a moment of guilty realisation, she continued. "Look, we can't tear ourselves to pieces, we did what anyone in our blood-stained shoes would have done. We'll just have to tell the others that he's a genuine peado and we've saved a load of young boy's innocent souls by taking him off the streets. They assume that anyway so they'll buy into it. Martin on the other hand, will sing like Bob Marley at a karaoke bar after a blast on his peace pipe. We have no choice but to take him with us. Before we do anything though, we need to get that God damn USB stick before the rozzers get their mitts on it!"

I stood, impressed by Sarah's new-found confidence. "Fair point. I'm loving the cut of your jib. Count me in. Now let's go and tell 'the peeping Martin' the plan."

Martin waited patiently for our return like a naughty school boy, sitting on the bench outside the headmaster's office. A hardship that he'd clearly endured many times in the past. On this occasion, he knew the discipline was warranted. The heavens opened and a downpour dampened his spirits further. With the car locked and no other option of cover, he allowed himself to wallow in the wet weather. By the time we'd appeared, it had stopped, leaving him with the scars of the destined deluge. His adversaries had taken shelter in a bus stop while we finalised the finer details of our plan. With little or no sympathy, we downloaded our thoughts to Martin. We offered him the hand of a begrudged friendship, a hand that would lead him away from danger and into the bosom of a couple that had had their lives turned upside down by his misgivings. He nodded as he bowed his head in shame at the upheaval that was discussed. Trying hard not to show any excitement for the new adventure that lay ahead. His escape path was being mapped out for him. A new life, a new beginning, starting afresh and leaving his demons behind. It all sounded honourable but could it be achieved? Could he trust his disciples or would we stab him in the newly tattooed bullseye, inked on his back? Could he trust the wronged, the servants of honour who he'd so unfairly persecuted? Maybe not but what choice did he have?

"Now, fuck off and get that USB stick, that's your road map to freedom." Sarah could feel the power swing and she embraced the feeling.

"Ok, I'll be quick and discreet. Shall I grab your passport Bobby?"

Sarah, maintaining control, barked further orders to the wounded soldier. "No, just get the stick and await our call. Now, off you pop like a good little boy."

After Martin had disappeared, I looked at Sarah with admiration. "And we danced on the brink of an unknown future, to an echo from a vanished past."

"Now, what are you going on about?" Sarah said looking puzzled.

"Come on, surely you know that one. "The Day of the Triffids!" Sarah smiled.

"God, if we are going to spend more time together, you've got to stop it with the film quotes!"

Escape from All That Jazz

As soon as Martin was out of sight, he disappeared into the rabbit holes of our minds. Our attentions turned to the act of chivalry necessary to clear our troubled souls. It was time to let everyone out. Did we have permission? Of course not but the tide was now on our side. Our arrival into the bunker was met with a cheer from the cherished few whose families prayed for their return.

"Ok guys, it's time to get you out of here." I knew that those words would stay with me for a long time. Just for that one moment, I would be a hero. A man honoured by his nation, a man loved and worshipped by his people. A man of his word, one who could be relied on to deliver. It was I who came to the rescue, my rewards would be in heaven or perhaps the vomit laden streets of the Costa del Sol. The rattling sound of jangling keys dominated the dimly lit space. Each rattle was greeted with whoops of joy, pats on backs and hugs of revelry as I basked in the gallows of gallantry.

Now, their time in the perilous pit was drawing to a close. Their bags were packed as the last candle of captivity was blown out. As I shepherded the flock out of their confinement and into the freshness of the freedom they deserved, arms were stretched, gulps of fresh air were stolen, sore eyes were wiped, musty smells were released and ruffled hair was blown. It was Winston who looked the happiest. The wag of a tail that had not flexed its muscle for a while, searching for a ball that had not been thrown for a few weeks but most importantly, the jump of a beast who knew the smell of freedom. The wounded infantry gathered by the entrance, not knowing where they were or which way to turn. Before the explosion of laissez-faire split our bonded nucleus, I asked them for a moment's hush. Circling the proverbial airport, waiting for permission to land, I delivered my plea.

"Listen guys, we did it. I promised you that this day would come and it has. We've made it out but before you all go back to your loved ones and the tranquillity of your lives, can I just ask you all not to mention our transgression. Sarah and I did what we needed to do to keep us all alive. Please understand this. Trust me, we will suffer in our own way. We will pay the price for the rest of our lives. No need for further punishment? Suggs was a paedophile, a danger to society. Maybe we had no right to take his rotten soul but maybe we have made the world a slightly safer place. Can we ask for your silence and your understanding? You will all have to agree for this to work."

It was Mr Bullock who dealt the disappointing blow. "I'm so sorry. I can't and will not guarantee anything. I have no loyalties to you and I have to fulfil my duty and tell the police everything. I refuse to cover for you. I really do sympathise and am grateful for everything but I'm just being honest guys."

"I understand." I said, expecting the worst. "You have to do what you think is right but you must understand that we now have no choice."

"Hang on, what are you saying? What will you do?" Asked Susan, moving closer to me in a clear sign of sincerity.

I held my head up high. "We've discussed it and decided to go on the run. We can't risk being crushed by a ton of legal weight. If I have to spend one more despicable day behind bars, I would simply crack up and Sarah feels the same. Before you ask, we are taking Martin with us. He knows too much and we need him onside for this too work. You all know that he won't rest until we're found. Plus, he's the one person who'll know where we'd hide."

Edging even closer, Susan continued. "But where will you go?"

"Come on my little buttercup." I smiled. "We wouldn't be very good fugitives if we told everyone who asked where we intended to run. What I can say is, it will be a long long way from this hell hole."

Susan looked down at her feet. "Fair point. Hey, maybe they'll make a movie about us!"

"Now you're talking my language. If they do, it will be much better than my favourite prison film "Escape from Alcatraz." I said lifting her chin.

"Hey, Bobby, Sarah, come here a minute." Dennis began wandering aimlessly away from the group. We followed and after a few dozen feet out of harm's way, he whispered the delights of the connected few. "Listen, I know people. Don't ask me why or how but I do. Take this number down." I grabbed my mobile and inputted the cryptic digits. "His name is Big Elvis. Tell him that you're a friend of mine. He'll get you what you need. A new identity, dodgy passports, the full works. You get caught, keep my name out of it. Comprende? Hopefully, you'll let me off that drink I promised you now?" With a bout of new found pessimism, I gave him a proper man hug. "Thanks mate. You might have just saved us."

As we returned to the group, Doug asked, "now, where is my boy?"

"Never mind him." I said nonchalantly, "He's damaged goods, past his prime, the leftovers of a dogs dinner. Let him go. Let him walk the path of the doomed. Guys, do what you need to do. We will leave you to it. But please, do us one favour and at least give us a few hours head start to give us a chance to escape."

We were friends from a day gone by. Brought together to cleanse the tarnished pallet of a man's deleterious diet from a dark and murky past. We said our final goodbyes. Emotional though they were, we all felt relieved to admonish our acquaintance. We were never destined to be together, nor were we primed to embrace the chemical formula of our involuntary friendship. It was time to separate the manmade atom knowing that's its splitting would generate a chain reaction of events that none of us deserved. A schoolboy's experiment that had badly gone wrong or one of life's natural disasters, it was irrelevant now. It had happened and it was over.

We left them standing there, silent, puzzled but high on the anticipation of putting back on the comfortable slippers of their lives. We walked fast through the woodland as they followed slowly. We had said our farewells and we knew that they had no other option but to hand us in. We had fed them the food of freedom only to get our hands bitten off.

Once we arrived at the car, we jumped in and sped off like the reckless boy racers we were to become. I could see them emerge from the forest in my rear-view mirror and I gave them a final wave of despair.

"So, where now?" I asked Sarah. I might have been in the driving seat but it was Sarah who would map out our new journey. It was she who would take the reins and gallop to our new life of anonymity.

"Just drive while I call Denny's mate." She dialled, she talked, she schemed, she arranged and she confirmed. She was a natural, taking on a voice from the underworld, a gangster in the making. Her voice grew deeper, and her answers monosyllabic. Was she rehearsing for a role in our new drama? A role that didn't generate many applicants. Maybe because the returns weren't that great. It didn't matter, all I knew was that I had no choice but to offer her the part as well as her dues.

"Right, we are meeting tomorrow afternoon in Oxford. We need to send him some passport photos and he'll sort the rest," she said, with a casual wave of mafioso magnificence and a triumphant blag of the tale.

"So, what's my new name? Can we not choose? I don't want to be stitched up!"

"Look." She said placing her hand over mine on the gear stick. "Who cares? It's bound to be better than Simon Dingle!"

"Alright, alright, enough already. Let's head to West London, there's a nice little hotel in Chiswick that I know. We can finish off our 'Game of Horns' there. I'll let you slap me if I can give you a tickle."

"Deal, now any chance you can stop driving like an old granny?"

Malice in Hunting Land

As Martin walked onto his residential road, he ground to a sudden halt. Three cop cars, half a dozen uniformed officers and a couple of plain clothed Noddys taking out stuff from the flat in see through carrier bags. Almost in rewind, he about turned on to the main street and into the nearest cafe. His back to the window and a cappuccino in hand, Martin turned back on his mobile only to see multiple missed calls from the same number, He didn't need to ask Siri, Google, Alexa or any other mother fucker who the perpetrator was, he knew that already. Six cups of coffee deep at the greasy spoon and the act of peering through the window over his shoulder gave him the green light to start the race of his divine decree. One by one the patrol cars convoyed out of his street. It was time to throw the dice, to turn the card and witness the cookie crumble. Since starting his sorry affair with jeopardy, he made sure that his normal life passed without further anxiety. Speed limits were adhered to, road crossings were obeyed, arguments were avoided and cafe bills were paid. Once this was administered, Martin darted out, hood placed over his guilty menace and at pace, he entered his once loved abode, potentially for the last time.

"Wankers, what a mess!" His belongings were left strewn across the once polished wooden floors. Drawers hung loose, cupboards left open and once hidden objects lay on display. Martin could tell that things were missing.

Laptops, files, notepads, some clothes, hairbrushes were amongst the objets d'art of lost household treasures. These things were collateral damage, surplus to requirement, Martin only had one item on his mind. The laundry basket had been tipped empty, dirty clothes sullied his bedroom floor. Socks everywhere but his prized Christmas tree specials stood out like a bald man on a barbers sofa. Martin grabbed one, the hope in his heavy heart sank to the bottom of his stomach. "Fuck, it's bloody empty." Almost in despair, he trod on the other. There was something there. Something small and hard. "That's what she said." Fifty percent of the worlds population wouldn't have been happy to find something small and hard but Martin was elated. He delved deep into his hiding place and pulled out his object of desire, the one thing that would bind the three runaways forever. Holding it tight, he ran out the door, not even bothering to seal its fate. Just like a genie in the bottle, out of reach wishes were granted and in a puff of smoke, all evidence vanished into thin air or maybe in the first rubbish bin he could find.

Martin's final instruction for the day was to obtain a set of passport photos. The local tube station offered the booth he needed. He studied the self-portraits as they dried. "God, I look old and weathered." He thought to himself as a message on his mobile focussed his mind.

"Meet us at Tipsy McStumbles Bed and Breakfast in Chiswick tomorrow morning at eight am sharp." It was Bobby bleating out his final order of the day. Martin called Tipsy's straight away. There was a room available. "I'll take it, I'll be there within the hour."

Meanwhile, back at Tipsy's, Sarah and I were making ourselves at home. "The room looks great my sweet." I said as I took off my jacket and placed it over the obligatory desk chair tucked into the mandatory desk table, cluttered with the requisite old-style house phone, the one with the turning dial.

Sarah noticed the glint in my eye. "Down boy! And before you ask, I mean let's go downstairs to the bar so I can have a couple of glasses of fanny flutter before we enjoy the headline act eh? Anyway, have some mercy, you know I need a tidy up before we tee off."

"Whatever you say my darling." We giggled and locked the door behind us.

The Inns drinking area offered a rather salubrious vibe. Two elderly gentlemen with flat caps adorned the bar. They perched on stools that they'd laid claim to over the past couple of decades. Seasoned pros with the odd titbit of small talk but on the main, happy in their own lonely bubble. A couple of tradesman looked focussed, enjoying a game of arrows post an arduous shift. A small gathering of the shirt and tie brigade sat in a dark corner. Perhaps lost, perhaps not. Three old age pensioners hunched over a table, enjoying their discounted steak and ale pie with a bowl of 'weekly gossip' for dessert. A middle-aged gent, stood alone, propping up the bar with a newspaper, perhaps anxious about his wife out shopping, armed with his credit card. We ordered a pint and a half of Guinness and sat amongst the orderly madness of the traditional Irish hostelry.

"I'm scared." Sarah sat uncomfortably, staring at the four leafed clover imprint in her drink.

I put my arm around her and eased her head back on to the sofa. "Ditto, my sweet, but it is what it is. Let's just crack on and make the most of the hand that we've been dealt. It's a pretty shit hand but a decent player can still win the poker game. We'll make a new life for ourselves, one enriched with happiness and sangria. We'll be fine. Trust me. Anyway, let's forget about all that for a moment and play a game. Right ok, I have a question to ask. Would you rather have sexual intercourse with Martin every night for the rest of your life or wake up one morning with a beard. One, that if you shaved off would grow back within ten minutes?"

"Oh, fuck off Bobby, you're making me feel sick. I'd take the beard every day of the week. I could make a fortune as a circus performer."

"Ok, your turn. Would you rather allow Martin to bang you up the chocolate starfish for one night only or have the words 'I love cock' tattooed on your forehead for the rest of your life? Sarah smiled triumphantly.

"You have a sick mind and here's me thinking that I'd met a pure and innocent girl." I pulled her close and tickled her.

"Stop it, you weasel and answer the question." She squealed.

I sat and pondered for a moment. "Ok, but I have one question before I can make my decision. Will anyone know that I've been violated?"

"Depends whether Martin's proud of his conquest, so probably not."

"Oi, you cheeky monkey. I'm a good catch, I'll have you know!"

"Well, you can ask him yourself. He's just walked through the door. I thought you asked him to come tomorrow morning?" Sarah gestured towards the entrance and then proceeded to down her drink in one unfeminine motion.

"I did! That boy is a diabolical liability!" We ushered him over. Love, hate, feel sorry for him, it was now irrelevant. We knew that he was an integral part of our future, our survival and a stalwart in our journey to the path of redemption. We discussed the finer details of our plan together. The three of us had an equal share in its success. Bygones were flushed, anger was swept away and remorse was tidied up for another day. We drank together like three old chums cradling the butter that couldn't melt. There was no reminiscing about the good old days. They have been erased, scratched from our memory banks. It was about the future, about the precarious voyage that we were about to embark on. "One for all and all for one." We ended our cordial palaver when the final bell rang. A sound that startled us.

"Time please ladies and gentlemen. Haven't you got homes to go to?"

I wanted to stand on the table and shout, "no! That privilege has been taken away from us by the idiot that is sitting right here!" But I couldn't muster the energy or courage. We said our phlegmatic farewells as we retired to our respective rooms. I knew that Sarah wouldn't be in the mood but if I was honest, neither was I. "Bobby, sorry honey. I've got a bit of a headache. Do you mind if we take a rain check?"

"Of course baby. We've got the rest of our lives to cosy up. Don't you fret my gorgeous. I want our first night to be special and a memory that we will cherish for the rest of our days."

Once Sarah had brushed her teeth and nestled into the bed, I found myself turning on the shower and inviting Palmella to shake hands with the unemployed. All this waiting around was breaking my balls, quite literally.

The three of us were tied by the strings of despair and not one of us slept well that night. Caught in the depths of a misapprehension that our futures were full of promise and devoid of any remorse, we awoke in the middle of our bad dreams of reality. Trapped and hopeless in the arms of fate, we cradled our hopes and burdens. The story of our three-legged race for survival would never be told with any bravado, our grandchildren would never wish to emulate our success and our parents would never hold their heads up again with pride. We were bound by the curse of duty, a commitment to prosper and eek out any happiness that didn't fall through our sieve of self-loathing.

We bathed and cleansed the hearts of a once previous life. The one job of the day, shedding the skin that was no longer fit for purpose and metamorphing into the decent people we once took for granted.

There were no words spoken at the breakfast table. We barely touched our stale cornflakes and burnt toast. "Is everything to your satisfaction?" The waitress spoke with genuine concern.

Sarah jumped in before any masks slipped. "We're ok, thanks, just a little hungover." She was right. Hungover from the poison of a man who had walked past the point of no return. We would journey with him into the pious garden of self-imposed turmoil. We wouldn't be eating one poisoned apple but pressing an orchard full and quaffing its cider until we passed out.

Once on the road, a deadly silence filled the car and accompanied us on our drive to Bristol to meet Big Elvis. A silence only broken by directional commands. "Take the next left off a cliff edge, head straight on for approximately ten kilometres and speed up when you get to the collapsed bridge, take the third exit on the roundabout of Russian roulette and don't ever pass go or you'll die a tortuous death." We didn't need to turn off the radio prior to calling our 'fixer' with the advanced warding of our arrival, as it played no tunes. Our departure out of this failed life would come without serenade. We entered an industrial estate, parked by a reclamation yard and together walked into a portacabin office.

"Morning, is Big Elvis around? Denny sent us." I enquired meekly to the frail skinny chap behind the counter.

"Yeah, he's expecting you. Go through to the back." He replied in the deepest of Welsh accents. No eye contact but a hand waved us through.

There was no mistaking Big Elvis. He was a man mountain, tightly squeezed into on old battered two-seater sofa. Clearly in his sixties, with a dyed black quiff, lacquered by a couple of cans of hairspray, a shirt as chequered as his darkened past and the blue suede shoes of a time only remembered on vinyl record sleeves. "Got the cash?"

What, that was it? This man had the power to change our lives forever. Washing out the stains of a former existence and offering us names that our parents never signed off. Surely, he had some advice, some help in limboing under the illicit bar of criminality and into the party that awaited. "We have." I passed over an envelope. I'd purchased a brown one as it seemed appropriate in these circumstances. He flicked through its contents and returned a white one.

"Now, get the fuck out of 'ere. I wish you good luck but remember, we never met. If this does come back to bite me, trust me, you'll regret that you ever crossed me. Don't forget, I know your names!"

We didn't open that white envelope until we were halfway to Dover. "You've got to be kidding me. Do I even look like an Alice?"

I jumped in before Martin had the chance. "In all fairness, you do a little. Anyway, what's wrong with the name Alice? I quite like it. It has a noble ring to it. What are our names? Don't tell me that I'm the Mad Hatter and Martin's the Cheshire Cat?"

"Dickhead." Hailed Sarah with contempt. "Ha-ha, you're Brian and Martin's Harvey. You two should start a band. Why not call yourself West 5?" Sarah couldn't contain herself. Throwing around a London postcode joke tipped the balance and sent us into hysterics. I loved her sharp wit but she clearly loved it even more.

"Alright, don't cry too much or you'll be drowned in your own tears." I giggled but only to myself as Sarah didn't twig on the loose Alice in Wonderland quote.

"Hey, but Brian! Fuck a duck. That's a crock of shit. Are there even any famous Brians?" I asked in distain.

"May, Cox, Bloom and didn't Monty Python do a film about a Brian." Martin roared from the back seat.

"Oh yes, I guess it could have been worse. He could have named me Biggus Dickus!" We all sat and laughed together. Bonding over our new identities, our masks of deceit, our shiny armour protecting us from the law.

"What about the surnames?" I asked Sarah.

"We are all Smith's, original eh? We'll have to be a married couple and Martin can be your brother, no actually you don't look anything like each other, make that second cousins."

We nervously checked in at the ferry port. It must have been apparent that we were not smooth criminals, we were clearly flying by the seat of our pants on a wing and a prayer. Thank God the port was extremely busy and its staff flustered. We were rushed through and returned to our vehicle, which we quickly drove into the mouth of the ship.

"We don't even know whether they're looking for us yet. Why was that so scary?" Sarah asked as we walked to the bar area. Sarah and Martin surprisingly talked freely and slurred their way through a cheap bottle of French wine. While I sat and studied a book of European maps that I'd purchased at the tacky on-board souvenir shop, easily located between the Eiffel Tower keyrings and the plastic toy telescopes. By the time we'd arrived at Calais, I had the route of our escape firmly etched on my mind.

"Don't forget to drive on the other side of the road Brian!" Sarah and Martin simultaneously shrieked as we exited the ferry. We started our pilgrimage, full of the joys of spring but by the time we'd arrived in Montpellier for our stop over, the winter of discontent had kicked in. We pulled into a budget motel, grabbed three cheese baguettes from the nearest café, ate them on the bed in our double room before all three of us succumbed to the exhausting and stressful first leg of our journey.

I awoke to Martin's croaky voice. "Buenos dias."

"We are still in France, you cretin." Bobby cursed.

All three of us had crashed out on one bed. Three very different people, three lost souls, three friends tied together, beginning an adventure, a journey of discovery. We were three people who were new to the world. We had to find ourselves all over again. We could be whoever we wanted to be. Defined by no one but ourselves. A fresh start, wiping away the damage of a time gone by. We were free, freer than ever. Our scars would heal, our memories forgotten, time to move on and break bread.

After a croissant and café latte, we continued our expedition into the unknown. Locals skins got browner, leaves lighter and the sky bluer. Before we knew it, the warming sun had tipped the scale and we were parking up next to our new home. A two-bedroom villa, just outside the beautiful Spanish town of Alicante.

"Wow, Sarah." I exclaimed with enthusiasm. "This place is a bit of alrighty then. Don't bother getting a job as a saleswoman. I was expecting a shithole. Undersell and over deliver eh? Talk about managing expectations. I had a vision of an old dilapidated barn with a couple of chickens in one corner and a dusty old pig in the other."

Martin must have had ants residing in his underpants. No sooner than we emptied the boot, he'd stripped off and was two lengths deep in the rather generously sized pool. "Come and join guys, the water is amazing."

Sarah and I ignored our travelling partner and took the little luggage we owned into the villa. The white washed two-story building was set back in around half an acre of sumptuous gardens. Orange and lemon trees prettified the baked lawn, large terracotta pots, filled with hibiscus and lavender sprinkled the colours of summer and welcomed us into our new abode. Bluebells and carnations lined the path to the opulent front door. Sarah lifted an ornamental frog which guarded the entrance and pulled out a bunch of keys.

"Blimey, this gaff has the same intricate security system as Fort Knox." I snorted, nearly tripping over the front step.

"This place is completely off the radar. The area's full of holiday homes. So, don't worry, no one really knows each other, let alone wants to bother anyone. We are all strangers here, there's no inclination to make friends or disturb the peace, not even for a cup of sugar." I took off my sandals and placed my feet on the old limestone tiles that welcomed the eyeline as I walked through the substantial oak door. Cold to the touch but beautiful to the eye. There wasn't a huge amount of furnishings, just the odd authentic piece of paraphyllia. A dark oak cabinet dominated the entrance hall. The downstairs was open planned, with a flow that worked well and would surely have inspired Señor Feng Shui.

"Sarah, I absolutely love it. How long do you think we can stay here?" I enquired, half hoping not to hear the answer.

"My Aunt and her family came here around a couple of months ago, I think. She only comes on an annual basis, so we should be ok for nine months or so."

The loud knock at the front door startled us at first but it didn't take long to fathom out that it wasn't our uncontrollable paranoia but our third wheel, Martin. I opened it slightly and passed through the car keys. "Mate, go and find a shop and buy a truckload of stuff for the kitchen. Meat, fruit, veg, snacks, some booze and a box of you know what."

"Ok you dirty dog but can I dry off first?" Had he forgotten that the tide had turned? Of course, I denied his request and slammed the door shut. Skipping back, I playfully picked up Sarah and threw her down on the old battered leather sofa that lay abandoned and unloved in the centre of the lounge. Nothing would stop me, I was a man possessed and judging from the look on Sarah's face, my efforts would be well rewarded. "Time to christen the place before bonehead trashes it." I smiled while ripping off my unwanted wrapping and uncovering my housewarming gift. It didn't take long to enjoy my bounty. Four minutes and forty seconds to be precise and that was twice. I didn't examine the instructions that came with my delivery. I was a man in a hurry, a man who knew what he wanted and who craved the fruits of his harvest. After the deed was done, I stared at my trophy. I deserved my prize. It glistened in a coating of perspiration. I had been to hell and back. I had endured the pain of my race, making considerable sacrifices along its route. It had taken its toll. Surely nobody could deny me my reward. It was clear that Sarah felt the same as we held each other close and caressed each other's naked bodies.

"Is that it? That was well below par and I don't mean in a good way on a golf course. You need a lot of practice my friend. You can put away your paint by numbers set. It's time to try the water colours. Next time, I expect a masterpiece." Sarah teased as she bathed in her warm glow.

I convulsed, almost chocking on the quality of her delivery. "Fuck off Alice and put the kettle on my sweet. Mine's a café con leche."

"Oh, and here's me thinking that you'd invite me to the Mad Hatters tea party! Anyway, there's no cow juice and before you ask or throw any more film quotes at me, let's be clear, I don't think there's any point in milking your udder just yet."

"Fair cop gov." I said as I grabbed my boxer shorts off the chandelier. "Wait here while I get some fruit from outside. If life throws you lemons, make some God damn lemonade as my mum used to say."

The Guy Who Loved Me

My performance improved across the next few days as I became accustomed to Sarah's sexual needs or was it the practice? Either way we were growing closer. The blossoming relationship certainly took away the dark thoughts from our minds which in turn allowed us to settle into a fairly decent existence. Sarah and Martin had managed to secure jobs at a local bar in the evenings and I'd bagged daytime employment at the nearby waterpark. With money trickling into our recently established Spanish bank accounts, life was fairly good and our anonymity, well preserved. The fine weather baked our pasty complexions and gave authenticity to our carefree disguises. We made an effort to ingratiate ourselves into the locality. Our Spanish language improved and we became experts in the art of ordering cervezas and patatas bravas.

We ditched the car, burning the hell out of it on the foothills of the Sierra Nevada mountain range. I cried as I watched the symbol of my past burn to a smouldering ember. Mopeds and bicycles became our only mode of transport. We darted through the streets of nearby towns and villages on two wheels, familiarising ourselves with the local landscape. Sarah and Martin preferred lounging by the pool whereas I relished the hustle and bustle of the beach. Martin and I enjoyed watching the odd game of English football whereas Sarah preferred the local karaoke bar. Sarah and I savoured long and romantic walks in the woods whereas Martin appreciated a scenic jog along the coast. It didn't matter, we'd moved on and we worked. We worked as friends, helping one another forge a new path. We worked as companions, never leaving one to dwell in their turbulent past. We worked as a unit to feed, clothe and put smiles on our faces. We had one another's backs and things were going pretty well.

Don't get me wrong, it certainly wasn't easy fitting into our newly found circumstances, there were plenty of bumps along the winding coastal road. The main obstacle to our newfound freedom was our newfound freedom. Temptation was everywhere and it was so easily accessible. We certainly tried to keep ourselves away from the crowds, but the local fiestas were far too enticing. A week into our arrival, we decided to pay a visit to the The Fogueres de Sant Joan Festival which celebrates the arrival of Summer solstice.

"Fuck the solstice, it will be a great excuse to party and celebrate our arrival." Screamed Sarah as she read the flyer that had been thrust through our letterbox. We didn't take much convincing and before we knew it, we were watching bonfires, fireworks and cries of joy light up the night sky. We ate and drank in the exuberant atmosphere it offered and as strangers, we welcomed its unbridled anonymity. We danced, we laughed and hugged on the first night of the celebrations.

"Let's go back again tonight!" I mumbled as Sarah opened the bedroom blinds and welcomed in the morning sunlight.

"Yeah, I'm up for it as long as this hangover clears."

Right, I'll get the coffees on!" I replied taking the hint.

Later that evening, as we sat and watched a rather comical effigy being tossed onto a bonfire in one of the town's quaint little squares, Martin turned to face me. "Looks a bit like Suggs eh?" Within half an hour we were back at the villa, our joyous moods extinguished. It took a couple of days of silence before we reconciled with Martin. Being a tad over sensitive was par for the course and had to be accepted. A house meeting was called, and all was forgiven, that is until the following week! I'd taken a day off work and we all decided to spend the day down at the beach. "Life's tough for you sun hardened criminals!" I hear you cry but you have to realise that we were just trying to fit in. After we'd settled into our very own picture postcard, we all let out a sigh of relief together. The sand underfoot stimulated every sense in my body, the sun on my face enhanced every emotion in my soul, the colour of the sky aroused every feeling in my heart and the fresh feeling of the rippling waves, washed through all of the guilt in my conscience. Well, as long as I didn't dwell on my misgivings. In reality, it was the music that clogged my self-condemnation. I took it with me everywhere. Earphones plugged my failings and speakers drowned out shame. This occasion was no different. The drum and bass played and rocked as gently as the light breeze ruffled our hair. After a couple of hours, the odd snore and three layers of factor fifty, I jumped off the sun lounger and took to my feet.

"I'm sure that kid is struggling." I shouted, waking up Martin and causing Sarah to miss her mouth with her ice cream.

"Shit, I think you're right." Sarah muttered with a concerned tone, wiping the cream from her face.

"Martin, you're the best swimmer, Quickly, go see if he's ok!" I called out, not taking my eyes off the poor lad who was now thrashing around in the waves.

"Hang on. Let me have a ciggie first." Replied Martin nonchalantly, pulling one from his packet.

"Are you fucking stupid or something, the boy's drowning!" I shouted with panic in my voice as I grabbed his cigarette and tossed it in the sand.

"All right, keep your wig on." Martin said, finally kicking into life.

It turned out the boy was just doing some exercises in the water and was not too happy when Martin dragged him out. After using some colourful language to describe his dismay at being manhandled against his will, he wandered off back to his parents. Believe me, it wasn't long before his father came over. "Oh no, here we go." I whispered.

"He looks like a thug. Leave this one to me." Sarah said standing up and trudging through the soft sand towards him.

"We thought he was struggling in the water. We were just trying to help." Sarah was left flummoxed, as the guy simply ignored her and walked on as though she was not even there.

"What's thee name, dickhead?" The strong Yorkshire accent directed itself towards Martin, accompanied by a ferociously wagging finger.

"Martin Bunratty. What's yours?"

"Doesn't matter what my name is lad. Touch my son again and I'll rip thee bollocks off and shove them up your arsehole! Understand?"

"Err, yeah, sorry." I thought Martin was going to start crying there and then but his trembling bottom lip began to subside as the menace returned to his family.

"He'll be getting his oats tonight." Sarah giggled.

Never mind that! Martin, you idiot! Why did you give your real name?"

"Oh shit! Yeah sorry, I didn't think. Anyway, he's as thick as two short planks. He won't remember anything in the morning." A huge argument ensued followed by two more days of silence and another house meeting before we got back on track.

Oh, and before I forget, there was also the time when we sat and enjoyed a moonlit Greek meal in a cosy little square off the beaten track. After devouring a few kilos of slow cooked lamb, Martin loaded the straw that finally broke the camels back. "If you guys had to throw six people into an underground bunker, who would you choose and why?"

"Are you being serious?" I remonstrated.

Sarah looked at me as though I'd just stolen the same camel's hump. "No, come on Bobby. It's only a game. This is a good question."

I downed my brandy and declared them as a couple of sickos, but Sarah continued. "Well, firstly and top of my list would be you Martin. You deserve to know how we felt down there and out of anyone that has crossed my path, you've hurt me the most. Secondly, I'd throw in my ballet teacher François, the lecherous old git. Then I'd chuck in Hitler and Mussolini."

Martin quickly raised his hand. "Stop, they have to be alive and you have to know them."

"Oh, ok, fair point. Then perhaps my bitchy school friend Amanda and her sidekick Tabitha. Now, who else. Aha, a little similar to you Martin, my geography teacher would get it. Mr Tibbs. He had it in for me the first day we met. And finally, I'd put my sister's boyfriend in there but only until she met someone else. God, she could do so much better. What about you Bobby? Who would you choose?"

I didn't answer and remained in a mood for a few hours but soon all was forgotten again. It's true that we had to whack a few moles, but our new lives marched on and we embraced it, but what choice did we have?

It wasn't until the autumn leaves began filling the pool when our bubble finally burst. Only one hundred or so days into our Spanish adventure. I was halfway through a shift at the waterpark when a headline in an English newspaper left on a bench, caught my attention.

"Police Hunt the Horsleys Green Three." Our mug shots were plastered all over the front cover. After the initial shock, I grabbed the discarded tabloid, jumped on my moped and dashed home. Sarah and Martin were sunning themselves in the back garden. Sipping beer by the pool without a care in the world. My unexpected appearance broke the serenity of their pleasure.

"What are you doing back? Aren't you meant to be at work?" Sarah asked, looking quite startled.

"Here, clap a load of this." I threw the paper down next to them in disgust. "Front fucking page! There in black and white for every Tomas, Diego and Horacio to see!"

Sarah began to read the article out loud. "Police are looking for three individuals suspected of kidnapping English test cricketer, Dennis Folks (30) and a number of others. They are also responsible for the murder of Peter Sugden (67), a retired headmaster from Grimsby. Police are offering a reward of twenty thousand pounds for information leading to their arrest. If anyone comes into contact with these highly dangerous criminals, do not approach them but contact crime stoppers on 020 CRIMESTOPPERS. Their names are Martin Bunratty, Simon Dingle and Sarah…"

"Enough already!" Martin shouted. "We get the message. They're looking for us. We knew this would happen. What's the sudden panic? Why are you jumping overboard just because someone has lit a match with the sole intention of smoking a cigarette? Calm yourself down dear boy or you'll give yourself a heart attack."

I took a deep breath. "You're right, Martin. I know, it's just hard to see our names in a national newspaper. It caught me off guard, that's all." I perched next to the pool and dangled my legs into its comforting cradle. Martin threw me a can which I opened and devoured until my nerves had calmed. I couldn't help but think about what evidence Officer Mary Blackthorn was piecing together. By now, she would know the full hair-raising details of our horrendous crime. The hard facts would have unfolded on the pages of those involved. All she had to do was find us. Surely it wouldn't be long before someone recognised us after a few investigative stones were overturned. Was it not a cliché in disguise? Brits wanted by the law, hide away in a Spanish villa. Were we being too complacent? It almost felt like a holiday before starting a new job, only there was no job, only a lengthy spell in another dingy cell to look forward to.

"Guys, I'm not going back to work today. I feel like it's only a matter of time before we get caught. We can't just go through the motions; we need to camouflage ourselves with better war paint. Any suggestions?" I said thrashing my legs around in the pool.

"Maybe you're right." Sarah looked annoyed as she placed her bookmark inside her novel of choice and threw it onto the floor.

Martin slammed down his can and watched its contents drain out before looking up with indignation. "Oh, come on, you're being far too suspicious."

"I find I live much longer that way! Well, that's what James Bond said in The Spy Who Loved Me."

"Really? You're comparing our situation to a Bond movie?" Martin continued, rather unimpressed. "It's in your eyes only. No one in this town cares! Everyone's on holiday. They've come here to get away from all the bad news at home not wade knee deep through its stench! Listen, I've got an idea. How about you go to the local DIY store and buy some yellow paint for your belly!"

"Fuck off Martin. At some stage, the sky is going to fall in on us so take your goldfinger out of your ass! Don't ever forget that it was you who got us into this ungodly mess and shit jokes like that ain't going to get us out of the cess pit that you've so kindly dropped us in!" I shouted, eyeballing Martin with resentment.

"Sorry bud, I'm only messing. As it goes, I think you're spot on. Look, here's an idea. You only live once, or twice in our case. How about we shave our heads? Go all out, total grade one. Sarah, to sympathise, you can dye your hair red. Hey, we could go even further. A couple of goatees and the odd tattoo will turn Bob into your uncle or Fanny into your aunt. Hey, to top it all off, I'll even get one of my ears pierced if Sarah gets her nose done."

"Look, I'm not sure if you're taking the piss but if not, let's go into town and do it now. It might just allow us to live another day!" I said with authority, pulling Sarah up from her sun lounger. "I understand your point about being over cautious, but you know that it's not just holiday makers here, some of the expats will have the three of us rolled up under their arms. Let's go separately, Martin, you go to the tattoo parlour first and we'll head over to the hairdressers."

Martin almost jumped into his shorts and wasted no time revving up his clapped-out second-hand scooter. He was out of sight before we could say, "and don't bother coming back." After a quick shower and change, Sarah and I linked arms and began our romantic stroll into the town centre together. Five hours later, we were all back at the base, our criminal headquarters, with our new looks. Sarah complimented me on my skinhead but thought my Saxon band tattoo was rather outdated. I felt that Martin looked like a refugee with his crew cut although the dragon inking wrapped around his bicep seemed quite remarkable. Sarah looked like a Disney princess with her long silver curly locks. So strikingly beautiful that I couldn't take my eyes off her.

"Martin, it's your turn to mow the lawn." I voiced without averting my stare.

"I did it last time."

Martin, it's your turn to mow the lawn!" I raised my voice a few decibels.

"Aha, I got you, you dirty buggers. It should take me about thirty minutes." Martin replied with a cheesy smile.

Twenty-eight minutes later, Sarah and I tumbled out of the villa and returned to the pool area only to witness Martin sweeping up the final few clippings. He looked across at our guilty, slightly embarrassed faces, "fuck me, I wondered who you were for a minute."

An Inspector Falls

Mary Blackthorn sat with her head in hands as Sergeant Parry left her office. His words still ringing in her ears. "There's nothing more we can do for now. We've spent enough time and resources on this case. Let's leave it to the big boys. It's time you went back on the beat."

With an emotional tie to the crime, Mary simply could not let it go. Admit defeat and return to her previous routine? How could she ever get excited about helping a cat get down from a tree or assisting an old lady in crossing a busy road? She'd tasted the big time and her hunger had not yet been satisfied, she wanted more. "What can the big boys do that I can't." She thought to herself. Finding 'The Horsleys Green Three' was her plight, she was the expert in this investigation, and it was her job to bring them to justice. "Fuck Parry, I'm not going to just leave it there. I'll work behind the turncoat's back." She was often out on the field alone and if not, she could always trust her partner Mick to be discreet. Having been in the office at the crack of dawn, coupled with the lack of senior support, she was feeling rebellious. Well before her shift was due to finish, she grabbed her jacket from the back of her desk seat and started her journey home.

"Where could they be?" She painstakingly examined the options as she sat behind her wheel. "The bastards have made it abroad. I just know they have but where could they have gone?"

With a newfound injection of determination, she dialled her mother's mobile. "Could you keep Alice tonight? I've got to work." This was no unusual request; her mother understood the pressures of her job and her appetite to succeed. The question was always taken as a statement.

"Ok dear, she can stay overnight, and I'll take her to summer camp in the morning. I hope all's ok?"

"Yes mother, just busy, that's all. I'll call her before bedtime and pick her up after work tomorrow. Thanks so much. Love you. Bye."

Within minutes, she was home and sat in the corner of her darkening sitting room, mentally studying the evidence she had so carefully obtained. There had been large cash withdrawals from all three suspects on the day of the big release and then nothing. No traces of their 'sorry, good for nothing' existence. They'd literally erased anything that would substantiate their carbon footprint. "They have to be overseas but where would they hide? How did they get there? What names are they using? Surely, they'd slip up soon. Contact a family member, a friend or a neighbour." All those connected to them had been informed that not passing on any information as to their whereabouts would be considered as aiding and abetting a criminal. They were all told, in no uncertain terms that the punishment for this unlawful deception would be severe. Unsurprisingly, all had agreed to play ball, but long-established bricks of loyalty were always hard to knock down. Mary woke up in the same place the next morning. Her back aching from the crumpled position her body had taken. Her head sore from the heavy burden she carried. The sun pouring shame over her face through the half-closed curtains.

"Fuck, I forgot to call Alice before bedtime. I hope she's not too upset with me." Mary didn't see her beloved daughter for another two days. Her obsession engrossed her like a cluster of nimbus stratus clouds engulfing the fruits of her arid brain. She feared failure, feared being hoisted onto a pedestal and being knocked down by the gust of a criminal wind. She had to succeed or die trying in order to create her legacy. She'd given up too much to enter the force for one significant case to cause her shoelaces to untie themselves. She had not been elevated up the ranks, of course not. She had achieved nothing. Back on the beat, walking between shopping centres and tube stations, her mind relentlessly telling her that she'd missed something. "If only we'd managed to track Martin's movements after we let him go! Could I have saved the old headmaster? Have I got his blood on my hands? Why did Sarah leave with them? Something just doesn't add up!"

A shower, a large dollop of makeup and a cup of caffeine did not improve her state of mind as she headed off to work. Her trusted sidekick Mick picked up on her negative energy immediately and challenged her mood. "Come on Mary, snap out of it! You did all you could! You have to let it go. Don't let this sorry saga haunt you forever. They'll catch the chuckle brothers and their muse soon enough."

Mary knew that he was only trying to help but his tone only rattled her cage further. "Yeah, I'm sure they'll do a better job than I could!"

They were tending to a 'snatch and run' handbag incident when the call came in. A young buck, knee high to a grasshopper, barely out of kindergarten, had gone into the back of a refuge lorry and was attempting to justify his actions by claiming that the service vehicle was driving too slowly. It didn't take long for them to arrive at the scene and witness a full-blown argument, well under way.

"It's a forty mile an hour road you buffoon! You were driving your truck at walking speed and then you have the nerve to slam your brakes on. It's no wonder I went into the bloody back of you." The angrier the teenager got, the lower his 'ripped to next to nothing' trousers fell, exposing more and more of his well-worn neon boxer shorts.

"We are not buffoons sir, we are waste management and disposal technicians and we're just doing our jobs you imbecile," snorted one of the binmen as he picked up a black bin bag.

"That's a load of rubbish!" Claimed the juvenile as he made a half-hearted attempt to cover his illuminated posterior.

"Correct!" The rubbish comedian appeared to take a bow at his unimpressed audience as Mick burst into a fit of laughter.

"Sorry Sir but you have to admit that you deserved that one." Mick adjusted his game face and asked for names and licences. As he called through to see if the flashy high-end Beemer had been stolen, Mary asked him to confirm if he'd driven into the back of the truck.

"Yes, but that's not the point." He remonstrated.

"I'm afraid it is. Now, the law states that it's your fault. You should always give the vehicle in front sufficient space in order to brake safely when required. You clearly did not and drove into the back of him. Full stop!" Mary said firmly, as she ignored a call coming through on her mobile.

"There appears to be no damage to the council vehicle, but I suggest, you apologise to your daddy for the damage you've caused to his fancy car. Oh, and pull up your trousers or I'll have you for indecent exposure!"

The youngster looked beyond startled in the headlights of his own stupidity as he drove away into the naughty boy's corner of his embarrassment. It was the first time that his father had entrusted him with the keys to his pride and joy and probably the last. "I hope he gets those ridiculous boxers pulled down and receives a good hiding when he gets home." Mary muttered under her breath, as she returned to her missed telephone call. She didn't recognise the number but gave the caller her professional curtesy and dialled it back.

"Hello. This is Officer Blackthorn, returning your call."

"Hi, this is Mrs McKay, Sarah's mother. Sorry for calling you directly but we are really worried. We haven't heard anything for a while, and we are concerned that you're not focussing enough attention on our missing daughter. Surely you must have some news for us? What's the update? Are you any closer in locating her whereabouts?"

Mary was caught off-guard and unconsciously found herself walking out of Mick's earshot before she spoke. "Hello Mrs McKay. I'm so sorry that nobody has kept you up to date. Are you at home at present? I'm keen to speak with you and let you know where we are with everything."

"Of course! That would be very much appreciated. I'll be at home all day." Came the despairingly hopeful reply. "See you later."

"Who was that?" Asked Mick as Mary returned to their patrol car. "Just my mother, asking what time I'll be home tonight."

The bluecoats came to the aid of a further two incensed members of the public before they clocked off. An exasperated shopkeeper who praised the lord on their arrival, after a group of school children had stolen an assortment of his confectionary. Details were taken and a brief discussion on what the world was coming to saw them on their way to their next assignment. A distinguished looking gentleman had thrown himself onto the bonnet of a car which had stopped to allow him onto a zebra crossing. After screaming blue murder and complaining about severe pain in his back and neck, he was halted in his anguish after the innocent driver pointed to the dashcam inside his vehicle. "I feel much better. Can I go home now officers?" Mary didn't even reply, she nodded a farewell to the bemused driver, looked at her watch and told Mick that it was a quarter past home time.

An hour later, Mary was at her destination. She wasn't entirely sure why she'd instigated the visit apart from a guilty feeling that she'd let a fellow mother down. Mrs Edna McKay lived alone. The rather glamourous woman had recently separated from her cheating husband who she'd caught red handed, with his trousers around his ankles. The front door swiftly opened before Mary had chance to ring the doorbell.

"Hello, I thought you'd forgotten about me," Mrs McKay mumbled unapologetically as she ushered Mary into her cluttered but charming end of terrace, two up two down. Mary followed her into the sitting room and took comfort in an old floral settee that looked like it had been passed down from one generation too many.

"Now, would you like a cup of tea? Or, perhaps some wine? I've just opened a nice bottle of chardonnay if you fancy a glass, mum's the word and all that malarkey."

Mary smiled warmly. She was officially off duty but hadn't as yet cleared the work tension from her bones. "I could murder one, but I'd better not, tea will be fine. White with one please."

As Edna wandered off to complete her hosting obligations, Mary stood up and surveyed the room. "Oh God, why did I use the word murder? Was that a Freudian slip?" The furniture was a mish mash of old and new. She felt a sense of guilt as she paced the cream carpet in her work boots. Perhaps she should have asked whether it was ok to keep them on? The curtains were undrawn, and a streetlight enhanced the illumination that the solitary lamp cried out for. There was a musty smell to the dwelling, one that she was familiar with. The damp patches on the walls almost reminded her of home. "I must get someone in to sort that out." She thought to herself as she was drawn to a sideboard full of framed family photographs. They were gathered like a little shrine to poor Sarah, who was the central figure in each one of them. Baby Sarah wrapped in swaddling clothes on her mother's knee. Sarah as a chubby toddler riding a tricycle, looking excited about her new-found freedom. Spotty teenage Sarah playing hockey in her school team. Academic Sarah, throwing her mortarboard into the air at her graduation. "An ugly duckling to a swan fairy-tale." Mary smiled with affection as she picked up the most recent one of Sarah in her bikini, lying on a sun lounger by a pool.

"That was taken last year in Spain at my sister's villa." Edna placed a silver tray filled with fine bone China on the coffee table. Sat perched on the sofa, she proceeded to pour the contents of the delicate teapot into the two elaborate cups. "There's some ginger snaps if you fancy?"

Mary declined the offer and returned to the settee. "Now, listen Mrs McKay, I want to be very clear and assure you that we have not given up on finding your daughter. In actual fact we have increased our resources. We have senior teams in the Met police looking for Sarah."

Edna sat back with her teacup on her lap. "And, have you any news?" She said expectantly.

"No, not yet but rest assured that we won't give up until we find her. Our understanding is that she is still with Simon Dingle and Martin Bunratty. From what we have been able to ascertain, it appears that she left with them consensually and we are confident that she is in no immediate danger."

Edna dug deep into the detail that didn't exist. Mary skirted around the truth that there was no detail. Edna asked questions and Mary drank tea. Edna asked more questions and Mary drank more tea as she knew that when her cup was empty, she would be pardoned from this fruitless interrogation.

Mary drove home feeling slightly battered and bruised from the verbal assault; all she could hear ringing in her ears was…. "Let the big boys deal with it." What did that even mean? That the best police officers were all male? That she was a little girl and could not be expected to solve such high-profile cases. Did women have no place in senior law enforcement apart from wearing out leather soles on battered high streets? In all the best detective films, the famous crime fighters were men, except perhaps Miss Congeniality. But did the words ring true or were they just the modern-day starting pistol, showcasing the race to resolve her own insecurities? She had to prove them all wrong, but how?

The Cheat with No Shame

Hours rolled into days, days rolled into weeks and weeks rolled back into the settled comfort of their new lives. I was always the first up in the morning, making breakfast for my two amigos before I left for my shift at the waterpark. Martin and Sarah would have dinner on the table on my return before disappearing for the evening shift at the town's traditional English bar, The Battered Bulldog. On the odd night, I'd find myself at a loose end and journey down to see them. The shift work wasn't ideal but being able to spend time and see my beloved behind the bar made it more bearable. I'd always pay for the first drink but that's where my evening's financial commitment would end. Although, a large tip would always be expected and who was I to deny them. You own your own Euro until you give it away. I'd never moan, it was kind of a loan and anyway, it's always nice to give a dog a bone.

Apart from the lazy American owner, they were the only two members of staff at the establishment and that meant that they pretty much ran the place. They worked well together, serving drinks and bar snacks with great efficiency and cheerful courtesy. Like a wrestling tag team, when one was front of house the other would be knee deep in the kitchen, cleaning the dirty pots and pans. The regulars took to them as they took the regulars retirement funds off them.

Martin flirted with charm and charisma with the old dears while Sarah had the elderly gents wrapped around her little unwedded finger. I applauded their newly found partnership from the outside. Admiring their Phoenix mantra as they rose from the flames of the burning injustices they'd endured. Their friendship was clear for all and sundry. Their wounds had healed and were forgotten. Distant memories of a much-maligned past. Oh, how I wished that I could have had the same resolve. Music was played, orders were made, drinks were served, food was prepared, and the till rang a merry tune, albeit minus a few of my coins. A fine experience was always enjoyed by all. I envied them. I could have worked at the bar in place of Martin, but not only did I think that it would be bad for our relationship, I also felt the need for Martin to feel part of the team if this merry dance was going to be successful. I sat on my usual bar stool. Free drink in hand and gave myself a pat on the back. Mission accomplished. A success of fine proportions, we'd overthrown the devilry of our foreboding and carved a steady and almost enjoyable life from the darkness of our hiding place.

We all had Mondays and Tuesdays free from the binds of work, consuming the fruits of the local landscape by cycling, walking and swimming around its carnal allure. Picnics, snorkels, frisbees and high jinks filled the contents of our day bags. We never talked about our demons and our demons left us alone to our own unique devices. We had eked out an existence, a routine, that worked for us and solved our predicament. The dark clouds of our past had cleared, and the sun shone on us until self-doubt got the better of me. Ironically, there was a fire at the waterpark.

Given that the grounds held over one million gallons of water, this high alert emergency initially did not concern me until the announcement. A call to evacuate the premises.

The subsequent official company statement was one that shocked me even further. The park would be closed for the remainder of the day while the safety of the complex would be assessed. With no other option, the staff were given an early bath. Given that this unprecedented action had caught the miserly manager off-guard, we were told that our spontaneous time off would be unpaid. Feeling a little aggrieved, I headed back to the villa, keen to make the most of an expensively free afternoon. A formulation of planned activity on my ride back teased my mood and uplifted my spirits. It was an unforeseen opportunity to take Sarah for lunch at the new harbourside restaurant that had recently opened with rave reviews.

On my arrival, and after parking my bike in the carport, I wandered around the back of the villa, anxious to give Sarah a spirited surprise. I knew she'd be delighted to witness my early arrival. As I turned the corner and entered the swimming pool area, I froze at the sight of my girlfriend lying totally naked next to her former abductor. No t-shirt, no swimsuit, no kaftan, nothing, nada, niente, absolut gar nichts! Were my eyes deceiving me? I was glad that they had formed a close bond but surely this was one item of clothing too far. A game of bat and ball would have been more appropriate. Maybe scrabble or a game of chess but not snakes and ladders! What would she think if I'd conducted myself with the same shameful indecent exposure? In the dusty shadows of the unwanted image, I hung back, not sure how to approach the situation. Their pool loungers lay close together, their naked bodies glistened in the sun from a recent dip in the pool. My report had been filed, this was irrefutably a betrayal and was absolutely not acceptable. As I considered my diminishing options, Sarah thrust her arms aloft in order to exercise an unjustified yawn. As she brought them down and before they came to rest, she stroked the length of Martin's arm which hung off the side of his sun bed. Did this miniscule action speak a thousand unfaithful words? Had I been naive not to notice their growing familiarity? Was I reading far too much into the whole episode of a fictitious romantic comedy? Surely this was not the start of a salubrious affair. Deciding that it was all too much to handle, or not wanting to see my worst nightmare unfold right in front of my eyes, I slipped back, unlocked my bike and headed for the tranquillity of the calming rugged coastline to gather my thoughts. With the expensive toll that my brain couldn't afford, I just had to untangle the potential web of deceit that my mind was whirling up into a storm of dishonesty. Was I making a three-course meal out of a slice of bread or was this the wakeup call that would end any possible dreams of a happy life? I had to fathom out the truth either way. I would not be betrayed again. I sat on a rock overlooking the beautiful bay and considered my next move.

An hour later, I was back at the villa, making the noisiest of entrances to alleviate any embarrassment. "Hi honeys, I'm home!" I screamed, as I wheeled down the front drive. The two of them were in the same positions as I'd left them but this time, swimwear adorned their bodies and relief plastered their faces.

"What the fuck are you doing back so soon? Do you ever do any work?" Did I notice a glint of guilt on Sarah's face as she gave me a kiss?

The following couple of days didn't give me any great cause for concern. I monitored the situation very closely and even strengthened my status as a loving boyfriend. Complimenting her at the drop of each feather she laid out before me. There were no debates or leading questions about feeling comfortable naked next to the ones you are attracted to. If I was correct, I had to be sure. Being paranoid was understandable given the recent events, but false accusations would only lead to further misery. If I was being led down the garden path, then I had to be prepared to mow the lawn. If I was being led a merry dance, then I would have to be capable of turning off the music. I needed evidence, if it existed, or I needed to bury the almost pornographic image deep into my locked and gated memory bank. I knew that they wouldn't parade their affections in front of me, so I decided to adopt the element of surprise, combined with the essential fly on the bedroom wall tactic. I plotted this course with inordinate skulduggery and masterminded my endeavour with the conviction it deserved. My plan was made, my trap was set, and it was now time to execute it.

We were all sat having breakfast when I announced. "I have to go to Valencia this afternoon for a company health and safety event. Turns out that the fire was badly mismanaged, and a couple of staff members got their fingers burnt. The course is compulsory, and it involves an overnight stay. They've booked us in a low budget hostel, the cheapskates! Do you guys need me to bring you anything back? I hear they are famous for handcrafted stuff. Martin, a wicker basket perhaps? Or maybe I could buy you a new bikini Sarah?"

"Err, no thanks. A course eh? Well considering the circumstances, it makes sense. No problem sweetheart. I'll miss you but needs must." Sarah said casually as she furtively looked across at Martin.

"I still think that it was you who started the fire. You pyromaniac you. I wouldn't be surprised if we saw the cathedral in Valencia go up in smoke by the end of the night." Martin turned to Sarah as they smiled warmly at one another.

"I'll scorch your arse if you're not careful. Oh, that might have come out wrong!" I forced out a laugh as I hugged Sarah, kissed her on the cheek and asked her to call me later.

Of course, there was no seminar, in fact there was no work commitments full stop. I'd taken the day off for the sole purpose of investigating the depths of my own sorry insecurities. Having invested in three separate outfits that I could disguise my disguise with, I was ready. I'd installed two cameras. One facing the pool and one displaying the open planned downstairs, both strategically hidden. The one outside, buried deep in a plant pot between some leafy plumage and the other squeezed at the top of a bookshelf, between 'Lady Chatterley's Lover and 'Fifty Shades of Grey." The veil of mystery would be uncovered, and the course of my new journey would either take a sudden turn for the worse or the autocruise would be turned back on.

I took my seat in a café on the outskirts of the town. Confusing the waiter, as I returned from the bathroom with a stuck-on beard and thick black rimmed glasses. Who was he to ask any questions? Questions that I probably wouldn't be able to answer anyway. Why did I need any guises? I was hardly hiding in the loft looking through a spy hole. I really wasn't sure but feeling the part and wearing the chainmail could potentially protect me from any poison arrows of deceit. The place was filled with eccentric holidaymakers who when at home would be steady Eddies but when abroad, would turn into flamboyant Freddies. A fun-loving family on the table to my right, filled the outside space with laughter. A couple of cyclists on my left, taking a break, created some adventure. A group of dark suited aficionados in front of me, gathered some mystery and a kind looking lady behind me generated some much-needed normality.

The two hidden cameras displayed their contents on my phone screen. Sarah was washing up the breakfast plates and Martin was already basking in the cheating sun of the mid-morning betrayal. Cigarette in one hand and a book in the other, nothing seemed unusual. He was even wearing his swimming trunks. After drying the pots, Sarah grabbed her reusable shopping bag and headed out of the villa, unaccompanied. What was I doing? Wallowing in my own self-pity. How could I have ever doubted them? But as Alec Stiles says in the movie The Streets with No Name, "what's the use of having a war if you don't learn from it?" I finished my coffee, gestured to the waiter and paid my bill, quickly before the woman behind could beat me to it. I then decided to take a trip down to the beach. Feeling completely stupid, I ripped off my synthetic facial hair with the distain it deserved. "I must stop this nonsense! I'll go back in the afternoon and just say that the course had been cancelled." My father's famous saying rang true. 'Throw a grenade in haste and repent without any legs.'

After gathering my thoughts and finding a suitable spot on the sand, I rested my paranoid head on a self-styled sand pillow and took a siesta, albeit an early one.

Three hours later and after awaking to a missing rucksack which created an even higher level of paranoia, I headed back to the villa. The perpetrator would have been less than impressed with the stolen treasure of a black curly wig, tatty baseball cap and my spare pair of florescent green rimmed sunglasses. As I wandered on my merry way, I began to untangle my knotted mind. "I'm so lucky to have Sarah, she's such an amazing individual. I shouldn't have doubted her, although at some stage, we do need to have a conversation about the naked sunbathing!" But I felt a lot more relaxed and was looking forward to giving her a big hug.

On the journey back to the villa, my spirits were raised even further. I admired a little boy wearing the full Arsenal football kit hand in hand with his father, who shone brightly in the Spurs strip. "You've got to love the Brits abroad." I thought, smiling at the father who, after noticing my amusement, told me to fuck off and followed up this standard English profanity by requesting that I stick a large chorizo sausage up my arse or something of that ilk.. "Charming." I replied. I wasn't going to lock horns. What was the point? He was probably having a bad day. Letting his family down by not getting up early enough to put his towel over a sun lounger next to his hotel pool. Or perhaps the bacon wasn't crispy enough with his full English. Could have been sunstroke, who cares. It didn't matter, I was off to surprise my lovely loyal girlfriend. Gathering some wildflowers along the way, I took the scenic route back home. By the time I'd reached my destination, I had a lovely assorted bunch of colour in my hand. I walked straight to the back of the villa. Half expecting to see them both sunbathing by the pool. Maybe this would be my chance to raise the roof off the naked sunbathing debate. I had to get it off my chest at some stage but to my surprise, there was nobody there.

I walked into the villa through the back door, only to find that there was nobody downstairs. Flicking on the kettle, I took off my trainers and sat down on the sofa. Slightly exhausted with the worry of my relationship imploding but extremely relieved with the lack of evidence to support my fears, I tipped my head back and closed my eyes for a second. Wait, what was I hearing? A grunt, a whimper, a loud sigh, a submissive moan! I was not completely sure but there was definitely a cacophony of chaos occurring from the upstairs chambers. "Oh! My dear God! This can't be happening." This was it; it was the moment of truth. If I had to hit the eject button and crash the relationship, then so be it. I owed it to myself. I would not be deceived again. Yes, the consequences would be horrific, but I would pick myself off the cold hard floor and start all over again. I'd achieved it before and was capable of doing it all over again. It was time to take control.

Not wanting to raise any alarm, I relieved the kettle of its whistle blowing duties and crept up the stairs, my bare feet cancelling the noise of my footsteps. Once I'd reached the small inadequate space of the landing, I placed my hand on our bedroom door handle and inhaled sufficient oxygen to satisfy my needs. The noises became heightened, I could distinctly hear Sarah's voice. Was she mumbling the incoherent words of a cheat to her accomplice? I was about to stumble on the state secrets that would blow the back door off my new life. My world was about to turn upside down yet again. Just for a moment, I considered backing down and running. But not facing my fears would never take the pain away from the once contented child, who played gleefully with a hydrogen filled balloon. No! I would never trash my integrity even if it meant bursting that much-loved balloon. I turned the handle and threw myself into the room.

"You dirty cheating whore! How could you do this to me?" I screamed as my face contorted with anger.

Sarah's face sprung from under the sheet. "Bobby, what are you doing here? I thought you were in Valencia?" A look of abject horror etched across her dishevelled face. I was lost for words, a broken man who was in the mental process of accepting his fate.

"It's not what it looks like!" Sarah grabbed the sheet and wrapped it across her naked body revealing Martin in his full glory. Within seconds, it dawned on me that it wasn't actually Martin but a completely bald headed, middle aged, slightly overweight stranger.

"Who the fuck is he?" I shrieked with unexpected stupefaction. The somewhat embarrassed cad grabbed his clothes which were scattered across the floor and with the expression of a squashed rabbit, who hadn't seen the headlights in time, grabbed the clothes nearest to him and ran past me without uttering a word. I took an imaginary swipe at him, but my fist never had the intention of making contact. My actions were simply for the cameras and to prove my manly worth to the woman who had just taken it away.

I composed myself, "I'll ask you again, who the fuck is he?"

Sarah sat up against the headboard, head in hands. "Nobody, somebody, I don't know. I'm sorry Bobby, I've messed up badly. Please wait downstairs and I'll come down in a minute and tell you everything."

Police - A Tragedy Too

Mary wasn't happy about being forced into a two-week period of leave, but at least it was offered with full pay. Once word got out to her superiors that she had paid an unauthorised visit to Mrs McKay, Parry had no choice but to persuade her to accept the break as opposed to being forced to explain herself in front of a panel of no reprisal. Mary had to sign a report that detailed her induced bout of stress caused by the high-profile case. She accepted her black mark and saw it as an opportunity to wash through the scourge of the last few weeks. The opportunity of spending some quality time with her daughter Alice was high on her agenda. Her prescribed vacation fell nicely within the school summer holidays. "Oh, Alice will be pleased!" Before the sun rose that morning, trips to Madam Tussauds, Legoland, The Natural History Museum and Thorpe Park were placed in the diary. "Some long overdue family time will be the perfect tonic." She thought to herself as she beckoned over her little bundle of joy who had awoken from her slumber.

"We'll have a blast Alice. I'm all yours for the next fourteen days. Work have acknowledged my recent achievements and have given me some well-earned time off. Are you excited? We'll have super time. Just me and you!" She snuggled Alice as they lay together in bed.

"Yay! About time. I thought you'd forgotten who I was." Alice smiled and tightened her grip around her mother's neck, planting a sloppy wet kiss on her forehead.

"Oh, how could you ever think that, my love? You mean the world to me. I'm sorry mummy has had to work lots of extra hours recently, but she's only doing it to make the world a better place for you to live. Anyway, let's forget about the bad guys for now. They can wait! I've got some great treats planned for you. Do you want to know what they are?" Mary returned the favour and blew a moist raspberry on Alice's bare stomach.

After the excited little lady stopped laughing, she looked into her mother's eyes and exposed her best puppy dog face. One that had never failed her, her trump card and the skeleton key that she knew could unlock her dear mummy's heart. "My friend Samantha is going to Portugal on holiday, she's been talking non-stop about it for weeks. They have a holiday home there. Can we go too? Her daddy said that she's allowed to invite a friend as long as they come with a parent. Please mummy, please! That would be the best present ever!"

Mary froze for a second, as the lightbulb flicked on in her muddled mind. She then placed her hands adoringly on Alice's cheeks. "Oh my God! You clever girl. Wait here, mummy has something she needs to do. I'll be back before you can say, donde esta mi pasaporte."

"Eh? But what does that even mean?" Alice spluttered, looking rather puzzled.

"Ask Alexa my darling, I won't be long." Mary walked downstairs and looked at her large train station style clock that hung above the Victorian fireplace in the kitchen.

She'd bought it on a whim and was perhaps too hasty in her choice as its time always ticked by too quickly, one minute for every hour. Eight fifteen was its display. "Just before eight then! Was it too early to call?" Before working through an answer, she dialled the intended number on her mobile.

"Hello, this is Mary Blackthorn. I'm so sorry to call you this early but could you tell me where your sister's Villa is exactly?"

Edna McKay rubbed the sleep away from her eyes and gave her the information. "Why do you ask? Do you think she might be in Spain? Thinking about it, it wouldn't surprise me, she was always at her happiest there."

"Probably not, I really don't want to get your hopes up, but it's worth checking and if nothing else, we can cross it off our list. Please don't mention this to anyone or it might hamper our enquiries. I need your word on that Mrs McKay. It's really important. One sniff of our tail and they'll make a run for it. Trust me on this and don't worry, I'll keep you posted." After some gentle pleasantries, Mary ended the call, ran back upstairs and flung herself back onto Alice's bed. "Go pack your suitcase, we are going to Spain!"

"You mean Portugal, you silly sausage."

"Your friend's family won't want us tagging along with them. Anyway, Spain will be much more fun, and the ice cream tastes much nicer there. Oh, and I've heard that your friend's daddy smells of old socks. Don't worry, we'll have our own adventure. Just the two of us, my little chorizo."

Instantly forgetting the name of her friend, Alice could not contain her excitement as she bolted out of the room. "Yippee, I love you mummy. You're the best!"

Mary felt a surge of anger which soon overtook her heightened mood. How had she missed this obvious breakthrough? Of course! 'The Horsleys Green Three' were holed up in the Spanish holiday home of Sarah's Aunt. It wasn't brain surgery, it wasn't even litter picking, it was as simple as the two times table. Even a blind man in a solar eclipse could have found the key to the mystery. Clearly, they no longer resided in this country. There was absolutely no evidence of their existence here. Nothing to track, nothing to trace. They haven't just disappeared into thin air. "How could I have been so stupid!" Mary muttered, as she flung brightly coloured clothes into her suitcase. "Their moral vision might be impaired but they're not short-sighted. Of course, they had no choice but to go abroad and what better place to start their new life than an empty holiday home in a predominantly English-speaking Spanish resort." She was given the initial task of solving this case as her reputation for detail had always been her saving grace. Yet her saving grace had let the victims and their families down and resulted in her failure. An oversight or simple aberration? "I shall not and will not pass this information on. The bastards will push me aside again and give it to the 'big boys' who will only mess it up. I'm not taking that risk and going back to square one. Who wants square one when the whole board is available!"

Mary remained firm in her conviction. "If I find them, I'll do the right thing then and only then." She knew that she was fighting against all of the police training that had resonated so well with her, but it was her case and her responsibility to bring the criminal bacon back home, even if it was a little crispy. As Alice packed her tiger print Trunki with 'God knows what,' Mary went online and booked the earliest possible plane tickets and a relatively posh family hotel which overlooked the main beach in Torrevieja. "That's close enough, I need Alice to be safe." Mary thought considering her priorities as she inputted her bank details and made the bookings.

The journey over to Spain was a trip within a trip. Alice could not contain her elation. The smile of anticipation did not leave her face. She'd been abroad before, but only on a school trip to Paris. This was to be her first real holiday overseas with her precious mother. A mother that she realised was full of morals and principles, hardworking and determined but starved of any time to take a bite out of the apple of her daughter's time. It was going to be special and she knew it. On the plane they talked of sun-drenched walks along the coast. Of building complex sand fortresses on the beach and of singing along to tunes by the hotel pool. By the time they arrived and checked-in, they'd worked through a playlist which would have made the finest DJ from the greatest club in Ibiza proud.

The hotel room was spacious and clean but showed signs of long and arduous holiday seasons. "Just like me." Thought Mary as she walked onto the balcony overlooking the pool area. "This is just the ticket, Alice my love. Just check out that view." After unpacking and freshening up, they loaded up an assortment of beach necessities and headed out into the early afternoon sunshine. Mary basked as Alice beached. Mary practiced her surveillance techniques while Alice practiced her paddling prowess. A Police Academy film at its finest. Mary studied each individual's face and potential life history, while Alice brought her seaweed and shells. One apprehensive, the other excited and animated. Their skins pinkened as the minutes ticked and the white catholic church bells tolled. Before long, they had become the last holidaymakers standing by their sandcastle. As the waves swept away their efforts, they begrudgingly packed up and slowly walked back to their temporary home, discussing what to have for dinner along their merry way. But Mary's mind wandered as she toiled with the guilty pleasures of the real job at hand. "This day is yours my beautiful angel, tomorrow will be mine."

The hotel laid on an Abba tribute band after the Italian themed buffet. They looked nothing like the real McCoy but had the crowd singing along and tapping their feet. A few of the youngsters, including Alice, got up and danced to the hits which flowed one after another. Mary ordered a bottle of wine after she'd finished her cheese and crackers. "Why not? I'm on holiday after all," she said, trying to justify her actions to the waiter, who just smiled, not understanding a word she had just muttered, and if pressed, would have said that he didn't really care. Grabbing the tour rep, Mary enquired about the children's club. "If you want some time off, we'll take your child and immerse them in a morning or full day of amazing activities, ranging from mini golf to pool aerobics. Trust me, you won't be missed. Do you want to sign up? It's ten euros for a morning and eighteen for the full day which is nine am to six pm." The well-presented woman, caked in makeup, who clearly took advantage of airport duty free, thrust a clipboard into Mary's lap. "If you book your child in this evening, I can offer you a half price Valencia City Tour that might interest you?" Mary had absolutely no enthusiasm for feeding her touristic cravings. She was here for one reason only. "Just the kid's club for my daughter Alice. Book her in for the next two full days please."

Back in the room, Mary nicely sold in the 'fun and games' package, well enough to get Alice excited and looking forward to the morning. "You're going to have a great time. I bet you make some new friends too." Feeling a tad guilty, she continued her sales pitch, unaware that Alice had fallen asleep in her arms.

The next morning, the sunlight streamed through the cheap curtains and woke Alice up. "Mum get up lazy! We have things to do!"

After a hearty breakfast consisting of far too much fried stuff, Mary dropped Alice off at reception. There were a few children already waiting and before the clock struck nine, Alice was chatting to a couple of them. After filling out the consent form, Mary snuck away, not wanting to give Alice any chance to change her mind. A day bag was packed, and a taxi ordered. It was her time to shine in the midday sun.

Mary's loose plan was to head to Alicante town centre first and get her bearings. She'd never been there and was almost excited when Mrs McKay said that the villa was located in the popular resort. "No point heading straight to the villa," she thought, deciding that this was too high risk as she could not afford to be seen. "There's plenty of time.

Best to be uber cautious at the start of this undercover mission." It was time to place the final piece of the jigsaw. Time to add the icing onto the home baked cake but most importantly, it was time to step up on the podium and claim her medal.

It didn't take long to get there. Dropping herself in the town centre, Mary wandered the streets, took in the views and entered a number of bars, cafés and restaurants. Her soul intention was to familiarise herself with the surroundings. "There's no hurry. Patience is a virtuous priority, all bad people eventually come to shake hands with the devil who await their fall from grace." Mary's thoughts guided her through the cobbled maze which tangled holidaymakers and locals. She studied each passer-by's face with a mix of motivation and trepidation. Would she even recognise them? Was she looking for a Father Christmas at a Santa convention or simply buying fresh bread from the bakery? Time would tell sure enough. She knew roughly where the villa was located but could not be tempted. "Hold back, if they are here today then they'll be there tomorrow." After a few lazy hours of meandering, she felt a decent enough affinity with the town. She finished off her visit with a pleasant stroll along the quayside promenade, beautifully lined with rows of palm trees and tessellated with marble. Their imitation of the waves of the Mediterranean were impressive and had to be admired but not as much as what they were hiding. "Ok, that's enough for one day." She felt a sense of achievement and a strangely alluring presence. Enough to convince her that they were here. "Time to head back and get some rest. Tomorrow will be a big day!"

A taxi back to the hotel catapulted her into the arms of Alice. "Where have you been mummy? You've missed me dancing in the pool! Miss Molly said I was like a mermaid."

Mary couldn't sleep that night. Was it down to the anticipation of catching them or the fear of failing? "God, what if I've got it totally wrong and they're not even here?"

The next morning, after dropping an excited Alice off at reception and watching her hug her new best friends, Mary returned back to Alicante. She felt invigorated, a tad braver and a lot more determined to locate her adversaries. The town had a familiar feel to it. Clearly the previous day's efforts had not gone unrewarded. She'd even decided on her favourite café which she headed straight for after paying the taxi driver. The sun beaten local cabbie had spent the whole journey chatting her up. Even though he was old enough to be her father, the compliments had given Mary a further uplift. "Today is going to be a good day." She thought as she sat down at an outside table and ordered herself a coffee.

Mary settled herself and looked around at her fellow diners. A romantic couple linking hands, a loud family whose pale faces and luggage gave way to their animated emotion of arrival. An elderly gentleman who looked part of the furnishings and a young bearded fellow with thick rimmed specs, who was digging into what looked like a rather succulent pan de chocolat. Even though Mary had eaten, temptation got the better of her and she decided to follow suit. She wasn't disappointed with her decision after taking a bite and even winked at the young chap to show her approval at copying his selection. He didn't acknowledge her as he appeared 'knee deep' in whatever his mobile phone was offering.

"Another person who can't separate vacation from vocation." Mary, sympathised with her conscience. She was further annoyed when this very same studious guy beat her to gaining the attention of the waiter when requesting his bill. She glared at him, wishing to show her distain but alas, no eye contact was offered once again. "Don't allow this idiot to ruin your day. One bad tackle never stopped you scoring before. Anyway, he's probably overheating with those ridiculous mutton chops." At that very moment, he whipped of that very same beard and put the facial mask into his rucksack. Mary almost gave out a shriek. She swiftly turned away, out of the reach of his vision but she could not contain her bewilderment.

She froze and shivered in the midday sun. Were her eyes playing tricks? No, she was sure. It was definitely him, skinhead or no skinhead, it was Simon Dingle. She sat still, one hand covering her face knowing that she couldn't give the game away now and jeopardise the whole case. She had not anticipated this dramatic and sudden reveal, but she knew that she had come too far to be complacent. From the corner of her eye, she could see him leaving the café. Mary, transfixed by her target, let out a relieved sigh. "Thank God he hasn't seen me. Fuck, what are the chances eh?" Throwing down double, maybe triple her bill in cash, she edged forward, slowly but stealthily and in his direction. Not wanting to be unveiled or create any unwanted attention, she hung back and took out her sunglasses and a newly acquired Panama hat from her bag. "OMG, I was right. They are here alright." The adrenalin pumped through her veins. "I'll follow him to the villa, just to be sure and then pass this damn case over to the Spanish police." She confessed to herself, knowing that her work was done, and huge success would be awaiting her on arrival back home. She wanted to shout and scream, "I've only gone and done it! I've only snatched a leaf from the tree of adversity. Fuck all of you who thought I'd failed. Who's the 'big boy' now?" Simon led her straight to the main beach. "Damn, ok, stay calm, I'm happy to wait. There's no hurry. No one is in any immediate danger."

Mary considered her options as she found a bench and basked in the glory of her find. She discreetly took out her phone and took a few photos of Simon behind the guise of the perfect holiday snap. Ones that would take pride and place in her memory's album. "No point putting that hideous piece of facial hair back on now, Sonny Jim. It's too little too late boyo. You've just nibbled on my bait and I'm about to reel you in. I can't wait to see the look on Parry's face. They'll promote me for this, once they've slapped my wrists a couple of times. I'll be on the front cover of all the Nationals! Oh, what a relief. I just knew it and now I've proved it. Of course, I had the makings of a decent detective. How proud I'll make Alice." Mary waited and waited but the time didn't matter. She'd smashed it out of the park, hit the home run to end the game. "Bang to rights my dear boy." She watched intensely as Bobby built himself a sand pillow and stretched out for a nap. She was even impervious enough to observe a small boy stealing his rucksack. Carefully and slowly, lifting Simon's arm from the straps, he ran off into the distance. Who cared? He would not be needing a day bag where he was going. As

Mary's eyes felt heavy in the afternoon sun, she eventually noticed Bobby stirring. He looked startled, annoyed and eventually browbeaten when realising his loss. Looking resigned he finally stood up and began to leave the beach. "It's only going to get worse for you my friend. Ok, come on Mary. The final hurdle before the finishing line. Where's the keep net, lets land this little fucker. Come on son, lead me to your demise."

Mary followed her suspect back to the villa. Its magnificence was not justified in the photo she'd admired on Mrs McKay's sideboard. Setback in a leafy mangrove of olive trees, it oozed the splendour of a miniature temple. Glimmering white marble pillars adorning its entrance, it basked in the glory of Spanish resplendence. Even though Mary was a good few yards behind, she could clearly see him walk through to the back of the dwelling. In slow pursuit, she tailed his every step and before she knew it, she found herself creeping into the kitchen and listening to a huge argument that bellowed from upstairs.

"What the hell am I doing? I shouldn't be here. It's just too risky." Mary fought with her conscience, but it was Sarah's voice that drew her closer. Was it her? She couldn't be sure. "This is stupid and far too risky. I need to leave." Before Mary had time to react, a door slammed shut and a half-dressed burly man bounded down the stairs. It was too late; she had been seen. Frozen in the still of time, she closed her eyes, half expecting a verbal or even a physical assault from the shady looking character. To her shock and amazement, he didn't even give her a momentary glance. He simply ran past her, unphased by her presence and leaving no mark of his very existence. She looked behind and watched as he fled through the back door and into the shadowy grave of an experience to be forgotten. Her attention again reverted to the goings on from the upper floor. She could hear unsavoury murmurings as the argument began to lose steam. "I must get out of here; I've done my bit."

Before her thoughts could guide her further, she turned to face the back door. Their eyes met like a couple of startled deer, paralysed in the headlights of an out of control eighteen-wheeler. It was Martin, as clear as the driven snow, right there obstructing her only exit. Once the initial surprise of her presence had faded, his face displayed the anger of a free-spirited fly caught in a dastardly web.

Pretty God-Awful Woman

"Please, for fucks sake, I won't tell you again, go downstairs Bobby, I need a minute!" Sarah smothered her face with the sheet she held so closely for comfort. Not wanting her accuser, who had knocked her dirty secret to the canvass, to see her guilty appearance.

"You've ruined everything Sarah. I thought we were close, two protected peas in a single pod. I thought we had one another's backs. How did I get this so wrong? I just don't deserve this." A tear rolled down my cheek as the realisation of deception smothered my betrayal. "How long have you been seeing this old sweaty excuse of a man? For God's sake, how could you! And in our bed!"

"Please Bobby! Wait for me downstairs!" Sarah pleaded, peering over her flimsy sheet which now offered little or no protection from her sins.

"Ok, but you'd better tell me everything or I'll blow this whole damn sham life of ours apart. I don't care what happens to me." I proceeded, on the instruction of a once admired partner in crime, to about turn and leave the room. Muttering profanities to myself as I did so. Stomping with all the anger of a castrated bull, I marched down the marble steps to a scene that would define the final chapter of my downfall and weaken the last threads of normality that I had so desperately clung to.

"Martin, what the fuck! Oh, my dear God! What the hell are you doing?"

Martin, who was grappling on the floor with a woman underneath his heavy masculine frame, looked up from his misdemeanour and delivered the final verbal blow which would end the forced relationship of three underground criminals once and for all. "Bobby, help me to teach this bitch a lesson!"

It didn't take me long to uncover the identity of the person in question. "You have got to be kidding me. Is that Mary thingamy... Blackthorn?"

Martin didn't feel the need nor the ambition to answer, he was too busy holding down his arch enemy. The ticking timebomb that was about to blow up everything we'd work so hard to gain.

"Mary, what the fuck are you doing here? Let her go Martin, it's over. I can't do this anymore!" I moved towards the assailant with the sole intention of freeing the one person who would end my guilt and sanction my demise. My efforts were short lived, as Sarah who had dressed, joined the commotion and pushed me to one side with the force and shrill of a woman possessed.

"What are you doing girl? Don't you think you've done enough damage for one day?" Still laying on the floor, I watched as Sarah, without remorse, grabbed the masking tape from the cupboard under the sink and proceeded to help Martin secure his prisoner. The binding was unravelled around legs, wrists and across the screaming law enforcer's mouth until she was silenced.

I stood, non-complicit in their punitive misbehaviour, simply watching two hardened criminals stealthily acting out their next move. "So, well done guys. What, in King

Nebuchadnezzar's name are you both going to do now? Go to the Gardens of Babylon to pick some fruit?"

Martin stopped for a second. "What a strange thing to say?"

In normal circumstances, I would have agreed, maybe corrected myself at the very least, let out an embarrassed chuckle but we were in unprecedented times. "Oh, and this is normal is it? God, can this day get any worse?"

"Bobby, don't get self-righteous on my tanned arse, we are just trying to protect ourselves. Surely you realise that? I wasn't the one who invited her. One thing's for sure, she's not here to give our home a spring clean! She's here to rob us of the only thing we hold of any value, our bloody freedom! There is absolutely no chance that I'm going to let her take that from us. Listen, you'll thank us for it later!"

Sarah's words ripped through me like a knife through granulated sugar. "You'll thank us for it later!?" Could she hear the demented words that gathered like storm clouds above our illicit piece of paradise? What had happened to my beautiful Sarah? How had she turned into this monster? Why was I surprised given the horrendous experience she'd involuntarily been through?

Mary, looking like a mystified mortified mummy, was taped to a chair and shuffled into the cupboard under the stairs. I looked at her startled face and felt empathy towards her. I had walked in her bejewelled beach sandals once and knew exactly how she felt. As the cupboard door closed and the inevitable darkness fell on her, I thought to myself, "At least I was not alone."

"Right, team meeting methinks. Bobby, put the kettle on please." Ordered Sarah after she'd low fived Martin and sat down on the sofa.

Had the landing gear of our 'out of control plane' been deployed? Were the doors set to manual and the cesspit of a cabin been prepared for a descent? Was the plane plummeting to signify the end of our adventure? How fast was it tailspinning and just how bad would the crash landing be? Was there really anyone at the controls or had we been out of control for a while? The two people who I now relied upon with my heavy heart were normalising the most heinous of crimes. Their criminal qualifications had taken on a whole new level. One that I was morally incapable of reaching. I knew that my time was up but how could I survive without them? Was it time to 'cash in' and take my chips off the table? Hand myself over to the authorities? The very thought of another room with bars terrified and chilled me to the core. I knew that my mental state would not carry me through any further punishment. I needed more time. Surely it had to be my prerogative to consider my options. If nothing else, they owed me that much.

"Ok, so what do you intend to do with Mary?" I felt calm, there was no point fighting the rusty links that held my charm. The secrets we held, bound us together no matter what.

"Never mind that bitch! Let's go for a walk, we need to talk." Sarah motioned me towards the door and like an abused puppy, I followed her outside. Everything was different now. I felt different. I didn't recognise the beautiful girl who less than an hour or so ago, had meant so much to me. As we ambled down the driveway, I hung my head in defeat as she hung hers in shame.

I'm waiting." I said, not really wanting to taste the rotten food I was about to be served.

Sarah cleared her throat and tried to hold my hand. A gesture that I immediately spurned. "I'm really sorry that you had to see that." She articulated without compassion.

"What, you shagging a sweaty, old fat bloke or you tying the hands of a police officer?" My venom wasn't meant to hit the intended target but just give her a sense of my disposition.

"Listen Bobby, you know how much you mean to me." Sarah looked shocked as I lashed out.

"You've got a great way of showing it!"

"Bobby, you're not going to like what I'm about to tell you, but you deserve the truth."

I was about to be cast aside. Thrown on the relationship scrapheap. Shoved down the river on a rudderless leaky boat with a broken paddle. A heavy weight sank through to the pit of my stomach. I was a dead man walking on a tightrope in the stormiest of conditions. I took in a deep breath, maybe my last in the sunshine, knowing that as I exhaled, I would be single and alone in a world that had passed me by.

After a few moments of pause for notable effect, Sarah delivered her opening salvo. "I'm not sure how to tell you this, so I'll just come straight out with it. Bobby, please don't judge me. What I'm about to say is going to hurt." She grabbed my arm and held her gaze. "I'm a lady of the night, a prostitute, a hooker, a brazen hussy, I have sex with men for money! I'm not the woman you thought I was eh?"

She threw the capricious words like stones, hitting my body with great force, one after the other. I was left speechless as my mind struggled to absorb the contaminated disclosure.

Sarah continued to walk but slowed her meander. I've done it before you know, in the past. How do you think I got through Uni, debt free? As we are completely skint with no official home, I thought it was time to start up again. Look, believe it or not, this doesn't have to be a big deal. I'm doing it for us. We need money for our future if we are going to survive this God-awful situation. I'm really sorry that you found out this way. I didn't want you to know, just to protect you, if that makes any sense. Of course, you're going to judge me. I get that. Why wouldn't you? But know this, we are in the middle of a shit storm and I'm just trying not to get skid marks on the white veil that hides my face from this mess."

"Sarah, we are earning money. We are surviving. We have made a new life for ourselves. Ok, I understand that it's not the life we would have chosen, but it's the only life we had available and I was happy with it. You've ruined everything!" I began to shake, shamefully. "How long has this been going on?"

Sarah took a significant minute before she answered. "A few days after we arrived here. Martin brings me the clients and takes a cut of the profits. I've saved three thousand Euros so far. There, that's it. No more questions. I don't need to justify myself to you but I do love you and if you want me to stop then I will. You are the most important thing in my life and I need you. Please Bobby, can we forget about this and move on? One days burden is enough for one troublesome day."

I couldn't believe what I was hearing. This life changing announcement, revealed with less emotion than someone asking you the time. How dare she chuck the L word into the mix? "Fuck Sarah, Martin was in on this! Martin, the man who has left us without family, without freedom and without remorse. This is too much to take in. I need some time to gather my thoughts. I'm going for a walk, alone." With that, I picked up the pace and left Sarah standing in a pool of shame and hopelessness.

She screamed like a wounded animal, frightened and trapped in the night only to be devoured by wild predators. "Bobby, please don't go. Bobby! Bobby!"

Her howls hung on the winds of the discarded. She was no longer the girl of my dreams. She had resigned herself from that post with her relationship violations. How could I ever trust her again? She was damaged goods. Tarnished by the sweat of sick, perverted men. I no longer wanted to hold her close as I would smell the tainted purity of a girl that once frolicked in the summer meadows of life. I walked further away from the rotten core of her lies and selfishness. As I absconded, I felt my faith in her dissipate. I was lost in a mist of deception but I knew that I had no choice but to find another way out.

I found a quiet spot on a secluded part of the coastal path that led into town. Looking at the sea, I wanted to embrace its cold and uninviting dangers. I wanted it to take me away from my nightmare. To swallow me up in my own self-pity. Wash away the pain and regret, allowing me to slip away in peace. I was too cowardly to face my fears and certainly too scared to feel my face lying on the sea bed. I sat for a while, knowing that I had nowhere else to hide. Knowing that my fate had sold me a dummy and it would be that dummy that would keep my silence. I could not and would not give myself up and I knew that being alone was not an option. That left only one solution. I would have to forgive and return to my living hell. Was this karma, asking me to roll over on my belly while it gave me a tickle? Of course it was. Karma was our fourth wheel and we had to accept this, just like any other criminals on the run. God knows how long I sat alone but as the night fell, I felt the need to return home to take my medicine, whatever shape or form it took.

As I walked through the back door, I was welcomed by Sarah who ran towards me, arms outstretched. "Bobby, thank God, I was so worried you'd done something stupid." She embraced me without return. "Please Bobby, come and sit down. I want to tell you how sorry I am again. I know that I've hurt you and I want to make it better." As I surrendered to her instruction, she poured me a glass from the bottle we'd been saving for a special occasion and stroked my face as I took a sip. Mary's plight weighed heavy on my mind. I managed to drown out the sounds of the muffled groans, it was tame compared to what I'd endured in the bunker.

"I don't want to lose you Sarah but I just don't know how I'm going to be able to get past this. I feel like you've stabbed me in the back with the same knife that got us into this mess. A knife, that I'm sure, you now want to use on the police officer. Someone who is just trying to do her job? What, the fuck do you intend doing with her or should I be asking your tin hat dictator friend? I'm assuming that he's the captain of this stinking sinking ship?"

Sarah fought to maintain her composure. Her battle would not be won tonight with high emotions running free from any scrutiny. "Come on Bobby, that's not fair. Blackthorn gave us no choice. It was her, walking into our bad dream, not the other way around. Anyway. It's been a long day. Let's call it a night and discuss it in the morning. I realise that I've tarnished the only thing we owned that was pure but I do know that sunlight is the best disinfectant."

I took off my shoes and lay back on the sofa. "Fine, but I'll be sleeping here tonight. You surely can't expect me to sleep in your place of work and lie in your earnings."

Sarah accepted the marking of her cards. She deemed it to be a written warning with her P45 hanging in the balance. As she walked upstairs and looked down on her wounded prey, she wished that she could turn back time to an era of normality and serenity.

"Hey Sarah, how about a freebie, it's my birthday." I just couldn't resist the dig.

"Fuck you Bobby. How dare you throw your stupid film quotes at me when I'm throwing myself at your mercy." Came the unsurprising reply.

"You know the difference between you and Julia Roberts' character in Pretty Woman? Well, I'll tell you, she didn't pretend to be something she wasn't!"

When one door closes another one opens and it was certainly true in this instance. The moment Sarah locked herself into her temporary sanctuary, Martin released himself from his criminal laboratory and stomped down the stairs with the pretence of pouring himself a glass of water. "Bobby, you ok mate?" A false sincerity echoed through his tone.

"What the fuck do you care?" My anger slicing through his pretence. How dare he come down and pity me. "You knew what Sarah was doing, in fact, you were encouraging and supporting her dirty secret. Making money from my girlfriend's desperation. Shame on you! Don't you think you've caused me enough hurt and misery to last a bloody lifetime? We were meant to be turning over a new leaf. You lack any integrity. You're a malicious idiot who'll never change. I wouldn't even have the audacity to call you a leopard as you don't even deserve any spots."

Martin maintained his distance. "Mate, I was just trying to protect you. She told me in confidence and begged me not to say anything. Having thought about it, I completely understand how that was the wrong call but it was never my intention to cause you any more pain. We have to stick together now more than ever. You and Sarah need to get through this or we are toast, brown bread, absolutely dead and trust me, nobody will sing at our funeral."

Shaking with anger, I found myself clenching my fist. "Don't you start blaming me for this burning building. I didn't start the fire and believe me, if our decaying world crumbles, it'll be you who is the architect of our demise. No one else!"

Martin, having finished his water, topped up his glass with the fine whiskey that had just been opened. "Ok, I understand how angry you must feel but that doesn't change the maths. We are in exile and we have a bloody policewomen tied up under our staircase, for fuck sake! They are going to be looking for her. She says that nobody knows that she's here but do we believe her? She's bound to have told someone. Of course, her whereabouts will be logged on some desk clerk's computer. It ain't looking good eh? We need to decide on what to do next, and fast!"

I sat up from my pointless slumber. "She's your problem. You'll have to deal with her. I don't want any part of it."

"So you agree that we can't just let her free?"

Not wanting to be an accomplice to any further wrongdoing, I just ignored Martin's attempt to ingratiate me into his dereliction of civil duties. "I'll be at work tomorrow. When I get back, I want the pieces of broken glass tidied up, capiche? This is your mess, now own it!"

Martin nodded before sulking upstairs, cradling the nightcap with his tarnished hands. Hands that had strangled the life out of his once greatest friend and leading light. His mind at war with the pain of his sins. How could he redeem the vouchers of his conscience? There was only one thing that was clear to him. His loneliness would be the drug that seduced his predictable demise. On his bed of withering roses would he lie, offering the only solace to his regrets. His dreams being the only escapism available. A gift from God after his dealings with the Devil!

There's Nothing About Mary

When Martin opened his eyes and parted ways with his disorientated slumber, he considered the stark reality of his actions, and found himself alone. Alone in the villa and alone in his pursuit of happiness. He sat up on the sofa with buttered toast and tea to contemplate and consider a plan to take away the newly brewing threat, in the shape of a busman's policewoman. She simply had to be taken out of the equation. He had to honour his betrayed friend's wishes and deal with the situation. Surely, it would help to payback some of the stolen peace that he had taken from his friend. The act would perhaps cement a single brick in the building of a new bridge. A starting point, an initial attempt to pull down the barriers that his callous behaviour had erected between their friendship. Of course, he didn't invite the officer to his doorstep, but what criminal does? As he thought carefully and pondered his options, Sarah walked through the back door. Sweat dripping from her brow and onto her running vest.

"Right Martin, what's the plan?" She panted out the words as she regained her breath.

Martin admired her glistening body for a moment until he realised that she awaited an answer. "We simply can't entertain the idea of keeping her hostage. Been there and done that and nobody, but nobody gave me a t-shirt! I'm sure that you'll agree that we can discount that option. So, that leaves us with two choices. We can either smash her over the head and bury her in the back garden or run as far away from this mess as is humanly possible. Disappear to another country, start again! We've shown that we are capable of doing it. I know that it's not ideal, but that's what fugitives do. What do you think?"

Sarah had run further than she had intended. Beating out her troubles against the hard surface of the coastal road. She stretched her muscles as she considered the implications of the two-sided coin. "When I was running, I wanted to continue and never stop, but my legs could take me no further."

Martin leapt to his feet. "I understand." With that he walked past her with purpose. She followed him to the shed that lay abandoned in the back garden and watched as he took out a large garden spade. Walking to the far corner of the back yard, Martin drove the shovel into the hard baked soil. "Right, let's do this! I promised Bobby that we'd clean up this mess and that's exactly what we are going to do!"

Sarah stood in amazement. "Jesus, you were never this confident at work. As I recall, you used to be a bit of a softy. Hardly the makings of a psychopath!"

Martin continued unflustered. "Yeah, and never forget that that's what got us into this poisonous predicament. I'm not that person anymore! Anyone that crosses my path will be crucified and hung out to dry!"

"If I'm honest, I quite liked that person." Sarah about turned and headed towards the safety of the villa, only for Martin to pause his demonic demeanour and call out.

"Where the fuck do you think you're going?"

"I'm getting showered and changed, if that's ok with you?" Her posthumous sarcastic remarks bounced off

Martin's thickening skin and left no dents on his growing ego.

"When you're finished, bring some rope or a belt with you. We need to move fast before Bobby gets home!"

Sarah's temptation and inquisitive nature got the better of her and as she approached the staircase cupboard she opened the door to expose its guilty secret. Mary looked scared. Startled by her abductor, she struggled against the binds that tied her. Rocking her chair from side-to-side like a mad woman scorned. Urinating herself into a damp frenzy, she'd heard the whole conversation that had taken place. She knew her fate and battled its implication. Sarah's face gave her feelings away, like a child who had asked for a games console for her birthday but been given a colouring book instead. After an initial wave of sympathy, Sarah slammed the door shut, not wanting to witness the blithering mess that sat before her. She continued with the pressing job at hand, washing away the grime that had become her daily routine. As she felt the warmth and comfort of the deluxe shower, she wondered whether it would have been fair to ask Mary if she'd like a coffee and perhaps some breakfast, but soon relinquished the thought and replaced it with venom. "That bitch should never have come here. We owe her nothing!"

The deep grave of condemnation was dug and Martin sat back and admired his handy work. Six feet below the bar of adequacy and three feet wide of the mark of humanity, the deed was done and it was time to bury the evidence of the unspoken word. With blistering hands and a formidable determination to wrongfully right his transgressions, Martin realised that it was his redeeming fate to get this particular job done, irrelevant of the consequences. A man reborn, all debts paid, he had promised his troubled friend that he would hide any animosity alongside the body. After throwing down the spade and his gardening gauntlet, he marched towards his victim. The muffled screams of Mary's madness balanced the screeching sound of her chair being dragged across the white marble flooring and through the open doors to her burial chamber.

Not wanting to leave any grooves on the scorched soil, Mary was carried for the rest of her funeral march and thrown next to her final resting place. There she lay, wriggling in the morning sun. Expending energy that she knew, very soon, would no longer be available. The energy that had allowed her to live a good and decent life. One that she hoped would live on through the eyes of her beloved Alice. She tried to scream her name, as she pictured her running around in the hotel gardens with her new found friends. Lost in her last dalliance of childish innocence and soon to feel her whole world crumble around her. Would her mother's final impassioned moments be etched on her heart forever? Time was lost to her struggle and as the sun cradled a cloud, Mary's blinded vision was no more. Was this to be her final memory, Sarah looking down on her, rope in hand? She froze and stared into Sarah's soul.

She tried to transfer the love for her daughter into a silent impassioned plea for her survival, but her failure was marked by the rope wrapping itself around her neck. As she felt it tighten, she knew that it was time to say her final goodbye. A farewell to the many people who had crossed her path with the sweet smell of friendship and compassion. A valediction to the peace and tranquillity that had guarded her through the brambles of her journey, but most of all, a cheerio to the one jewel in her crown of life, her gift to the world, Alice. She closed her eyes and pictured the apple within. As she felt the rope tighten, her thoughts warmed her spirits. "I will take the image of your beautiful smile with me Alice, I love you so very much. Look after yourself and make me proud!" Her body started to spasm. Was it the last tumbling frolic of a spring lamb before slaughter?

"No, stop, don't do it! Get off her immediately!" I cried as I entered the shocking scene. "Thank the Lord I came home early!" As the rope loosened around Mary's neck, she took a huge gasp for air and she felt the energy of life once again running through her veins. "What the hell are you doing!" I shouted as I pulled Sarah off the relieved but petrified innocent officer. "We can't do this! There has to be another way! Martin, give her something to drink and put her back under the stairs. This is not the answer!"

Martin protested with little conviction. "But, I thought that this is what you wanted?"

"Just do it! We can't have any more blood on our hands. This woman has done us no harm. She's only doing what she's paid to do. We have no right to take her life. God, what were you thinking man?" I grabbed the spade off him and started to replace the dirt into the unused hole. Sarah fell to her knees and wept. She cried the tears of a demented woman who had lost her way. One who had misplaced her conscience and respect for the living. I stopped for a moment and held her close. "It's ok my love. Everything is going to be alright. Trust me, this is not the answer. If anything, this whole experience will make us stronger."

Could one ever replace the twin towers in New York, close down the McDonald's standing close to the ancient pyramids or wipe clean the pollutant stains off the once impressive Taj Mahal? Could three insignificant acorns, which lay abandoned be placed back onto the magnificent oak tree? Probably not, but hurricanes do rip through towns and cities only for time to rebuild them, bigger and stronger. We had become disjointed, emotionally frail, our friendship strained and our trust lost. Best China crockery we were not, handles glued, cracks showed and stains showcased our vulnerability. Battered and bruised by circumstance and bad judgements, we had to regroup and recharge our survival batteries. Each read chapter had to be ripped out and forgotten forever, but what would be the conclusion of the cacophony of connotation?

When Martin returned outside, we all hugged and reconnected our allegiances. Apologies were thrown around like confetti at a royal wedding. Landing everywhere and for the few moments that they covered our hallowed circle, we were as one, until the wind of reality swept them away.

The lighthouse of honesty lit up our destitution, the flames of our future were clear as day as I sounded the alarm. "We are fucked! It's only a matter of time before Mary is reported missing and the bright sparks rain on our parade. We need to work up a plan and quickly. I think we're all agreed that Mary isn't going to meet Suggs any time soon?" Nods from my right and left concluded that conundrum. "Ok, great. At least we all agree on that. So, what other choices do we have?"

Sarah and Martin looked at one another and almost said in unison. "We've got to go on the run, again!"

I took a step back. "I know, but where?"

After a moment of deep deliberation, Martin broke the silence. "Mexico or Thailand? Those are the usual faraway places where outcasts like us are welcomed. We know that our fake IDs work, so why not? As far as we know, our new identities have never been revealed and I don't think that anyone has suspicious minds. Unless Elvis has started singing Jailhouse Rock! Oh, and let's not forget. We have some cash, thanks to Sarah."

I took umbrage to Martin's insensitive interjection and felt all shook up. He'd just physically dug up old ground, so why do it metaphorically? "Shut up Martin, a little less conversation from you lad! Look, if we are to continue together then Sarah's past has to remain buried instead of Mary. Got it?"

Sarah held out a hand and I clasped it tightly. As she spoke, she drew me closer. "Martin is right, let's head to Thailand. It's a bloody beautiful haven for delinquents like us, plus the food is amazing. We could teach English to ladyboys or organise excursions for weary backpackers."

Who was I to deny the textbook cravings of a gap year student? "Ok, sounds like we are all agreed. Let's get this place clean and tidy for Sarah's Auntie's sake, then we can book flights and accommodation. We must be gone by tomorrow afternoon at the latest. Once we are there, we can alert the authorities as to Mary's whereabouts."

Martin looked around the garden. Unsure, whether he was surveying the amount of work needed to make it spotless or saying his final goodbye, I pushed him in the direction of the villa. As he broke into a firm stride and left us behind, he shouted, "you two get started on the cleaning and I'll make a big 'fry up' for us all. I might even offer Mary a 'peace' of my bacon butty." With that, the kettle was on and the dusters were out. Music played as we worked, each one of us contemplating a new life in the Far East. With a nervous energy we mopped, polished and scrubbed away our memories of the villa. Bin bags were filled and suitcases repacked until it was time to settle down to a meal that may not be on the menu ever again. We sat in silence, broken only by Martin force feeding a sandwich into Mary's mouth, resulting with tomato sauce dripping all over her cream blouse.

Returning a half-eaten slice of fried bread back to my plate, I cleared my throat and addressed my audience. "Careful Martin, they'll think we've shot her. In Heinz sight, brown sauce would have been a better option."

Sarah broke into hysterics, but Martin gawked, "I don't get it."

Not wanting to miss an opportunity I continued, "oh, come on Martin, do ketchup."

To which Sarah nearly choked on her gourmet sausage, but still managed to mutter the words, "Bobby, you are saucy."

I couldn't be sure, but I was convinced that even our threatened victim spluttered out the faint stifle of a snigger.

The laughter was short lived when Sarah threw out the question that would hasten the analysis of our dire situation. "Hey Mary, how did you know that we were here? It can't possibly be just a coincidence. How the hell did you follow our carefully placed steps?"

"Yeah, come on, open up a whole can of whoop ass, why don't you?" I cried, almost choking on my coffee.

"Oh, that's your best film quote yet. Even I know that's a line from There's Something About Mary. Clever, I like it!" Martin said almost begrudgingly.

Mary didn't answer immediately. She pondered her crime craft and the implication of any statement. Would they be panicked if they knew who had given the game away? If so, what would this cause them to do? She quickly concluded that her disappearance, perhaps over time and further questioning, would result in them locating her whereabouts. "It was your mother who gave me the clue. A simple framed picture on her sideboard. She knows where I am and if I don't report back soon, I'm sure that she'll let my Station know. Give yourself up and they might go easy on you. Don't do anything that will cause you further trouble. Sarah, Bobby, we understand that you committed your crimes under duress. You did what you did to save the lives of others. Denny Folks has gone on to score a couple of Ashes centuries. What jury in England wouldn't have mercy on you for that alone? Martin, we are aware of your background. The courts will take this into consideration. Let me free and allow me to take you in. It's for your own sake. Please! It's not too late to come clean. There's no point in running. We've found you once and we'll find you again. I'm offering you a hand of friendship. Take it and end this foolishness!"

Martin quickly replaced her gag. "Don't listen to her guys. They'll lock us up and throw away the key. They'll show no mercy on our sorry asses. It's a life in the sun versus a life as Attila The Hun!"

Sarah threw her arms aloft. "Stabbed in the back by my own family. Fuck 'em! Fuck the lot of them! We must stick to the original plan. Where's that laptop. Let's get the damn tickets booked!"

Martin's face brightened, as he waddled off in search of the search engine, while I sat and digested Mary's impoverished speech. "End this foolishness?" Was she right? Would the courts understand the method of our madness? It was too risky. The price of failure was just too high. Would Denny's success soften the blow? Maybe, but our middle stump being knocked out of the ground would be little solace and hardly keep us warm at night as we lay on a hard mattress in a cold cell.

"Come on, let's check out Koh Samui!" Martin called out excitedly.

"Sssh." I whispered, motioning towards Mary.

Martin closed the staircase cupboard door as Sarah tapped away on the key pad of optimism. With no remorse, the three of us basked in the glory of images of sandy beaches and bhang lassis. It was time to charter our next course. Offers were discussed, hotels appraised, travel arrangements signed off and toasts to our future, made. The morning would open the door to a new fool's paradise and allow the stars to twinkle upon our terminal pain.

Sex, Lies and Text Messages

The night screamed the agony of the day ahead and by the time we lay our scrabbled minds on the pillow, the Spanish dust had been swept away and the Thai sunrise was almost visible. The villa had been our hidden secret, uncovered by the dark but disingenuous forces that had unlocked our unpublished mystery. It was time to flee the roost. Time to migrate to sunnier climates, spread our wings of freedom until we couldn't smell the stale fragrance of our past. I could hear the light patter of the last summer shower against the window. The first rain we experienced since we'd arrived in Spain. Was it a sign, a call from the gods to leave our tarnished sanctuary or simply the bitter sweet pill of the summer's end?

As we lay our weary heads, my embrace with Sarah was disturbed by her mobile phone. A text message at this time of night, and from who? "I must be dreaming." My sleep wrapped its warm blanket around my tired body and before I knew it, I was out like an expired lightbulb. I drifted into slumber but one thing wrestled with my mind. "Who could be sending my girlfriend phone messages at this ungodly hour?" The heavy weight of my dilemma held me in a Boston stranglehold until I slapped the canvas in order to surrender its strain. The bedroom window was slightly ajar and the damp smell of the long awaited rain filled the room. Its overdue familiarity sharpened my consciousness, and as I attempted to wrap my arm once again around my unrequited beloved, I realised that half the bed was empty and I was alone.

At first, I was not disturbed. A trip to the bathroom in the depths of the night was commonplace for a woman with a week bladder and nervous disposition, but as the moments ticked by, I began to get fidgety. "Sarah?" I whispered, not wanting to raise the alarm to my paranoia. No answer. I flicked on the bedside lamp, knocking her mobile to the ground which nudged the faint memory of the text message. I didn't look at the screen intentionally, or did I? "Meet me downstairs when that clown has fallen asleep." I read it twice, three times and again until it had lost all of its meaning. Why would Martin want to speak to Sarah alone and without my knowledge? What were they hiding? Why was he referring to me as a clown? Banter, or pure and simple downright nastiness? There was only one way to find out, investigate for myself. I slowly crept out of the bed with the sole intention of listening in on their furtive conversation. "I'm sick and tired of dirty secrets." I thought to myself as I rolled out of the bed.

On all fours I edged forward, moving stealthily and closer to uncovering the enigmatic nature of their midnight verbal feast. Creeping through the bedroom door and down the landing, I peered through the staircase baluster. It was dark, but the gentle glow of the moon cast a dancing shadow against the white walls. It was difficult to make out what was causing it, but as the sleep left and allowed my eyes to focus, it soon became crystal clear as to exactly what I was witnessing. "Oh, dear God, no!" It was happening again! Karma biting chunks out of my happiness. Two naked bodies intertwined, writhing in the heat of passion on the Moroccan rug. Sarah's womanly curves were unmistakable, but who was the grabbling imposter? "Surely not another customer at this time of the night? When does this shop close for business?" With my thoughts running away with me, I rubbed my eyes and accustomed myself to the dimly lit nightmare. It soon unravelled my demon. It was the one and only, Martin Bunratty! "I knew it! Bastards!"

With my world once again blown apart and the murder weapon firmly lodged in my back, I withdrew to the bedroom. That was it, the final straw. The hump that had grown far too big for the mentally dehydrated camel. My anger soared, reaching peaks of uncontrollable fury. I had been cheated on by the only two people in my new life, but why? Why were they doing this to me? What had I done to deserve this? Martin had kidnapped me, starved me, tortured me, lied to me, insulted me and if all of that wasn't enough, here he was, shagging my girlfriend right in front of my eyes. As for Sarah, she wasn't the person I thought I loved. We'd been through so much together, but none of that mattered to her. She had the heart of a black widow. Our relationship had been thrown off a motorway bridge onto the rush hour traffic, that was for sure. But how could she sleep with the person who would have happily left her for dead? Surely, I had got this wrong? Pinching myself for clarity, I found myself retracing my steps for confirmation.

The second viewing left me scarred for life. Sarah sitting on top of the person she'd have, without a second thought, pushed off a cliff only a few months ago. Swinging her arms around as through she'd just beaten her record on a bucking bronco ride at the local fairground, I had seen enough! Enough to know that I could no longer stand the thought of being around these abhorrent individuals, let alone start another new life together with them. It was time to jump ship and go it alone. But before I jumped, I knew that I'd have to spring it a leak and allow it to sink to its watery grave.

As the rain stopped and I gathered my thoughts back on the bed, I heaved out a loud cough. Then another one along with an over emphasised guttural clearing of my throat. I couldn't allow it to continue in my head or downstairs. Within two minutes, Sarah had crept back into the room as though nothing had ever happened. "You bitch, I hate you!" Wrestling with my inner self-conversation, I knew that I despised her. Even more so than my once trusted friend. She was now my betrayer. She had once held my fragile happiness, which had been harnessed by her confidence and thrust for life. She'd cut me loose, leaving me exposed to the harsh and lonely conditions that lay ahead. Now was not the time to confront her or seek my revenge, that time would come soon enough.

With my wounds raw and my thirst for survival unsatisfied, I began to work through a plan of retribution and a route to escape. I was dealing with dangerous people who had little appetite for loyalty. Having deserted our band of warriors, they had become strangers to me, perhaps enemies. Being a threat to their freedom put me in a perilous situation. One that could be life or death or at the very least, hazardous. I knew that I had to tread carefully amongst the broken glass of our relationships. I could just run, but where would that take me and should that always be the answer? I needed time, but alas any seeds of extension had long been thrown to the vultures.

The morning would map out my future and I needed to be ready. Tossing and turning the night away with angst, left me exhausted as I arose for the last time from our bed of iniquity. As I paced the length of the villa, they slept on with their heavy crosses of deception to bear. They had been judged and their 'no comments' would not save them from their awaiting sentence. I knew what I had to do but pathing a way for resolution did not make it any easier. "You have to be strong, you have to be strong!" I repeated it over and over again as I heard the rumblings of electric toothbrushes and the spluttering's of the doomed. They would feel my wrath, but I needed them to be taught a lesson in respect first.

Like two lemmings, they poured down the stairs, one after the other. "Morning, would you guys like any breakfast? I was thinking of making some French toast." I cracked an egg as I awaited their response.

"Excellent. Are you sure? This better not be a yolk" and "yeah, cracking, that would be exquisite," came the scrambled, but expected replies. Like wounded soldiers, hard boiled lines were our way of softening the heavy load.

Not wanting to show my distain and walk on egg shells, I joined in with the early exchange. "Enough already or you'll have egg on your face!"

As I prepared the damned breakfast, I began to whisk my plan. "Our flights are not until the afternoon. I'd like to take you both for a picnic before we leave. There's a beautiful little cove that I've been told about. It's meant to be stunning. It would be a great setting for us all to say our final goodbyes to Spain and a great stepping stone to our future. You both ok with that? I think we need to take our minds off the drama for an hour or two. Don't you agree?"

Sarah's eyes ignited a warmth that heated the vengeance in me as she whole heartedly agreed.

Martin wavered, "are you sure that we have time?"

Almost snapping to his tune, I banged down the pan on the stove. "Yes, there's plenty of time. Now, ask Mary if she'd like some eggs!"

"Oh, I'd nearly forgotten about her." He sneered as he opened the stair cupboard door and took off her gag.

"Please! My daughter is alone in the hotel! She will be scared! Please, just let me go!" Mary pleaded.

Without deliberation, I asked Mary for the details of the hotel, and ordered Martin to call and let them know that she'd been unavailable waylaid and would return before the day was out. He moaned and protested but I put my size nines firmly down. "Get it done and have a heart just for a moment! She's an innocent kid, for God's sake!"

After taking guidance from Mary, Sarah dutifully shouted out the relevant number from her internet research. Clearly under duress, Martin nervously dialled. "Is that the San Sabastian Hotel? I'm calling, just to let you know that Mrs Blackthorn, from room 101, apologises profusely for not picking up her daughter from the children's club yesterday. She will be back at the hotel at some stage tonight. She has asked me to say that she's very sorry for any inconvenience caused. Thanks, bye." After snapping shut the call, Martin threw his mobile down on the kitchen table. "There! Satisfied?"

After the hearty breakfast, Sarah took charge and gathered a suitable selection of drinks and nibbles. Basically emptying the fridge and patching together what looked like a fairly appetising picnic. Ham sandwiches were decrusted and cut elegantly into triangles. Carrots and celery sticks were caressed into shape and placed in a Tupperware box alongside various dips. The whole content of the now redundant fruit bowl was thrown into a carrier bag along with crisps, chocolate bars and coke cans. Finally, as per my request, half a block of fancy but smelly Spanish cheese, was partnered with a dozen or so crackers in cellophane. As these antics occurred, Martin and I sat outside and consumed the final two cans of lager from the cool box. There was an effort to converse but the image of them cavorting was firmly etched in my mind, making any small talk extremely difficult. The only thing I could think of was the execution of my plan and the chips being removed from my shoulders. Things were taking shape, and with a splash of imagination, I felt confident that it would be my finest hour. The sun caressed my vision of revenge and before long, it was time. Time to hail down the bus of redemption, time to pay the devil for my one-way ticket and time to enjoy the overpriced ride to vindication.

Sarah, three bags to the good, joined us outside. "Right, are we ready? By my reckoning, we've only got three hours before we need to be back at the villa to collect our suitcases."

Feeling rather nervous and grabbing two of the bags, I began slowly walking down the driveway. "That's plenty of time. Come on, follow me. We need to hire a boat from the harbour. It's the only way to get to the cove." The clock of impending indemnity was ticking with every beat of my stride. Time was of the essence, if I was to gain satisfaction from my gratification. "Hurry up guys, I don't want to rush the lovely feast that my darling has so kindly prepared."

Once we arrived at the harbour, I treated the troublesome twosome to a cappuccino as we waited for a rather flash motorboat to be prepared for our excursion.

"Throwing Sarah's hard earnt cash around, eh Bobby?" Martin said sarcastically as we boarded the vessel.

"Only the best for my bessies. We deserve this treat and there is nothing that I wouldn't do for you guys." I responded, as we stood to attention and listened to the weather-worn seafarer, whose job was to hand over the keys, detail the health and safety protocols, and give us a short verbal manual of the basic controls.

As he exited, I rotated the key, smiled, pulled down the throttle and shouted. "Aye aye me hearties. It's off to sea we go."

It took a few moments to gain my shipmates confidence as I meandered through the undulating waves, throwing our bums off our seats until I found a suitable speed. Not really knowing where my destination lay, I hugged the coastline. Was that the only flaw to my plan? Mechanically, we weaved our way through the obstacles of my poisoned chalice. Was the end to my pain in sight or was this the next level of anguish? Time hadn't been my friend for some time, but its analysis would be welcome. Whoever scored my efforts would be held in the highest esteem. The tangled web of deceit had scaled the mountains of madness. The piper was awaiting payment on its summit, but my pockets were empty.

As we gathered momentum, it wasn't long before I found what I was looking for. A small cove, locked in the sheer backdrop of a rugged cliff. Its entrance surrounded by the heavy weight of the sea. A hidden cavern, unfit for human inhabitancy. Waves guarded its darkness, winds warded its secrecy and its very presence cast a spell on its uninvited guests. I slowed down the boat and drifted towards its opening.

"Why are you stopping? Surely, this can't be the place you had in mind? There's nothing here but a gloomy sea cave. Hardly a great spot for a picnic. It's more like a prison!"

"Looks familiar, eh Martin?" I thought as I cast down the anchor by the tiny exposed beach that lay inside the cave. "Trust me, a few of the guys from the waterpark have been here. It's meant to be really cool inside. Lots of mighty stalag thingies."

Jumping overboard and walking into its dark eerie mouth, I beckoned to the others to follow. My torch lit up a sinister expanse. Dark, jagged rocks plastered the gloomy walls, small pebbles lined the floor and a damp rancidity welcomed its intruders.

"Are you sure?" Sarah said bemoaning its existence. "It looks like a shithole to me! The stalactites might be here, but I'm not sure that I want to be."

Ignoring her and opening my backpack, I threw down a blanket and lit candles around the camp. Some of floral fragrance and some of dancing flame. "You see, ye of little faith, looks better now, eh? Why don't we pour ourselves a drink and stick some chillaxing beats on instead of moaning?"

Martin unpacked the bags, and before we knew it, we had what looked to the naked eye like the foundations of a lovely family outing. "Let's get into the mood and play some Gipsy Kings."

"Fair play, Martin." Sarah said hesitantly as she sourced the music on her mobile.

As we sat, I threw beer cans to the two misfits. "We've got about an hour before the tide comes in. Plenty of time for a picnic and a fitting end to our time in Spain, eh?"

Sarah softened and laughed to the rhythm of the rumba. "If you say so, but do you know what? This is all a little weird, but nonetheless, I'm starting to like it. Thanks Bobby, what a thoughtful idea, especially after what I've just put you through." She started to sing along to Bamboleo. As her sweet voiced bounced off the cave walls and created an echo. Martin joined in, but I kept my musical distance. I just wanted to shout. "I fucking hate you!" And let the walls repeat it until their ears bled.

Time was against me and I'd had enough of the charade. Grabbing Sarah's arm mid verse, I made my solemn request. "Can we turn the music down a smidge? I want to propose a toast."

"I've only packed bread, sorry bud." Martin called out dismissively.

"Not now, Martin!" I snatched Sarah's phone and silenced the party. "I'd like to say a few words."

Martin objected and waved his arms in the air. "I was enjoying that," but Sarah halted the protest, "no, fair play. Go on Bobby, the floor is yours."

I took a deep breath before I delivered my closing statement. "Just before my father passed away with a tear in his eye, he told me how proud I made him feel. As I held his hand, he delivered a speech that I will never forget. 'You're going to go on and do great things son' he said to me, and I believed him. He reminded me of the moment that he knew I'd be alright in life. 'You were five years old,' he said. 'You won't remember, but your mum and I took you to our local park. A boy, around your age, was playing football. You asked if you could join in and he said no. Without complaint, you sat on a bench with us and watched him having fun. He knew it too, and with great gusto and an air of defiance, he kicked the ball so hard, it got stuck in a tree. The boy stared at his misfortune while his mother shouted at him in disgust. As he began to sob, you wandered over and started to climb that tree. Halfway, you lost your grip and fell, tears streaming from your sorrowful eyes. I bought you an ice cream to cheer you up,' my father continued. 'After thanking me, you walked straight over and gave it to the boy.'" I stopped speaking for a moment as I felt myself choking up. My audience just stared at me in disbelief as I regained my composure. "You know what, my father heard the boy ask why I was being so kind to him when he didn't deserve it. 'You made my heart swell with pride son,' he said, 'when you delivered the line that made me feel so honoured to be your father. I never forgot your words son. You told the boy that your bruises would disappear but he might never get his ball back.'" I paused again, remembering how minutes after he revealed that line, his eyes closed for the final time. "Martin, I trusted you. We were friends. You've stolen that boy from my father. If he's looking down on me, he'd be so disappointed in the person that I've become and the horrendous things that I've done. I will never forgive you for that!" Martin bowed his head in shame.

"I might have moaned now and then, but I loved my life. It was pure and simple. You know better than most that it was hard for me to settle in London. It took time and effort, but I forged myself a bloody good existence. Great friends, a decent job with prospects, a flat that I was proud to call home, and enough cash at the end of the month to treat myself to a night out. I was happy. There was no doubt that a fine lady on my arm would have been the icing on the cake, but I was young and that would have invariably happened in due course." I took another deep breath. "Sarah, no offence, but you were never that icing. Ok, I have no entitlement to judge you on your past, but I can score you on your present and as a girlfriend. It's a 'nul points' from the Dingle Jury. We are both the victims of Martin's poison. We quite frankly bonded in the wrong place at the wrong time. We did what we had to do in order to survive. A partnership, a team, we had each other's backs, or so I thought. Sleeping with perverts in our bed for cash, I struggle with, but shagging the maker of our misery and the thief of our liberty is definitely a bridge too far."

Sarah looked startled. "What are you talking about Bobby?"

"I bloody saw you both in the darkness! Sneaking around in the middle of the night like the sewer rats that you are. You two are pure evil."

Martin tried to stand up but I pushed him back down. "It's not what it looked like, mate." He remonstrated.

Sarah rocked on all fours like a demented dog with rabies. "I'm sorry Bobby, we never meant to hurt you. It was just a one-off, I swear! I don't even know why it happened!"

"Sarah, I remember reading somewhere that men learn to love the person that they are attracted to and that women become more and more attracted to the person that they love."

"You didn't read that Bobby, you've never read a book in your life. I bet that's another one of your stupid God damn film quotes!"

"Oh, now you understand me, Sarah! You are right, Sex, Lies and Videotapes. I'm surprised that you haven't seen it!"

Martin, pointing in my direction, shouted, "mate, the tide is turning!"

"You are damn right, the tide is turning. I am no longer prepared to be a passenger in your out of control car! As far as I'm concerned, it's run out of petrol and so have you two!" I screamed.

Martin pointed his finger with more aggression. "No Bobby! I mean the sea tide is coming in! Look, we need to leave this deathtrap before it's too late and we're all well and truly finished!" He shouted with nothing but sheer panic on his face.

Turning around to address his concern, I could see that he had a point. The waves surged into the cave, each one crept an extra inch towards us. With haste and a determined strength, I grabbed my backpack, took out my predetermined weapon, a hammer. With the force of a mad axemen, I wheeled it in the direction of Martin. Smashing it against his knee cap with an almighty force. He doubled up and howled with the pain of a thousand decibels.

"Bobby, what the fuck!" His screams drowned the sound of the boat hitting the entrance to the cave. One by one, the gushing sea water doused the candles, darkening the atmosphere, but the fear in his eyes lit up the true extent of the situation.

The realisation on Sarah's face was clear to see. "Bobby, please! This is not the answer!" As she looked on with astonishment, the hammer pirouetted on a sixpence of pandemonium before finding its second target. The sound of Sarah's right arm break echoed through the cave. The deed was done. The heavy hammer of castigation had inflicted its intended punishment. The two desperados writhed on the cold and now wet floor. It was time to leave them to their own guilty consciences. I threw down my bludgeon and paddled through the rising tide before jumping on the increasingly battered boat. As I hauled in the anchor and pushed away from the cliff edge, I delivered my parting gift.

"The two of you are mavericks, wildcard entrants in the race to the bottom. Any sane runner would rest and recover, take a drink of water, maybe have a stretch or two once they'd passed the finishing line, but you two have continued running instead of placing a medal around your God damn necks. Reaping havoc and misery along your journey. There's no turning back, your race is over. Nobody is safe with you around. You deserve your threesome with the Angel of Darkness."

Turning on the engine and steering the boat clear of any hazards, I stopped and listened to their screams until they were swallowed up and washed away by the sea. I sat there alone. The heavy weight of my heart had been lifted of its pain. I was free from the heft of their torture, free from their conditional reliance for happiness. I felt a profound feeling of relief until the loneliness washed through. For the first time in a long while, I was on my own with only their ghosts to keep me company.

The Young Man and His Plea

I just sat there and drifted. The tide cradling me in its arms and rocking my trauma to sleep. It could feel my pain as it caressed my hour of need. "What have I done?" The words rattled inside my heavily burdened head like a metal ball in a glass bottle. The bottle always smashes and the ball always attaches itself to a chain and the chain will always be wrapped around my neck. "What will become of me? Will I fry in the burning embers of hell? Help me, please, somebody help me!" There was no one around to hear my plea. I had ironically killed the only two people who couldn't judge me. Would I miss their devilish company or was I just too scared to face up to the next chapter of my life alone?

"Come on Bobby, you can do this!" I couldn't help but imagine the pain of the fisherman in the film The Old Man and the Sea. "Man is not made for defeat. Man can be destroyed but not defeated."

I couldn't take the boat back to the rental shop. It was far too battered and bruised. Just like my life, it would need a fair amount of tender loving care to restore it to its former glory. Just like my fair-weather companions, I dumped it by the cliff edge and left it to fend for itself against all of the climatic odds. Just like my own purpose, I left it there, abandoned and disrespected.

Making my way back to the villa was a tempestuous journey. Not knowing what to do or what my next move would be, laid bare my worsening prospects. With each stride, I moved further away from the epicentre of my emotional eruption. With each step, I moved closer to my destiny. With each tread along the hot coals of my future, I felt the same relief that a dry acrid plant feels when splashed by the first drop of a magnificent monsoon. My deed was done, it felt right. I had rid the world of two dangerous mortals. Two individuals who lost the tick to their tocks. Two unsavoury members of the public who would deal with anyone who crossed their path. Forgetting Suggs for a moment, I had done the world a favour, surely it was time to bask in the glory of my accomplishment. I was a hero, but would the masses celebrate my triumph?

As I arrived at the villa, just like a true Englishman, I put on the kettle and made myself a brew. Just like a man of chivalry, I also made one for my guest. Just like a softening criminal, I took off her gag and untied her hands.

"They're gone, Mary." What was I saying? Was I ready to confess? Take my punishment like a remorseful psychopath?

"What do you mean? Where have they gone?" Mary said almost nonchalantly as she cupped and sipped her tea.

"I don't know where exactly, but I know it's a long way from here." I wasn't ready to justify my actions to myself, let alone the untied arm of the law.

Mary didn't look surprised. "So, what happens now? Can I go and see my daughter? Hold her in my arms and tell her that I'm safe?" Her face softened as she stared into my eyes.

Her emotional strategy wasn't required. "I'll let you go soon enough, but first I need you to give me some good old-fashioned honesty. What will happen to me if I hand myself in?"

Mary held her gaze. "I'm really not sure. You've clearly come from a solid background and your actions were uncharacteristic. It's your first offence too. Obviously, giving yourself up will help your cause. You have committed murder, but from what I've been told, it was in extenuating circumstances and you had no choice. I'm confident that any jury would take that into account, especially with what you've been through. There's plenty of witnesses that will corroborate your story."

I walked to the window and looked at two starlings blissfully playing in the midday sun. "I know all that Mary, but what do you think I'll get for my crimes against humanity? Cut out the bullshit and tell me how it is. Please, this is really important."

"Ok... let me be completely honest, I think they'll throw the sanctimonious book at you. Not only did you cross over to the other side of the road, but you continued walking. When the clouds darkened, you stood in the rain when you should have taken cover in the shelter of justice. For that you'll have to pay the price. You've played in the park when you should have sat in judgement. There was an open goal, but you chose to pick up the ball and hand it to the opposition. As the hours ticked by and the film reached its conclusion, the credits started to roll, but you remained in your seat, awaiting the next screening. You're only giving yourself up because you've reached a dead end. They'll strip you of all your clothes of innocence and still take you to the cleaners. Sorry, but that's really how it is. But believe me, it's never too late to turn back and rewrite your wrongs.

Untie me, we'll get my daughter and I'll take you back for judgement. If you do that, they might let you keep your underpants and socks on."

"Fuck me Mary, don't hold back! Tell me what you really think!" My throat tightened as her words strangled my optimism. The weight of having to do the right thing played heavily on my mind. It was time to decide! Continue to run, or stare down my fate? Face the shame on my family's faces? Experience the hatred of Suggs' loved ones? Answer and relive the dark times of discontent? Or just run? Run away again from all of the tarnished limelight, the humiliation and the distain. I had a ticket to Thailand. There was still time to catch the plane. I could buy a new life and lose myself in the Asian hustle and bustle. It was time! Time to decide!

"Mary, if you were me, and we don't need to go into the nitty gritty of why you couldn't possibly be, but if you were, would you give yourself up?"

"If you're toying with the idea of joining the other two, I would really ask you to think long and hard. One day, maybe not tomorrow or next week, but soon, we'll catch up with you and believe me, things will be a lot worse. I mean, just look how easily I found you this time."

I sighed heavily, wondering how long it really would take? Bodies would be washed up and identified, surely they'd know it was me or would they? I didn't have a motive or did I? What did Mary actually know, what had she overheard? I took a seat, head in hands.

"Ok, but I want you to hand me into the English police. Escort me on the plane yourself. You can call ahead and they can arrest me in London. I have to have your word

Mary or I will not hand you my honour." With what seemed like a genuine acceptance of my terms, I untied Mary and passed her my phone. She rubbed away the soreness in her wrists and ankles and the confidence that rose through her, was plain to see.

"I need to go now and make sure my daughter is ok. Wait here, I'll be back as soon as possible. Do not go anywhere. My Alice comes first, but I trust you. You're making the right decision." With that, she was gone and I was alone. Alone, apart from the demons that danced on my contaminated conscience. I sat there, trying not to think of the tangled web of deceit that I had spun, about the irreversibly terrible decisions that I had made and about the deceitful people that I had trusted. I could hear the kitchen clock ticking away my freedom. It was the only fuss in the room, apart from the crashing sound of my dreams. Motionless I remained, thoughtless I stayed and regardless I waited. The passing noise of each passing motor caused my heart to skip a beat until one mechanical growl grew louder and became layered with the sound of a car door slamming shut. Fresh as a daisy, with a blossoming fragrance of self-assurance, Mary swept in to pick up the broken pieces of my aspirations.

"Ok Bobby, come with me. A taxi will take us to the airport. It's time to go home and face the music."

Alice was sat in the front seat. A mini version of her mother with a welcoming angelic smile on her face. Surely, she was unaware of my misgivings. I looked at her innocence and remembered that I too once owned that purity.

Guiltily contemplating why she had returned, knowing that she was putting her career before her beloved daughter, Mary tapped the taxi driver on his broad shoulder, "to the airport, departures please."

During the journey, Alice talked about the friends she'd met, about the fun she'd had and all the activities she'd enjoyed at the kids club. Her mother hung on to her every word while teasing compliments with each supportive gesture at every twist and turn. "Oh, that's great my love. Oh, wonderful, I wish I was there to have seen that. Oh, she sounds amazing. You are very brave." In a moment of bewilderment, I imagined that they were my wife and daughter, and we were fully immersed in our family holiday. "Sounds like you had fun Alice." With a grunt and a stern stare from my fictitious wife, the illusion was over before it had really started.

On arrival, we parked and headed into the terminal. Without a second thought, I found myself hauling and pushing their luggage. Mary paid over the odds for three tickets back to London. I didn't know whether to feel appreciative or blessed that someone was looking after my best interests or mugged off at my inevitable plight wrapped in a flight. Mary even shamelessly smiled as she opened my fake passport and uncovered my new identity.

I didn't have any bags with me. In fact, my pockets were bare. Just like my future prospects. What was the point taking home my belongings? I would be gifted clothes and basic toiletries on arrival at my new lodgings. Skipping through the departure gate with great guile, I almost felt a sense of the newfound excitement a traveller feels, returning home to familiar surroundings. Once through, I was treated to tea and biscuits along with Alice, before we sat down in the atrium, awaiting our gate number. I wasn't afforded a seat next to my new travelling companions, although I felt my new master's beady eyes fall heavily upon my every move.

As we waited, I watched mothers run after their wandering toddlers, fathers heading off to bring back treats for their offspring, couples sitting in silence after a week of exhausting all conversation, old folks planning their next trips, strangers comparing holiday photos, airport staff marching to the places they should have already been, but most shockingly, I saw them! Yes, them! Bloody Martin and Sarah!

"You ok, you look like you've seen a ghost?" A kind elderly soul who sat solemnly in a wheelchair having witnessed my reaction, offered me her bottle of water. Unaware of my sighting, Mary stared on with the ferocity of a disgruntled vegan who had been offered a hot dog. I looked back apologetically, fully aware that she needed this trip to go smoothly for her sake, but more importantly, the inculpable infant that held her hand so tightly.

"I'm ok, thanks. Just a little nervous about the flight." I smiled warmly to match the old lady's concern.

Employing her brake and leaning forward in my direction, the good Samaritan held out a hand of reassurance. "You'll be fine, young man. You know, when I was your age, I went on my first train journey. I was absolutely terrified but look at me now. I'm on my seventh holiday this year! You'll be ok and back home before you know it."

The genuine warmth calmed my initial shock. "You are so kind. I hope that one day I will be half as brave as you." She chuckled and muttered something about wishing that she was fifty years younger as she rolled herself back to the safety of what appeared to be her granddaughter's company.

I looked across once again. Having been through a traumatic experience, maybe I had got it wrong? Sat there, across the atrium awaiting their flight! A makeshift bandage holding up Sarah's right arm and the lack of colour in Martin's cheeks, confirmed my worst suspicions. I was bewildered in my amazement for I had left them not much longer than two hours ago, for dead. Trapped in a cliff edge cave with the sea sealing their fate. Broken limbs had clearly not broken their spirits. Had they found a shelf within their grave? Did they have time to call for help? Did the cave lead to higher ground? How on earth could they be sat there, showered and changed without a care in the world? They must have returned to the villa, that was clear, but how did our paths not cross? The details to their adventurous escape mattered not, what did impede my victory parade was what to do next. Could I let them go free having erased the four leafed clover that was tattooed on my back? Or, was it time to blow the final whistle on the tsunami that wrecked hell on their tumultuous pathway of disaster. I knew one thing, this was not a hand of friendship. A sign of forgiveness. An opportunity to reconcile our differences and move forward as one. I was done with them, if not literally, then certainly mentally.

Mary, who was completely unaware of the turmoil of my making, sat relaxed with one eye on the departure board. Was she the answer? Could I slip her the nod? Bringing back all three vigilantes would catapult her to police stardom and the courts would brandish me with a remorseful key to a reduced sentence. I continued to stare at the back of their heads. My mind was made up when I observed Martin's arm wrapping itself around Sarah's shoulder. I knew that time was against me, but when I stood up to declare my findings to Mary, half the airport got to their feet with me. "Oh, what timing!" Our boarding gate had been called.

Amongst the madness that ensued, I grabbed Mary's arm. "I need to speak to you. This is really urgent!"

"No Bobby, not now, you're coming with me. This is not the time to change your mind." Along with Alice's, she grabbed my hand and started to forcefully lead me through the flow of human traffic.

"But you don't understand, they are here!" I protested.

"Who's here?" She remonstrated without meaning.

"Them!" I pointed in the direction of my fellow fiendish felons. The look on her face was The Picture of Dorian Grey as her eyes focussed on the objects of her desire but my repulsion.

"Oh, dear God. I thought you said that they were long gone!" Mary screamed as she relinquished my grip.

Lock, Mock and Three Thought Provoking Grovels

Seeing a professional leap into action, really is an incredible sight to behold, but unfortunately Mary did not hold that accolade. To say the word panic was etched across the worry lines of her face would have been an understatement. The rusty piece of law enforcement machinery ground to a halt. It was clear that she was used to a superior pressing the buttons and directing her workflow. The tension in the air sparked as the surging boarding gate crowd disrupted her train of thought. I had sent the legal production line into disarray. The warning lights were flashing in Mary's eyes.

"Come on Sergeant, we need to do something before they get away!"

Alice seemed confused, almost disorientated, "what are we waiting for mummy?"

For some reason, maybe willingness and craving for her daughters admiration, Mary cranked up her intensity. "You two, sit back down and don't move. I have to go and do something. I'll be back in five minutes." Before she'd even finished her sentence, we were shoved into hard plastic airport seats.

This was clearly way above her pay grade and I knew that she was looking for the assistance of airport guards. I watched as she darted between unsuspecting holidaymakers, rushing somewhere, anywhere, until she'd find an official. As she turned a corner and disappeared out of sight, I reverted back to my nemeses. The two of them were unmoved, unaware and unsuspecting of their imminent downfall. It was only a matter of time before they would join me on the gravy train of repatriation. "But wait, no, not now!" The public address signalled the preparation of their flight and as they stood up, my heart skipped a beat. "Come on, Mary. Where are you?" Martin looked in absolute agony, limping, almost dragging his right leg with Sarah acting as a crutch. She winced with his every step, clearly feeling the effects of the hammer blow. Almost zombielike, they staggered in the direction of their boarding gate entrance. I knew their final destination but could not remember the transfer city. My mind scrambled with the amount of passengers moving at pace from place to place. I felt stuck between the rock of trust and the hard place of revenge. I couldn't let them disappear. They had turned down their maker's invitation, but they were not going to begrudge Karma his meet and greet. "If they disappear through that gate, they'll be lost in the mad rush of transit!" My mind raced faster than they moved. "I have to follow them."

"Alice, stay here. When your mother returns, tell her to come through to the departure gate lounge." It was my final hurrah, my last adventure before returning to a locked up, confined space. I glided through the crowded hall, always keeping my prey in sight. The bedevilment in me embraced being the hunter, haunting the hunted. I followed them through the barriers and watched them take their pews next to the window, at gate thirteen.

"Unlucky for some, eh?" I mumbled as I looked around for Mary. Of course, I should have returned and awaited her instruction, but I had to have the last laugh, the final foray in the extraordinary passage of our association. Lambs to the slaughter, sitting ducks or scapegoats, it was irrelevant now. They were in checkmate. Their king was about to be slain. Cornered in the inevitable chessboard of their chequered past, they had no more moves to make. His lady of the 'knight' could not save them now. The game was over and they were about to be knocked out of the competition by a mere novice. Two worthy players they were not, disqualified and abandoned by the very sport that turned their wheel of fortune.

The area was quiet, of course it was. Filled with anticlimactic families, who for the past week or so, had lived like royalty, but were heading back to the hum drum monotonous of their average lives. They blurred into insignificance. There was only three people worth any note and it didn't take long before our eyes met. The sense of shock, fear, anxiety and desperate emptiness was not lost on the moment. Martin and Sarah didn't move, maybe they couldn't muster the energy. Battle worn with their mouths aghast, they sat there cornered, confused and unclear as what to do. The panic in their faces was duly noted and an air of sympathy proceeded to engulf my anger. I mouthed the words. "It's over." Again and again until the Chinese whispered, "you're going to burn in hell!"

Wait! Surely not! Passengers were starting to board their flight. Was I to let them go? Maybe they had been tamed, like beasts held in captivity being freed into the wild? I had made my point, put them through great distress, taken my revenge, it was time to move on. Yes, perhaps that would be the right decision. It was time to break our bond once and for all. "Fly my friends, fly like the wind." As I held up my hand to wave a final farewell, I felt it tug behind me with superhuman force. "Fuck, that hurts!" I was being handcuffed. Two more officers raced towards Sarah and Martin. The crowds parted, the children were swept to safety in the arms of their guardians and the silence was broken by the shouts of the heavy-handed men. There were calls for mercy and cries of anguish, but within minutes we found ourselves in a small dingy back room. Real names were requested in broken English, photos were taken by antique cameras and fingerprints were smudged with sticky blue ink before we were thrown into an airport cell. Yes, a cell, another bloody cell! Handcuffs removed, the door was slammed shut, locked and once again, we found ourselves alone and together.

An immediate kick from Sarah to the proverbials left me in excruciating pain. I collapsed to the floor. Martin followed up with a limping drop kick to my head, which if it had connected, would have resulted in a certain three points. I awaited the next wave of physical attack, but it never came.

I looked up, already nursing a headache and a bloody nose only to see Sarah pushing back her new man. Once he'd settled and stabilised his outrage, he barked, "what the fuck, Bobby! How could you leave us there to die?"

"You what, are you joking? Have you been on the pot again? You can stick your black kettle up your arse. How dare you! Are you that stupid that you don't realise what you've done? What you've turned me into? What's my crime? I'll fucking tell you! Feeling sorry for a homicidal lunatic. I rue the day I asked you to go for that drink. The truth of the matter is that I just felt sorry for you. You were a sad loser then and you still are. I despise you. I abhor you both. You animals were made for one another."

Sarah stood over me, spitting her venom over my wounds. "Hey, don't tar me with the same brush. I was only making the best out of a bad situation. I'm not the one who tried to murder his friends!"

Edging away from her and into a corner of the room, a red mist was filling the air with insults. "Friends, is that what you really think we are? You people are mad! I'm done with you! The only thing that I'm sorry about is that I didn't finish the job off properly."

The raised voices accelerated my aggression and my rapid withdrawal from the room. As I was hauled back up from the floor by two uniformed men, my feet were dragged along behind me. I passed Mary in the corridor, before being thrown alone, into the room opposite.

"That's enough! Don't make it any worse for yourself." Mary snapped.

After the door slammed shut, I composed myself and called for her attention. She entered, protected by the same two officers who had manhandled me.

"Mary, you promised that I would return home to face my punishment. You gave me your word!"

Mary folded her arms with a sense of authority. "Your new flight leaves tonight. We are just waiting for the extradition team to arrive from London. Now, do you want a drink before I leave you? A coffee, perhaps?"

The entire British Empire was built on cups of tea. And if you think I'm going to war without one, you're mistaken." I said, forcing a smile.

"Lock Stock and Two Smoking Barrels?" Mary said, covering her face with one hand. I nodded, turning my forced smile into something more natural.

Five minutes later, she brought me that tea, but didn't stay to reassure me that everything was going to be ok, or that I had done the right thing by giving up my criminal gang. She simply left me to my own thoughts of desolation. Why was I surprised? I was a marked man, a murderer on the run, a fugitive who had flouted the law. After all, I was a reprobate who only deserved four cold stone walls for company. The room in which I found myself bore no fruits to the luxury I had grown accustomed, aside from a table and chair. With no other option, I sat down and waited. I'd accepted my fate. All I wanted now was to press the fast-forward button and see it through to its inevitable conclusion.

The moments ticked into minutes which tocked into hours. The waiting, coupled with the nervous upheaval of the day, had caused my bladder to swell. I crossed my legs, I paced the room, I ran on the spot, I imagined turning off a tap until I could take it no more. "Is anyone there?" I desperately banged on the door for assistance, which only resulted in bruised knuckles resulted. I shouted for help but there was no answer. I sat back down, but this just made things worse. I jumped up and down, but nature had to take its course. I banged on the door once again, shouted and pleaded, but nobody came. I don't know why, maybe habit or desperation, but I tried the door handle and to my shock and utter bewilderment, the door opened.

"Oh my God, no wonder the criminals head to Spain." I whispered. I looked down the corridor, left and right, but it stood empty. The black crow on my shoulder squawked, "just go, what have you got to lose?" My subconscious tried to push me back into the room, but the voice in my head was relentless. "Come on, this is fate. Just go!" I couldn't resist any longer and proceeded to walk, bold as brass towards a fire escape at the end of the hallway. "Come on son, make me proud. Everything is going to be ok." Pushing through it, without a second thought, I was met with the shrilling sound of an alarm, but I was outside and on the right side of the terminal building.

What was I thinking? The black crow or my father, I wasn't sure, but I was being urged on. "Keep going, it wasn't you who killed an innocent man! It was Sarah! You have nothing to be ashamed of. None of this is your fault son. Keep going!" I ran around the front of the building and bundled myself into an awaiting taxi. Before I had time for reflection, I was on my way. Heading back to the town of my woes. I looked out of the rear-view window only to see disgruntled passengers fleeing the building. Some with arms aloft, others grabbing onto their luggage, but all unaware of the misguided mayhem that I had just caused. It was too late to turn back. The fatherly black crow had delivered its shriek and flown away, leaving me to my own devices.

I travelled the Spanish mainland's scenic winding roads for the last time. Alighting from my escape by the boat that

I'd abandoned, battered and bruised. The taxi driver looked at me, puzzled and confused, but where else was I to go? I sat for a moment. Free now, from any shackles, I knew what I had to do. I jumped onboard, turned the key and its engine roared into life. My mind raced into gear, there was only one place I could go. I'd been to the party island of Ibiza before and I knew that its cascading irrelevance would hide my indiscretions until the time called for a new adventure. There was no other option and my course was set. I was a nomad, a wanderer, a hobo, my home was where the wind or my chartered vessel took me.

Selling my only asset, the stolen speed boat, would give me temporary relief and a roof over my confused head. With almost a full tank of fuel, my mind made up, and with the wind ruffling my new-found freedom, I headed towards my new home. As I directed the boat, full steam ahead, I imagined the look on the faces I'd left behind. Mary would have felt aggrieved and disappointed. Martin and Sarah would be furious but envious, no one else mattered. One man and his boat, one victim and his demons, one survivor and his plight for happiness.

As I ploughed through the waves, I thought about my old life. The safe routine, the build-up to the weekends and the unrewarded challenges of keeping up with society's expectations. The small treats that kept you going, the heavy knocks that made you stronger and the individuals that shared your memories. The family that kept you in check, the money that flamed your fire and the inspirations that kept you striving forward. That masterpiece had been painted, sold and carted away to its new owner. A new blank canvas had been delivered and it was time to start again, perhaps with a new style. A style that would be less conventional, but nevertheless, just as much loved and admired.

I don't know why, but I looked back. Maybe in the hope that someone was following me in order to haul me back to face my grand jury and my dereliction of duty. Maybe just to see the mainland getting smaller. But I think it was to say goodbye. Goodbye to everyone who had made me and to those who had broken me.

In my heart of hearts, I knew that I'd be back one day. Either in chains or adorned in a jewelled crown. A sense of satisfaction warmed my inner being. Martin and Sarah would pay for their crimes. They would go down in folk law. Being talked about across the breakfast table, perhaps in law lectures, but certainly in the dark shadows of the underworld. As for myself, a wanted man, a myth, an urban legend, what would become of me? Would anyone even care? Over time, would I be forgotten? Surely, I'd be tattooed on the minds of two people forever. Martin and Sarah! I basked in the glory of my revenge.

A tear rolled down my cheek as I turned back and focussed on the next chapter of my embattled life.

It was over, once bitten and twice shy. It was my time now. I thrust the boat into full speed and knew I could never look back again.

....   The End   ....

Printed in Great Britain
by Amazon

49346177R00192